Thrilled to Death

A Samantha Shaw Mystery

Thrilled to Death

Jennifer Apodaca

KENSINGTON BOOKS
www.kensingtonbooks.com

KENSINGTON BOOKS are published by

Kensington Publishing Corp.
850 Third Avenue
New York, NY 10022

Library of Congress Card Catalogue Number: 2005928270
ISBN 0-7582-0988-6

First Printing: February 2006
10 9 8 7 6 5 4 3 2 1

Printed in the United States of America

To magicians everywhere—
thank you for bringing a little magic to all our lives!

Acknowledgments

Laura Wright—thank you for sharing your insights into the world of magic, for pushing me when I slack off and for reminding me (often!) to believe in myself. But most of all, thank you for being a friend.

Marianne Donley—thank you for putting up with a year of my whining about this book while we did the Co-President gig together, for your keen-eyed critique, and most of all, thank you for all the coffee and laughter!

Susan Packler—thank you for your unwavering support from the beginning. You were there when Samantha Shaw was born, read through all my drafts and listened to my dilemmas with endless patience. I know this isn't "The Witch Book" but at least there are magicians in this book. I'm getting closer!

The Tale Spinners—thank you for giving me my start. You were my first "critique group" and stayed my friends. A very special thank you to Pat Bavardo who read my very first manuscript, then took me to lunch and gently told me that my heroine sat through the book and did nothing. Thanks, Pat! I think I learned the lesson!

My incredible editor, Kate Duffy—your reputation as a smart, savvy and wickedly funny woman is well deserved! Thank you for taking a chance on me and sharing your brilliance.

Thanks to Karen Solem, my agent and my rock in the wildly changing world of publishing.

And always, thank you to my husband, Dan, and our sons, Matt, Gary, and Paul. You four are the "magic" in my life.

Thrilled to Death

1

Grandpa was on a rampage. His fury had been brewing for months, but now it bubbled to the surface. "Shane Masters is a spoiler! A . . . a . . . ."

I poured my first cup of morning coffee and struggled to get my bleary eyes to focus. The sun streamed cheerfully through the sliding glass door to the kitchen table where Grandpa was reading the newspaper article about Shane Masters's upcoming show. After taking a careful sip of the coffee, I said, "I know. He's a traitor to all magicians." And I agreed with Grandpa. Shane put on a show that revealed the secrets of magic. I abhorred the man and his ilk—making money by revealing all the long-held secrets of magic so that the shows of honest, hard-working magicians lost their appeal. I walked to the table. "But Grandpa, you shouldn't get this upset." Anger darkened his balding head nearly to the shade of an eggplant. As Grandpa was in his seventies now, I worried that he'd have a heart attack or stroke.

I did not want to find out what the world would be like without my grandfather in it. He was the rock of my entire life. Though my two sons and I had originally moved in with him because we had been destitute, we now stayed to keep him company. I didn't want Grandpa to live alone.

Or die.

"Sammy." He glanced up at me, his milky blue eyes snapping flashes of blue flame. "I should be this upset! I went to the city council meeting when they first proposed having this charlatan in our town. But all they cared about was the money and prestige."

I picked up my coffee mug and muttered, "That and the national television coverage of his act. 'It'll make Lake Elsinore and our Storm Stadium, where Shane Masters will perform, landmarks,'" I mimicked. They just didn't get how *wrong* it all was. Okay, I was getting pissed off too. I drained half my coffee mug and sat down by Grandpa.

He flashed a grin. "I've arranged a boycott."

I blinked. "You did?" I didn't want to sound discouraging, but asking his senior citizen friends not to go to the show wasn't going to make much of an impact. Shane Masters drew more of the MTV crowd. This was why MTV was going to cover his show at Storm Stadium on Saturday night.

"Yes." He nodded, his crafty face relaxing. "I'm doing everything I can to destroy Shane Masters and his spoiler show."

Worry skittered up my back. Though retired, Grandpa belonged to a group called the Multinational Magic Makers, or Triple M for short. They all kept in touch on the Internet, and they had long-reaching tentacles. They could access information and secrets that reached deep into some rather scary places. What had Grandpa done? "But that's all, right? I mean all you've done is arranged a boycott?" I knew my voice thinned with worry.

His gaze didn't change. "Mostly."

My future flashed before my eyes: *Samantha Shaw, proprietor of Heart Mates Dating Service, aspiring private investigator, and frequent visitor of Grandpa in prison.* Just what I wanted on my business card. I fought down a groan. "What does *mostly* mean?" Grandpa was slick. But he was so angry that I was afraid he'd do something stupid. And get caught. Another worry popped into my head. I narrowed my eyes on him. "Where were you last night?" He'd been out unusually late.

His face closed up, and he looked down at his watch. "Hey, it's almost seven o'clock and you're not even dressed yet." He jumped up and shouted out for the boys. "TJ! Joel! Get a move on!" He glanced at me. "Gotta get my keys. Don't want the boys to be late for school." He disappeared down the hallway.

What the hell was Grandpa up to?

I drove to work and tried not to worry about Grandpa. He was smart and crafty, but he was not stupid. I pulled into the strip mall that housed Heart Mates and parked in the single lane of spaces across from the offices. I locked up my 1957 fully restored T-bird, took a quick look to make sure my short ruffled jean skirt and red top were in place, then I turned, ready to face the day.

I stopped and stared. The office suite next to mine had new stenciling across the windowpane: PULIZZI SECURITY AND INVESTIGATIONS. Beneath that in smaller letters read, GABE PULIZZI, LICENSED PRIVATE INVESTIGATOR.

It hit me that Gabe and I were really doing this. We were combining our businesses. Gabe had leased the suite next to mine. We were taking the wall down between the suites with the landlord's blessing. Then my assistant Blaine would move to the center and work for both of us, and soon we would hire any help he needed. In the meantime, I would continue to run my beloved Heart Mates, and Gabe would run his PI business.

So what was different? I was going to start training to get my PI license. I had to log a certain number of hours and pass a test to qualify for my license in the state of California.

More and more, Gabe's life and mine were becoming intertwined—something that scared me. I'd had a miserable marriage that ended when my husband died from eating peanut candy. Suddenly, I was a widow with two sons, and then I discovered we were broke and that thugs were after me, looking for money my dead husband had stolen.

I hadn't been paying enough attention in my marriage, and that left my sons and me vulnerable. I had vowed then to never again be passive and rely on a man.

I studied the stenciled name of Gabe's PI company and smiled. Gabe didn't try to make me dependent on him. Instead, Gabe supported my desire to grow stronger. Realizing that, I took a deep breath and went into my side of the building.

The threadbare, steel gray carpet was still there, but my cubicle was gone. I stood in a square area that faced a wall with a door. My office! No more cubicle for me. To the left was a second door that led to a long interview room.

The wall directly to my right was coming down beginning today. That would open up the reception area between the two suites. I had the paint and carpeting scheduled for Thursday and Friday. The furniture would be delivered on Saturday, and we'd be in business.

I didn't see Blaine anywhere, so I assumed he was over on Gabe's side. They were doing much of the construction to save me money.

There wasn't much else for me to do, as we had cleared our clients for the week. I went into my office where my oak desk fit perfectly facing the door. Once I sat down and stored my purse in the bottom drawer, I thought about working on paying some bills and figuring out where the money was going to come from to cover my half of the costs, but that seemed depressing.

I didn't want to sit there and worry about Grandpa either. So I did what any astute and savvy businesswoman would do: I pulled a romance novel out of my desk drawer and started reading.

Everyone needed an escape.

For a few minutes, I slipped away into a world where I knew how everything would turn out—HEA, or Happily Ever After. Although my own marriage turned out to be anything but HEA, I was perfectly willing to suspend disbelief and devour romance novels.

"Good book?"

"Ack!" I jerked, dropping the book on my desk and sending my chair back into the wall behind me. With my heart pounding, I looked up. A well-built, light-skinned black man stood in the doorway of my office. I'd been so engrossed in the book, I hadn't heard anyone come into the office. But as my romance-reading haze cleared, I recognized him. "Bo!" I jumped up and hurried around my desk, extending my arm to shake his hand.

He reached out, grasped my hand, and pulled me into his arms. Then he kissed my cheek and stepped back to study me. "You're looking good, Sam. Your new life must agree with you."

Bo was too suave to mention my new and improved bustline, but I knew he was sincere. "Thanks, I am happy these days. And you look wonderful as always." He had a slight resemblance to the movie star Will Smith, but Bo's best feature was his voice. It was rich, melodious, and tinted with a drawling accent. Bo used his voice to seduce audiences as a magician. Home for Bo was New Orleans. Grandpa had known his father, and he had often let Bo work in his shows when he toured New Orleans. "What brings you to California?"

"Good news, very good news. And I want to see you and Barney. I went by the house, but no one was home."

"How did you know where to find me?" I hadn't seen Bo since I bought Heart Mates.

Bo laughed. "Barney brags about you all the time when we e-mail or talk on the phone. I looked up your dating service, and here I am. Barney also said that you are expanding into private investigating."

A warm happiness blossomed inside me. Grandpa always supported my dreams. "I'm not actually a private investigator. I don't have my license. I just do a little work under my boyfriend's license."

Bo flashed his easy grin. "Boyfriend, huh? I wondered how you ended up doing PI stuff."

I smiled back and realized we were still standing in the doorway. "Come in and sit down. We're in the middle of remodeling. Would you like me to make some coffee?" If I could find the coffeemaker. I think it was in the interview room where Blaine took pictures and shot videos of our dating service clients. That was pretty much the only dust-free zone.

"I think I'll run over to the motel and see if I can get a room. But how about dinner tonight? I'll cook my famous jambalaya if you all don't mind me invading your kitchen."

"Sounds good to me." Like I'd turn down a dinner cooked by someone else? I thought of Kentucky Fried Chicken as my personal chef. "Come on over whenever you want. I'll tell Grandpa—he'll be thrilled. Now tell me the good news that brought you to California before you run off."

Bo shook his head. "I'll tell you tonight."

"That's not fair." I tilted my head back to see the sparkle in his chocolate-colored eyes.

"Life's not fair, darlin'; you just gotta deal." He stepped forward, leaned down, and deposited a swift kiss on my mouth. "See you tonight."

"Really?" A new voice intruded.

Uh-oh. I recognized that voice. I stepped past Bo and saw Gabe looming in the reception area. He had on faded Levi's, a tight black muscle shirt, and a tool belt strapped around his hips. All two hundred pounds of his tightly packed, six foot plus frame looked tense. He stood with his feet spread and his hands hanging down at his sides. His straight, jet black hair was brushed back to reveal his dark eyes under winged brows. His mouth had thinned, but he kept his expression blank. Just like the ex-cop that he was.

Bo turned easily and walked toward him. "I'm Bo Kelly. I've known Samantha since we were kids." He held out his hand.

Gabe took a moment to study Bo, then finally shook hands. "Gabe Pulizzi."

"Sam's boyfriend. She told me about you." Bo dropped Gabe's hand and glanced back at me. "Catch you later, Sam. I'll bring all the groceries I need." Then he looked at Gabe. "Hope to see you at dinner. Bye."

Gabe moved out of the way and Bo left.

But Gabe kept moving. We were in the boxy reception area, and I backed up a step. My back hit the doorjamb to my new office. Gabe came to a stop when the tip of his work boot was flush with the toe of my sandal. "Why do I keep finding you kissing other men?"

I had to tilt my head back to look up into his eyes. "You're jealous!" Gabe's Italian heritage showed in his olive-colored skin, the hard cut of the bones in his face, and his occasional temper.

"Damn right I'm jealous. Every time I turn around, some man is stalking you, in love with you, or kissing you."

"Sometimes they try to kill me, too," I added, just to keep the record clear.

The right side of Gabe's mouth quirked up. "That too. But let's talk about kissing. Why were you kissing him?"

"He kissed me. It was just a friendly peck, Pulizzi, not sexual. Bo's a longtime friend of Grandpa's."

"Friendly, huh?"

I stiffened my back to rise to my five foot five height in heels. "You're not going to let this go, are you?"

"It's a lot to ask of a man, Sam. You are a magnet for sex and murder." He stopped glaring at me long enough to draw his gaze all the way down my body and back up. "Fortunately for you, I happen to be man enough to handle it. And you."

I cracked a grin. "You are a stud, Pulizzi." I dropped my gaze to his hips. "And you wear a tool belt well." Obviously, Gabe had already been working this morning. He looked hot, the kind of hot that made me think of him in the tool belt and nothing else. Nada. Just Gabe naked in a tool belt.

Gabe lifted a hand and cupped the back of my head. "Don't try to distract me. So what kind of kiss would you call this?" Holding my head where he wanted it, he leaned down and pressed his mouth to mine.

I inhaled his scent of Irish Spring soap and sweat from this morning's hard work. I put one of my hands on his arm and felt his roped muscles beneath warm skin. And when Gabe slid his tongue inside my mouth, I forgot about everything but the two of us.

He lifted his head and said, "Well?"

"Huh?" I didn't want him to stop.

A slow half smile rolled over his mouth. It oozed male pride. "The kiss, babe. Friendly? A peck? Or are we talking sexual?"

Volcanic might cover it. But I had my pride, too. "Certainly more than a peck," I allowed.

Gabe leaned down. "Liar."

I took a deep breath and tried to control the sudden heated lust rushing through my veins. "Did you stop by for a reason?"

"I need to run home. I saw you pull up a while ago and thought I'd check in with you before I leave. Do you think you can keep from kissing other men while I'm gone?"

"Hard to say for sure, but I don't have anything like that on my calendar. Still, magicians will probably be showing up all week." I thought about why they would be showing up and frowned. "Grandpa's in a lather over the Shane Masters show Saturday night. I'm sure that Bo knew that. It's probably part of the reason he is here in town."

Gabe kept his hand on the back of my head. "Are you worried about Barney, Sam?"

I wondered if I was starting to lean on Gabe too much. The feel of his hand threaded into my hair and cupping the back of my head was both comforting and sensual. "A little bit. But he'll be all right. He just hates spoiler magicians."

"So do other magicians, I imagine. But are you saying

that magicians will come to town just as a show of support
for Barney?"

He seemed genuinely surprised by that. "Grandpa's had
a hand in a lot of careers, Gabe. Like Bo, for instance.
Whenever Grandpa performed in New Orleans, he'd usually have Bo appear as an assistant. Bo's dad is a carpenter
who used to build special set apparatus for Grandpa. Bo
was always interested in magic, and Grandpa supported
that interest. So when Bo started getting serious about
magic, Grandpa got him into the Triple M." Grandpa had
friends all over the world. I remembered something else
Bo had told me though. "But Bo also said he was in California because he had some good news. He'll tell us tonight. Can you come to dinner?"

"Probably. I'll let you know." He dropped his hand from
my head and looked at his watch. "I'd better get going
now. I'll be at my house if you need anything."

"Okay. Uh, before I forget, you know the painters are
scheduled for Thursday, carpet on Friday, and furniture
on Saturday, right?" Would everything be ready? My office
was done, but the wall between the suites had to come
down and the electrician had some wiring to do. So did
the phone company.

And I had to come up with the money. Gabe was wearing the sexy tool belt to help me save money by doing some
of the work himself with Blaine. I was also saving money by
not getting new furniture. Well, except for Blaine's new
desk; I was paying for half of that.

"Easy, Sam. You're tensing up. The wall will be down
today. It's only Tuesday. Tomorrow we will patch the adjacent walls and do all the electric and phone lines. We'll be
ready for paint on Thursday."

"Right. Everything is fine." I took a breath. "What if you

don't like the paint color? Or the carpet? Or the furniture I picked out for your conference room?"

He grinned. "Then you'll have to walk around naked a lot to help me take my mind off it." He leaned down and brushed his mouth over mine. "Later, babe."

I watched Gabe stride out of the office, noticing the way the tool belt was slung low over his hips and emphasized his tight butt. My phone rang and ruined the moment. Since my assistant was over on Gabe's side, I grabbed the phone. "Heart Mates Dating Service."

"Sam! It's Rosy."

Rosy Malone was a longtime friend of my grandparents and one of the seniors who gather every morning for coffee and gossip at Jack in the Box. Rosy was retired from the University of Riverside where she had taught literature. "Hi Rosy, how are you?"

"I'm mad as hell, that's what I am. You have to do something, Sam!"

I sat down in my chair. "I'll try, Rosy. Tell me what's wrong." Rosy wasn't typically the hysterical or dramatic type. Had Grandpa broken into her hospital files again? Last time Rosy claimed she was having gall bladder surgery, Grandpa broke into the files to find out she was having a face-lift.

"It's Barney, Sam. He's been arrested!"

I shot up out of my chair. "What?"

Rosy kept right on going. "That upstart young detective marched in here and hauled Barney off to the slammer!"

"Vance," I hissed through gritted teeth and squeezed my fingers around the handset of the phone. That sounded just like Detective Logan Vance. The man was so damned arrogant. And sun-god handsome. Not that I cared how handsome he was. Vance and I never saw eye to eye on anything.

JENNIFER APODACA

Rosy demanded in my ear, "What are you going to do about it, Sam?"

Kick some detective bootie, that's what I was going to do. "Don't you worry, Rosy. I'm on my way right now to straighten this out." I hung up and thought, *Grandpa, what have you done?*

The Lake Elsinore police and sheriff station was housed in a red brick building with green trim and looked more like a corporate office than a police station. I went through the glass doors to the receptionist behind the window on the left. "I'm Samantha Shaw. I understand that my grandfather, Barney Webb, has been arrested by Detective Vance." I took a breath and tried to clamp down on the urge to say that Vance had better get his sorry ass out here and explain himself. "I'd like to speak to Detective Vance and see my grandfather, please."

The receptionist listened, then touched some numbers on a phone and spoke into her headset. Then she looked up at me. "If you'll take a seat, someone will be right with you."

I went to the glass case holding photos of the local soccer and Little League teams. Okay, I was pissed at Vance. I thought we'd gotten past some of our animosity. Why hadn't he let me know if Grandpa was in trouble?

"Took you longer than I expected."

I turned around. Vance wore a light gray suit that fell in excellent lines around his swimmer's shoulders. He had on a shimmering black button-down shirt, no tie. His military short dark blond hair emphasized his stern brown eyes as his gaze zeroed in on me. "It was a little hard to get the story from Grandpa's friends." I put my hands on my hips. "Why did you arrest him?"

Vance's cop face softened and his dimples winked as he grinned. "I didn't arrest him. He came down to the station voluntarily."

"Oh." The heat leaked out of my outrage. I sucked in my lips, thinking about those old gossips. Now I started off looking like a fool in front of Vance. Again. Nothing to be done now but brazen it out. "Where is my grandfather?"

"In my office. Come on." He held the door wide open for me to walk through.

I passed by him, catching a whiff of his faint coconut and sun scent. Vance shut the door and led the way to his office, which was really a cubicle off a long hallway. Grandpa sat in the corner with a Styrofoam cup of coffee.

"Hi, Sam. Guess the gang blabbed, huh?"

I went into the cubicle and kissed Grandpa's weathered check. "Rosy called me. In her version, you were arrested and dragged off to jail."

"Sammy, no handcuffs can hold me. I came because Detective Vance asked me to."

I didn't like this. I turned so I could see both men. "What's going on?"

Vance sat in his chair with wheels. "A serious accusation has been made against your grandfather. It appears that someone broke into the place where Shane Masters was staying last night. Mr. Masters says the man had a gun and intended to kill him. But one of Mr. Masters's two dogs attacked and bit the right hand of the man. He ran off."

I gaped at Vance. "Shane Masters is accusing my grandfather of breaking in and trying to kill him?" What planet was Vance from? "Grandpa doesn't even have a gun!" He had a switchblade, but I figured this wouldn't be a good time to mention that. I turned to Grandpa. "Why would

Shane Masters accuse you of trying to kill him?" It didn't make a lick of sense.

"To clarify," Vance said in his highbrow voice, "Shane Masters said Barney *hired* a hit man to kill him. There's no dog bite on Barney's hand, so I'm pretty sure he wasn't the one who actually broke into Shane Masters's place."

I swung my head back to Vance. "What? A hit man? That's crazy! What do you think? That Grandpa hired a hit man at Jack in the Box over coffee and a Breakfast Jack?" Where does one go to hire a hit man? This was insane!

Vance reached for a piece of paper carefully tucked into a protective plastic sleeve and slid it across the desk to me.

I looked down at it. It was an e-mail, and it read, "Spoiler magicians are not welcome in Lake Elsinore." A spear of hot dread hit my stomach. I looked up at the return e-mail address.

It belonged to Grandpa.

Damn. Fighting to keep my face blank, maybe confused, I said to Vance, "So? No legitimate magician likes these guys. What's the big deal?"

Vance had a square-cut face with a strong chin. He met my stare. "It could be interpreted as a threat, particularly when Mr. Masters received hundreds of these. After contacting a few people who sent e-mails like this, they all said Barney Webb was behind the campaign to keep Shane Masters from performing his show in Lake Elsinore."

Dark, sweaty fear arrowed deep into my gut. "Grandpa, what did you do?"

He shrugged. "Just had some friends make their opinions of Masters's spoiler magic show known. There's no crime in freedom of speech."

Oh God. I should have called Gabe. He would know

what to do. I turned back to Vance. "See? It's all innocent. Can we leave?"

Vance looked past me to Grandpa. "Where did you say you were last night between nine and eleven P.M.?"

Grandpa fixed his milky blue eyes on Vance. "I didn't say." He took a breath, then added, "Am I under arrest? If you have any more questions, I want a lawyer."

Cripes. "Grandpa, just tell him where you were!" Where had he been? He'd gone out and come home late. I just assumed he went to play cards with his friends. Seeing the stubborn set of Grandpa's face, I shifted back to Vance. "What does it matter anyway? You know Grandpa wasn't the one who tried to kill Shane Masters." I could barely keep up with the situation or my own rattled thoughts.

"The attacker went somewhere when he left Mr. Masters's place. So far there's no report of adult males with dog bites at local hospitals. So maybe whoever hired him was waiting for a report and helped the attacker doctor up the dog bite."

Tension pulsed behind my eyes and wrapped around my neck and shoulders.

Grandpa set his Styrofoam cup on the desk and stood. "Am I under arrest?"

Vance stood, too. "Not as yet. But I'm working on it." He started out of his cubicle.

I caught Vance in the hallway and put my hand on his arm. His muscles clenched into granite. I ignored the warning signs and said, "Vance, you can't believe my grandfather's involved in this!"

He glared down at me. It looked like it hurt to unclamp his jaw. "Shane Masters is famous. He came to Lake Elsinore expecting to be welcomed, not attacked by a hit man. And your grandfather is involved in this, Shaw. Masters believes your grandfather hired a hit man, and he has thinly veiled e-mail threats to back up his claim. All your grandfather needs to do is answer a simple question about where he was!" He wrenched his arm from my hold and stalked off.

Probably to kick a kitten.

Damn, Vance was in a rare fury. Grandpa was in trouble. Serious trouble.

2

I had parked my white T-bird next to Grandpa's black Jeep outside the police station. The Jeep should have been a clue that Vance hadn't arrested Grandpa or he would have been brought to the station in a police car. We walked out of the police station and headed toward our cars. I took his arm when we reached the back end of the Jeep. "Grandpa, what's going on?"

His mouth was pulled tight, fanning out deep lines around his lips. "Don't worry about it, Sam. I'm handling it."

"Handling what?" I was really getting worried. None of this made any sense. "Why would Shane Masters say you hired someone to kill him? And where were you last night? Why didn't you just tell Vance where you were?"

He looked down at me. "I don't have to tell Detective Vance anything. I am not under arrest. I don't need to tell him where I was last night."

I couldn't figure this out. Okay, so he didn't want to tell Vance. "What about me? Will you tell me where you were last night?"

"I went to see a friend."

I'd never let my two sons get away with that answer. But Grandpa's thin shoulders were rigid with anger. Anger at me? At Vance? At Shane? I tried another avenue. "Have you met Shane Masters? Do you know him?" Grandpa had talked about him, but he'd never said he'd met him. Wouldn't he have told me that? I thought he detested Shane for being a spoiler magician, but it was becoming clear I really didn't know everything.

He didn't answer; instead he turned so that I dropped my hold on his arm. He looked to the street, past our two cars parked side by side. "You should trust me. I've always trusted you."

The disappointment in his voice cut me. "Grandpa, of course I trust you. I'm trying to help you!"

He turned his blue gaze back to my face. "Then leave this alone, Sam. Stay away from Shane Masters." He turned and walked around his Jeep to the driver's side door.

I was more baffled than ever. Rather than go back to work, I got into my car and followed Grandpa home. We have always been able to talk. If he was determined not to tell me what was going on, then I was at least going to tell him how much I loved him and that I'd be there when he was ready to talk to me.

But when we got home, I saw a small yellow truck parked in the dirt lot in front of our small three-bedroom house. There was a man sitting on the porch. Ali, our large German shepherd, barked and fretted from the backyard.

What now, I wondered, and parked my car between the truck and Grandpa's Jeep. Then I remembered Bo Kelly was in town. It could be Bo. The sun was in my eyes, so I couldn't make out the features of the man waiting for us on the porch.

Grandpa was already out and heading up the steps to the porch. I heard him call out, "Fletch!"

At the bottom of the porch steps, I jerked my head up and got a clear look at the man. About five foot eight or so, he resembled a goofy Tobey Maguire.

"Fletch Knight," I muttered toward the ground. "Perfect, just perfect. Maybe he can finish the job of getting Grandpa arrested." Fletch was one of the magicians that Grandpa had mentored over the years. Grandpa had taught Fletch to use his natural goofiness and boyish charm to create a comical magic act. It was the perfect combination for Fletch. He was in his element on stage, pretending to trip and fall and then accidentally pulling off fabulous magic acts. No one looked more surprised than Fletch. One of Fletch's trademarks was his disappearing assistant illusion. He was supposed to make some object disappear, but he would accidentally vanish his assistant instead. He made jokes about how he lost more assistants that way, and hey, maybe that was why he couldn't keep a girlfriend. At the finale of the act, Fletch got the audience involved to help him make his assistants reappear.

He was really becoming a popular magician.

He was a nice guy, too. But every time Fletch came to visit Grandpa, they got into trouble. It was Fletch's driving need to prove his manhood to his redneck, beer-drinking, contact-sports-loving father.

"Samantha!" Fletch loped down the four steps like a gangly Great Dane and hugged me. "Always nice to see you." He let go and looked at me with his big blue puppy eyes. "You ready to marry me yet?"

I couldn't help it. I laughed at the old joke between us and hugged him back. "I'm still sowing my wild oats."

Once inside the front door, Fletch let go of my hand and turned to face me. "Yeah, I heard about your boyfriend." Then he struck a pose like a bodybuilder. "Think I could take him?"

I fought back a grin. Fletch ran on the thin side, and though he had a wiry strength, I knew he didn't stand a chance with Gabe. "In bodybuilding or modeling?"

He laughed just as our dog, Ali, bounded in from the back door. Since she spotted me laughing with Fletch, she discounted him as a threat and came over to greet us. Ali sat by my leg. I reached down to pet her regal head. She turned her slim nose up to look at me, then she went to check out Fletch.

Fletch dropped to his knees, delighted to pet Ali. He was a dog lover, having grown up with all kinds of hunting hounds. He always had a way with animals.

While Fletch was occupied, I walked over the ancient brown shag carpet to the small corner dining room and hung a right to the long galley kitchen to check on Grandpa. He was adding water to the coffeemaker. "Grandpa." I went up to him, putting my hand on his shoulder. "You know I love and trust you. I just worry about you, that's all." I was desperate to help him, but he was shutting me out.

He closed the water receptacle, slid the coffeepot under the drip, and pressed the button to start the coffee machine. Then he looked at me. "If you trust me, then you trust me. Let me handle the police and Shane Masters."

"But—"

Grandpa stiffened his kind, craggy face into a stern look and pulled out his trump card. "Don't act like your mother, Sammy. I'm not an incompetent old man." Anger blazed in his blue eyes.

I shut my mouth and breathed in through my nose. My mother drove us nuts with her determination to change our lives. And she constantly insulted Grandpa by insinuating he couldn't live in his own home anymore but should move into a senior complex. And the flat truth was that Grandpa had trusted me, accepted me, and loved me. And he provided the boys and me with a safe place to land when our lives fell apart after my cheating, scumbag husband died. I was torn between the need to help and protect him and his request to trust him to take care of things. Love really was tough sometimes. "How about this?" I tried for a simple compromise. "What if you swear to tell me when you need help?"

His face softened. "You'd be the first person I'd tell, Sammy."

That would have to do for now. Except that I had enough of my mother in me that I was going to do a little checking around to learn all I could about Shane Masters. After all, I had a very cool PI boyfriend and plans to get my PI license—what was all that for if not to protect my grandpa?

"I smell coffee," Fletch said as he came into the kitchen.

I glanced at the clock on the microwave over the stove and decided I'd better call the office. But first I should make small talk with Fletch. "The coffee will be ready in a couple minutes. How long are you staying in town?" I tried to keep my voice light.

He leaned back against the counter with the coffee dripping behind him. "A week. I've been in LA getting ready for my appearance at the House of Cards next month."

I did know that, I just hadn't realized that Fletch would be in southern California a month beforehand. The House of Cards was a cross between a magician's clubhouse, a museum of magic, and a massive theater where magicians who caught the eye of the magic community were asked to perform by special invitation only. An invitation to perform at the House of Cards was on par with an actor being nominated for an Academy Award. This was going to be Fletch's big night. "You must be very excited. Grandpa managed to get us all tickets."

He actually blushed. "It's awesome." He turned to look at Barney. "I'm going to add a video backdrop to the show. They have two large screens on the stage. It'll be perfect."

Grandpa's look of pride turned stern. "Remember, don't try to change anything in your act. As soon as we have the video, we can go to the House of Cards and do some rehearsals. Any little difference can affect your timing."

He shook his head. "No, I'm not changing anything in my act. The backdrop is only for the intro and finale. The rest of the time, the screens will go to close-ups of my act. I'm just adding a little pizzazz."

"Pizzazz?" I didn't like that sound of that. Experience had taught me that what Fletch called pizzazz, I would call disaster. "What exactly is your idea of pizzazz?" I crossed the kitchen to the coffeemaker and took down three cups. Grandpa obviously knew what Fletch was up to with this *pizzazz* idea. Clearly the two of them were cooking something up, which was probably why Fletch was in the area so early. I picked up the coffeepot and started filling the cups.

"Extreme sports."

I sloshed coffee over the edge and onto the countertop. Turning with the dripping coffeepot in my hand, I said, "Extreme what?" I knew what extreme sports were, but that phrase and Fletch did not belong in the same sentence. Ever.

He didn't notice. His blue eyes sparkled. "It's going to be great! Lake Elsinore has a gnarly dirt-bike track I thought I'd try out."

Lake Elisnore did indeed have a dirt-bike track down on the other side of the lake close to the airport. It was a

successful venture by a private party. The city leaders for
some reason haven't figured out the absolute gold mine
they could have in that area. With Storm Stadium, the
lake, the dirt-bike track, and the skydiving airport already
there, they could make that area into a sports park play-
ground. I stared at Fletch in his oatmeal-colored pants and
silk black shirt and asked, "You ride dirt bikes?" No matter
how hard I tried, I could not picture Fletch riding a dirt
bike.

The tips of his ears darkened to the color of his freckles. "Well, no, but how hard could it be? Barney's going to
help me, right Barney?"

I pivoted while still holding the coffeepot and looked at
Grandpa. "What?! You can't—"

"I can't what?" he demanded, his crafty blue eyes shining with laughter.

I narrowed my eyes, then turned back to the counter
and finished filling the cups. "All right you two, spill. What
schemes have you and Grandpa cooked up?" After grabbing a sponge and wiping the counter, I picked up one
filled cup and walked over to hand it to Fletch. "Let's hear
it."

He took the coffee, then walked to the refrigerator to
get out the milk and said, "It's not a scheme, it's a spectacular idea. The twin video screens gave me the idea."

I picked up the other two cups, handed one to Grandpa,
and muttered, "I can't wait to hear this."

"During my introduction and the finale, the backdrop
screens will play videos of me doing spectacular stunts like
riding a dirt bike and skydiving. I already have added pyrotechnics to my shows. They are really cool, but this will be
awesome. The final touch."

I nearly choked on my sip of coffee. "Skydiving! Have
you lost your mind?"

Fletch flashed his goofy grin filled with big white teeth. "It's all arranged, Sam. One of the instructors will be holding a camera to catch my jump. It'll be super! For dirt-bike riding, Barney's going to videotape me on the dirt track. Oh, and wakeboarding. Barney can tape that from in the boat. I'm going to put it all together in an extreme video to backdrop my magic show!" His light blue eyes practically glowed.

Pyrotechnics, extreme sports...I finally got it. I narrowed my eyes and said, "Fletch Knight, you are trying to impress your father." His dad constantly belittled Fletch for not picking a manly profession. He thought magicians were sissies. Now if Fletch had played football or shot small furry creatures for sport, his dad would be back-slappin' proud. Of course, his dad was invited to the show at the House of Cards.

Both of Fletch's ears turn fiery red. "I am not!"

"You are too! And after the last time, you swore to me you wouldn't drag Grandpa into your . . . your . . . childish need to impress that Neanderthal!" Fury boiled up hot and ready to blow, both at Fletch and at his father.

Fletch hung his head like a little boy. "I didn't drag Barney into anything last time. He wanted to join the National Rifle Association. We took the safety classes and learned to shoot properly."

"You blew up the garage! Did you learn that in your safety classes?" I could still hear the explosion and taste the smoke and gunpowder in my memory.

Grandpa looked up, his blue eyes gleaming. "Sammy, we didn't blow up the garage. It was just a little fire."

"The fire department called out a bomb squad!" Was he kidding? I took a gulp of coffee and tried to calm down.

"That was just a precaution"—he waved his free hand through the air—"because the gunpowder we used to pack our own bullets was a little unstable." His face grew serious as he turned to Fletch. "I never did figure out what we did wrong. The directions off the Internet seemed clear enough."

Fletch answered, "For one thing, we should have had a fire extinguisher. I always have fire extinguishers when we use pyrotechnics in my act."

"Stop! Both of you just stop!" I slammed my coffee cup on the counter for emphasis. "No one will need a fire extinguisher! No one is packing bullets. Absolutely no gunpowder! In fact, no guns! Do you two understand me?" I sure hoped that Fletch had professionals handling the fireworks in his shows. He was dangerous around guns and explosives.

"Yes," Fletch said contritely, and he looked down into his coffee.

"Sure, Sammy," Grandpa said cheerfully. "No gunpowder. I don't have a gun anyway. But I have a switchblade." He turned back to Fletch. "Want to see it?"

Oh God. "No!"

Grandpa frowned at me. "Sam, are you all right? You seem a little uptight."

I glared at him. "What are you and Fletch up to?"

He set his coffee cup down on the counter. "All we are going to do is go over to that motorcycle place and look at dirt bikes."

I narrowed my gaze at Grandpa. "You are *not* riding a dirt bike."

He laughed. "Not me. Uh-huh. Nope, I wouldn't do it. But I am going to record videotape of Fletch riding a dirt bike. I'll wear a helmet while operating the camcorder if it makes you feel any better."

I gave up. I reached out, snagged my cup of coffee, and downed the last third of the cup. Then I set the cup down and said, "I need to call the office." I headed for the phone on the wall between the kitchen and dining room. "I should call a babysitter too, but who would babysit two magicians?" I grabbed the phone and dialed the office while watching Grandpa leave the kitchen and go down the hallway to his bedroom. Fletch set his coffee down and walked out too. I heard the hallway bathroom door close.

"Heart Mates Dating Service."

"Blaine, it's me. I had a . . . uh . . . situation and had to leave. But I'll be back in an hour."

"Situation. Okay, whose body did you find?"

My face tightened in a grimace. "I didn't find a body." Given that Grandpa's gray-haired friends were already out spreading the tale of Grandpa being hauled off to the slammer, it was silly not to just tell Blaine. "Detective Vance needed some information from Grandpa, and I went to the police station to support Grandpa."

Blaine's casual voice sharpened. "Information about what?"

Grandpa had headed down the hallway to his bedroom. I debated what I should tell Blaine, then shrugged and said, "Shane Masters accused Grandpa of sending a hit man to kill him." Then I held my breath while watching Fletch walk back into the kitchen.

The silence stretched for about fifteen seconds. "Have you told Gabe, Boss?"

"No. We only just got home from the police station. And Grandpa doesn't want me to interfere."

Blaine snorted.

"What?" I demanded, my back stiffening into a board.

"Yeah, that's you, Ms. Mind Her Own Business. That's why everyone in town thinks you are a private investigator. That's why you keep tripping over dead bodies."

I winced. "Don't say anything about bodies! And I'm

not the one who tells people I'm a PI." No, that was my two sons. They were convinced that having a mom who was a PI was way better than a dating service owner. Well, I might have contributed to that by doing a few side jobs for Gabe.

And now I was working with him to get my PI license.

So okay, I might have contributed to the PI rumor, but the dead body crack sent skitters of worry up my spine. Maybe I was a little superstitious, but I didn't want to tempt fate, especially with my grandpa involved.

"Whatever you say, Boss. It's not like you stumble into trouble or anything."

Sarcasm was the price I paid for such a competent assistant.

Office manager. Blaine was the office manager now, of both Heart Mates and Gabe's PI business. I had to remember that.

"Is everything all right at the office? Do you need anything while I'm out?"

"Nope. It's quiet here. I thought Gabe would be back by now."

"He's not?" I watched as Grandpa came back into the kitchen and refilled his cup of coffee. He held the coffeepot up to Fletch in a silent question.

Blaine answered, "No. And here I was hoping he'd be the kind of boss who actually hung around the office once in a while."

"Ha-ha. I'll swing by Gabe's house on the way back to the office. See you in a bit." Blaine's body crack had definitely stirred my superstitions. I wouldn't interfere with Grandpa, but there was nothing wrong with asking Gabe to sort of check around, right? Just in case Grandpa decided he needed help?

"Later." Blaine hung up.

I replaced the phone and headed for Grandpa. I kissed his cheek and said, "I have to go by Gabe's, then to the office. Please be good."

His smile lit up his face. "I'm a magician, Sammy. I can take care of myself."

"Maybe," I agreed lightly, though I meant every word. "But I need you." I stepped back and looked at Fletch. "*You* don't get him into any trouble."

Fletch reached out and touched my shoulder. "Barney is just helping me do the video backdrop to my show, Sam. Relax. Go to work. Besides, he's as important to me as he is to you. I wouldn't let anything happen to him."

That I believed. Fletch loved Grandpa. Grandpa stayed in contact with most of the magicians he had mentored over the years. They all adored him. But only Fletch got Grandpa into trouble. "Okay, I'm leaving. No gunpowder," I reminded them. Then I picked my purse up off the table, petted Ali good-bye, and started to leave when I remembered. "Oh!"

Grandpa was halfway to the kitchen table. "What?"

I smiled. "Bo Kelly is here! He came by the office. He said he'll come by later, and he's going to cook his jambalaya for dinner."

Grandpa grinned. "Bo must have good news."

"He said he did and that he'd tell us tonight. Do you know what it is?" I was really curious.

"Maybe. Now go on, Sam."

He wasn't going to tell me. Bummer. Grandpa was like that. He loved gossip, but he was stingy with the secrets of magic or magicians. "I'll see you later then." When I got to the door, I said, "And stay out of trouble!"

Once in my car, I turned left onto Grand. After talking to Blaine, I really did want to stop by Gabe's house. I assumed he was packing up more stuff from his home office to move to the office we were sharing. I wanted to see what he thought about the strange story Shane Masters told the police about Grandpa.

I made a left on Broadway, passing the park that connected to Terra Cotta Middle School. Then I took a right on Outrigger and finally came to Gabe's one-story house. His big black truck was in the driveway with his desk loaded in the back end. Clearly, Gabe had come home to move his desk.

As I turned into the driveway, I noticed a red truck parked on the street in front of his house. I didn't recognize the truck, but I imagined it was someone helping Gabe move the desk.

I got out the T-bird and headed around the front of my car and Gabe's truck, then up the side walk to the front door. I stopped when I heard a thud resonate from somewhere inside the house.

Maybe they were moving something else? Gabe's home office had a window by the front door, but the blind was closed. I moved up to the door and knocked just as I heard another thunk.

What the hell?

I was sure Gabe didn't hear my knock. Maybe they were moving a filing cabinet.

Or maybe something was wrong. My mom instincts immediately conjured up an image of Gabe trapped beneath a filing cabinet. That triggered an adrenaline rush, and I reached for the doorknob, turned it, and hurried inside.

A loud grunt came from my left, from the fourth bedroom, which Gabe used as an office. I left the front door open and rushed into the office. It was empty except for an opened box shoved against one wall and two men fighting.

Oh God! Someone was attacking Gabe! They were so

intent on one another, they never saw me. They were similar in size and coloring, but Gabe had on a black shirt and the other man had on a blue one. I opened my mouth to yell at them when the man in the blue shirt lunged, knocking Gabe to the ground.

Fear and rage slammed into me. Frantic, but cold with determination to save Gabe, I looked around and spotted the box filled with Gabe's plaques and pictures. I grabbed the heaviest looking one, dropped my purse, and charged forward. I raised the frame over my head and brought it down hard on the head of the man in the blue shirt.

I heard the loud whack, a crack of glass, then an oomph of expelled air as the man collapsed on top of Gabe.

3

The adrenaline blast still buzzed in my head as I stood looking down at the man collapsed on top of Gabe. But why wasn't Gabe moving, throwing off his attacker and doing something? I shifted my gaze to Gabe's face. His eyes were wide with shock, then suddenly those dark eyes crinkled, and he started to laugh.

Huh?

He shoved the man off him. "Get up, Cal. She didn't hit you that hard." Then Gabe rolled up to his feet.

Cal? My head spun, and a hot sick feeling blossomed in my stomach. I started backing up. *Cal?* I knew that name! I had dropped the frame when I hit the man, now all I had to do was grab my purse and run like hell. I reached down to snatch my purse and straightened up.

Gabe stood in front of me, blocking my path to the door. His dark hair fell over his forehead, and there was a gleam of sweat on his face. He raised a single eyebrow. "Why the rush to leave? You just got here."

"Umm, I forgot something. I have to go!" I tried to get around him.

Gabe shifted to block me. "Not so fast, sugar. I want you to meet someone."

I glared at him. "Let me by, Gabe."

"Or?"

He stood there taunting me with that single eyebrow arched up like a red flag. "Get out of my way, Pulizzi!"

He couldn't hold his expression and broke into laughter again.

"Damn it, Gabe! I thought someone was attacking you! It looked like he was going to hurt you!"

He stopped laughing and snorted. "Fat chance."

I rolled my eyes and gave up. I turned around and looked at the man watching us. Of course now it made perfect sense why he was similar in build, coloring, and looks to Gabe. He was Gabe's older brother. "Hi Cal, I'm Sam, and I'm really sorry for hitting you."

Cal grinned. "You saved my brother's sorry butt. He should be thanking you."

Cal had the looks that belonged on a fireman's calendar, except for the black eye and split lip that was oozing blood. "You're hurt!" Remorse joined all my other uncomfortable feelings. "God, did I hurt you?"

Gabe put his hand on my shoulder. "You didn't hurt him, babe. Cal got his ass kicked a couple days ago, but he still has shit for brains."

Cal's easy grin fell away. "Shut up, Gabe."

The tension sucked all the breathable air out of the room. Clearly, Cal had been in a fight. Then he and Gabe were fighting. I stepped aside and put my hands on my hips. "What's going on here? Why were you two fighting?"

Gabe said, "We weren't fighting. I was showing him how to take care of himself."

"Ha. That's why you needed your girlfriend to run in and save you." Cal used the back of his hand to wipe the blood from his lip. "By the way, nice job, Sam. My brother's a lucky guy."

Since Gabe nearly burst a blood vessel laughing at me, I decided to change the subject from me and my stupid attack. "Don't do that to your lip." I tried not to wince. "Let's go in the kitchen so I can clean it up." I turned and hurried out of the office. I'd find out from Gabe later what was going on between him and Cal.

I turned left into a hallway that opened up to a large family room and kitchen. I went directly to the white side by side and opened the freezer to get out an ice cube. I shut the freezer and tore off two paper towels. After getting one wet, I turned around.

Both men stood in the kitchen, watching me with the same amused expression. I looked at Cal. "Go sit down at the table." I pointed to the table at the end of the kitchen by the door to Gabe's backyard.

He went. I followed him. Once he was settled, I gently cleaned the blood from his lip. "You almost reopened this whole cut." The cut was across the left side of his lower lip. It was swelling a little bit.

"It's fine. Just a small cut."

I felt Gabe move up behind me and sit down, but I kept my gaze on Cal. His dark eyes were amused. I wondered why he wasn't mad that I hit him. "How's your head? Do you want some Tylenol?" I really felt bad, and added, "I'm so sorry, Cal. I just panicked."

He surprised me by wrapping his arm around my waist and squeezing me. "My head's fine, Sam. Stop worrying." He let go of me.

Gabe came from a touchy-feely family. But I was still surprised by the casual sideways hug. "Umm, okay." I set the bloody paper towel on the table and held out the towel-wrapped ice cube. "Hold this on your lip."

He took it, and I stepped back. Looking at the two of them, I knew this wasn't a good time to tell Gabe about Grandpa. But I couldn't stop worrying that Grandpa could be in trouble. I didn't know what to do. So I started babbling. "Blaine said you didn't go back to the office, so I came by here to check on you. Obviously you're moving your desk. I'll tell Blaine that everything is fine. Umm, do you know when you'll get back? It doesn't matter, he probably has enough guys to help him with the wall. And I'll be there. Not that I'll help with the wall, but for like, other stuff."

Gabe reached out, grasped my hand, and pulled me toward him. "Sam, what's wrong?"

My knees were flush against his jeans-covered thighs. I looked down at Gabe. "Probably nothing. And you have your brother here. I have to get back to work."

His eyes darkened, going nearly black. "Sam."

Cal stood up. "I'm going to go take a shower. Sam, great to meet you. I'm looking forward to seeing more of you while I'm here."

I shifted my attention to Cal. "You're staying for a while?" Gabe hadn't told me his brother was coming to visit. But from the looks of things, I wasn't sure Gabe had been expecting him anyway.

Gabe said, "Cal's on a time-out from work. He's going to give us a hand with the construction."

"Oh. Well thanks, Cal. And don't leave on my account. I need to get going anyway."

"Go away, Cal," Gabe added.

"Gabe!"

Cal laughed. "See you later, Sam." He headed out of the kitchen and down the hallway to the guest bedroom.

I looked back at Gabe. "That was rude!"

"Come here." He pulled me down to his lap.

I settled across his thighs, hoping his brother wouldn't come back out and see us. "What's going on with you and Cal? Why were you fighting?"

Gabe's mouth thinned. "We weren't fighting, we were sparring. And he's a pigheaded idiot." Then he grinned. "But I like you on top of me a hell of a lot better than Cal. Now tell me what's up."

I studied his face. The trouble with Gabe was that he made everything look easy. But I knew he had to be concerned about his brother. Should I add this weirdness with Grandpa and Shane to it?

"Sam?" He put his hand on my thigh and searched my face.

I faced the truth—I needed Gabe's input. "You remember this morning I told you that Grandpa's been all upset about the magician Shane Masters coming to town to perform his spoiler show this weekend?"

He nodded.

I tried to ignore the feel of his warm hand spread out on my thigh just below the line of my skirt. "Well apparently the place where Shane Masters is staying was broken into last night, and someone tried to kill him. One of Shane's guard dogs bit the attacker and ran him off." I took a breath.

Gabe didn't say anything. He waited.

I went on. "Shane told the police that he believes the man who attacked him is a hit man and that Grandpa hired him." I snapped my mouth shut. Just saying the words was absurd.

"I see. And you saw Vance because he brought your grandfather in for questioning?"

I nodded. "He apparently tracked him down at Jack in the Box and asked him to go down to the station in front of at least half a dozen gossip-loving seniors."

"What did Shane give Vance to back up his accusation?"
That was Gabe. Coldly logical. "An e-mail. Grandpa sent
Shane an e-mail that said something like Shane wasn't welcome in Lake Elsinore, and a bunch of other people sent
him e-mails with a similar message. And when Vance contacted a few of those who e-mailed Shane, they said it was
Grandpa's idea."

Gabe shook his head. "Barney didn't hire a hit man,
and Vance doesn't believe he did. He's fishing. But he
must believe that it's possible someone hired a hit man."

I was still annoyed about this part. "Grandpa wouldn't
tell Vance where he was last night."

Gabe's expression didn't change. "Do you know where
he was?"

I shook my head. "Last night he said he was going out,
and I didn't ask where. I assumed he was playing cards
with his friends. I was reading in bed when he got home;
he stuck his head in and said good night. I asked him
where he was today, but all he would tell me was that he
was with a friend and that I should trust him the way he
trusts me." I gritted my teeth and added, "And that I
shouldn't be like my mother." That had been low.

Gabe smiled. "Barney's smart. He knows how to keep
you out of his business. Maybe he's got a girlfriend."

"Why wouldn't he just tell me?" The idea felt odd, but I
wouldn't be mad. I know how much my grandfather loved
my grandmother, but she had been dead over two years
now.

Gabe's face shuttered. "Barney might be wrestling with
feelings of guilt or betrayal."

I studied the way his eyes lost focus and his jaw
clenched with his own dark memories—memories of his
wife who had loved and adored him. And depended on

him so much that she hadn't had enough of her own strength to save herself and their unborn baby. Did Gabe feel he was betraying her with me?

God knows I didn't feel I was betraying Trent. Not with Gabe. Trent had cheated on me in our marriage, and I had refused to see it. I had betrayed myself then, but now with Gabe? That wasn't a betrayal to Trent, that was taking a chance on love. A chance that scared the hell out of me, but it didn't make me feel guilty.

But Grandpa had been married to Grandma for fifty years, and they had a good marriage. What Gabe said made sense. "You could be right. That would explain why he was angry with me. If he is seeing someone, he might be dealing with some guilt." I hated that. Had I made him feel that way? I looked up at Gabe. "So what do I do?"

"I'll check with my source in the police department and see what all I can find out. It may be that the hit man theory has no credibility at all."

I shook my head. "But Vance questioned Grandpa."

Gabe smiled. "Because Vance is very smart. Didn't you say that this Shane Masters is pretty well known? This way Vance can show he's taking Mr. Masters's problems seriously. But it might have just been a simple break-in or something like that. Even a jealous girlfriend, or the husband of a girlfriend—any number of scenarios."

My shoulders dropped in relief. "You mean like someone scaring Shane Masters?"

"Could be. Let me get some more information, then we can talk. In the meantime, try to coax Barney into talking about where he was last night."

I put my hand over his fingers on my thigh and smiled in relief. "Thank you. I know you are worried about your brother, so I appreciate your doing this."

"Cal will come to his senses. And I'm sure Barney will be fine. As soon as Cal's done showering, we're going to get back to the office. What about you?"

"I have to get back. I'm already a half hour past when I told Blaine that I'd be there." Then I leaned down, putting my mouth on his.

Gabe reacted by wrapping his left arm around my waist and taking his hand from my hold to slide his fingers up my thigh to the edge of my panties. Then he plunged his tongue deep into my mouth. Heat rushed into my body, filling up every crevice. But I also could feel the tension in Gabe.

And that reminded me of his brother. I pulled back from the kiss. Grabbing hold of his wrist, I moved his hand. "Talk to your brother, Gabe. You two are too old to try solving your problems with violence." I stood up.

He grinned at me. "You're the one that attacked him."

I glared down at him. "A slight miscalculation."

"And funny as hell."

"Try to grow up before you get to work, Pulizzi." I turned and left.

Driving to work, I was still puzzling over Gabe and his brother. Had they been fighting? Or were they just messing around? Gabe was a very physical man, though with me his physical side ran to sex, or touching. He was never violent. Cal had been in a fight, and Gabe mentioned he was on a time-out from work, so what was going on?

Why didn't Gabe just tell me?

I didn't know the answer. I passed the lake, then veered right on Lakeshore and left on Limited, catching sight of the police station. That reminded me of Grandpa. That was even more confusing. Why would Shane claim Grandpa hired a hit man? The more I thought about it, the more convinced I was that Grandpa knew Shane.

More secrets. It was enough to give me a complex. So when my cell phone rang, I took my eyes off the road for a second to stare at my purse suspiciously. Now what? I came to the stop sign at Main Street and reached over to the passenger seat to get my phone out of my purse. The screen told me it was Rosy. I took a deep breath, put the phone to my ear, and turned right on Main Street. "Hi, Rosy. Grandpa is fine."

"Glad to hear it. Sam, we need to meet."

That comment struck me right in the center of my chest. Rosy had been a friend of both my grandparents for decades. And she had stayed good friends with Grandpa after Grandma died, just being there as a calm and steady friend. So the distress or worry in her voice urged me to agree to see her. "I'm on my way to the office, how's that?"

"How about McDonald's? Can you stop by there on your way to the office?"

Why not? My whole day was shot. Besides, I wasn't going to get any work done with Heart Mates currently a construction zone. "Sure, Rosy, I'll be there in five minutes."

"I'm already here," she said, and cut the connection.

That was the efficient side of Rosy that I knew well, and it also meant that she had something serious on her mind. Quickly, I dialed the office.

"Heart Mates."

"Hi, Blaine. I have to make another stop before I get to work. Everything okay there?"

"Nothing's on fire."

I took that as a yes. "Okay, I have my cell phone if you need me."

"Now I can sleep nights." He hung up.

Sheesh. A little respect would be nice.

* * *

The McDonald's on Mission Trail has historical pictures of Lake Elsinore dating back over a hundred years. They included the railroad, Main Street, and the Chimes that once boasted of hot springs used for therapy and relaxation. The Chimes has been renovated and still stands on Graham Street, but the hot springs were closed. McDonald's always struck me as an odd place to hang historical pictures, but on the other hand, more people would probably see pictures of Lake Elsinore's history in a busy fast-food place than in a museum.

Rosy sat below the picture of old Main Street, wearing a blue top stamped with huge white flowers, munching on a hash brown patty and drinking a large cup of coffee. I ordered a cup of coffee and joined her. Lord, I was tired. "Hi, Rosy. So what's up?"

After patting her mouth with a paper napkin, she met my gaze and said, "I want to hire you."

Surprised, I leaned my elbows on the small rectangular table. "Hire me? Or are you looking to sign on as a client at my dating service?" Maybe she was lonely? Rosy had lived alone since her husband died a decade ago. She regularly hung out with the seniors in Lake Elsinore, did some volunteer reading tutoring in the middle school, and met up with her old friends at the university regularly. But even though she had a full life, she might long for a little romance.

Rosy moved her coffee aside with her blue-veined hand. She had her short, neat fingernails polished a shell pink with sparkles. "I want to hire you to investigate Shane Masters to find out exactly which magician's act he'll spoil this Saturday night."

I didn't know what to say. In the last several years, Shane had made a huge splash by revealing the secrets of the magic behind the acts of magicians. It was usually a magician who was breaking out into big success. But why would Rosy try to find out whose act Shane was spoiling? Trying to think this out, I started with the obvious. "Rosy, he keeps the identity of the magician a secret. No one knows until Shane goes on and starts the show. And then he never says the magician's name, he always just says things like, 'This act is performed by a well-known magician.' And of course, it's all from a single magician's show. It's the media that names the magician." It was ridiculously clever. The damage to that magician was very real, while Shane gained more and more fame.

Rosy nodded and started twisting her napkin. "I know, but Sam, this is our town. Someone must know. Surely you can find out. We will pay your fee, whatever it is."

An uneasy sensation skittered down my back. "*We?* Who is the other part of the *we?*"

I heard the slap of rubber sandals on the floor just as a new voice said, "I'm the other part of we."

I looked up at a tallish woman in her twenties wearing a pair of baggy jeans, flip-flops, and a Harley T-shirt. She held a large bottle of soda and had dark circles beneath her hazel green eyes. Her short, spiky, black hair looked tortured by finger combing. I recognized her. "Nikki."

Rosy swiveled out of her chair and stood up to hug Nikki.

In the meantime, my mind reeled. Nikki Eden was Rosy's granddaughter and an up-and-coming magician. She was building her reputation by doing high-cost illusions that intrigued and mystified audiences. In her opening illusions, Nikki rode a motorcycle onto the stage, then she vanished the motorcycle. It got the audience's attention right away. Combined with girl-power attitude expressed with her leather stage wardrobe and expertise with a whip, Nikki was heading for hard-earned fame.

"Nikki, what are you doing here? What's this all about?" My brain was jumbled with possibilities. And I couldn't help but wonder if any of this had to do with Shane's accusations against Grandpa.

Rosy sat down, and Nikki slid into the seat next to her. "Hi, Sam. I'll give you the short version—Shane and I had an affair."

Cripes. I was astonished that smart and savvy Nikki would fall for someone like Shane Masters. I hadn't met Shane, but Nikki had to have known who he was when she'd met him. "What happened?"

She shrugged. "Hormones, pheromones, chemistry, brain damage, it's hard to explain. Probably arrogance," she added. She unscrewed the cap from her bottle of soda and chugged a healthy dose. "I need the caffeine and sugar." She flashed a grin, then went on. "I thought I could outsmart him. I arranged to meet him, planning to find out his weakness. Every magician is afraid of him, of becoming his next target. I was trying to convince some of them that we had to stop being afraid and stand up to these spoilers."

A small smile pulled at my mouth. That was so Nikki— not afraid of anything. Her parents had divorced when she was a teenager, and she'd turned into a hellion. At Rosy's request, Grandpa had taken her to one of his magic shows, and she'd been hooked. She held on to her rebellious edge, but she took to magic with a passion. "And then?" I asked.

She glanced at Rosy, then said, "He turned on the bad-boy charm, and I fell for the illusion he created. I thought he loved me. We had a secret affair."

It made more sense now. They were both rebels and edgy. And Nikki was still young, around twenty-six, while

Shane had to be closer to forty, judging from the recent picture I'd seen of him. "So he broke up with you?"

Her jawline, cheekbones, and nose all had knife-cut edges. The memory sharpened her face even more. "Yep. Right after I told him that I loved him and wanted him to give up doing spoilers so we could develop an act together." She picked up a paper napkin and unfolded it, then pulled it through her fingers like a scarf trick. "Then he told me to get out of his hotel room or he'd have security escort me out."

Ouch. What a bastard. But that made me look at Nikki in another way. "I bet you were furious." Furious enough to hire a hit man?

She dropped the napkin and drank some more of her soda. "If I wanted to kill Shane, I wouldn't hire someone to do it for me, I'd do it myself." She fixed her tired but vivid gaze on me.

Gotta respect that, I thought to myself.

"Nikki," Rosy said, reaching over to put her hand on Nikki's arm in a calming gesture.

"Sorry, Grandma." She smiled at Rosy, her face softening. Then she shifted back to me. "As soon as Grandma called and said Barney had been arrested, I got in my car and started driving."

"From Vegas?" She had a show in one of the newer casinos.

She nodded. "We knew it had something to do with Shane Masters. It just had to. Grandma called my cell an hour or so ago to tell me that we were right, that Shane Masters accused Barney of hiring a hit man." She twisted her mouth in disgust. "God knows there must be a long line of people who want to kill him."

I tried to stay on track. "So you think that Shane might

have used your affair to learn about your illusions so he could reveal them in his show this weekend? That's what you want me to find out?" And how would I do that?

Nikki nodded.

Rosy added, "And since not many high-profile magicians vanish a motorcycle in their act, we thought that maybe you could see if Shane has a motorcycle in his props."

Boy, nothing like an answer to my unspoken questions. "That's a possibility. Or I could ask around to see if anyone else has seen one, or knows if an illusion involves one." My mind raced along at a dangerous speed. "But what if I do find out Shane's spoiling your show, then what? How will you stop him?" Nikki had real reason to hate Shane. I had to be careful. If Gabe let me take this case, it was his PI agency's reputation that was on the line.

Calmly, Nikki said, "I won't stop him. I can't. But I do have a little revenge planned."

Uh-oh. "What kind of revenge?"

She smiled and ran a hand through her wilting spikes. "I can't tell you my plan. I've signed a confidentiality agreement. But it's legal."

Confidentiality agreement? What kind of things required that? My curiosity bubbled and oozed over. "Can you tell me anything?" I thought that might have sounded like begging.

She shook her head. "I'm not going to risk my chance by breaking the agreement. But I would like you to keep trying to find out whose show Shane is spoiling. Even if it's not mine, I want to know. And if some magician is trying to have him killed, I want to know that too."

I narrowed my gaze and studied both women. Did Rosy know what Nikki had signed the agreement for? Maybe.

Her face was determined. And Nikki? She looked dead tired, but a resolute tenacity was stamped over the fatigue.

I believed them. But I still had one problem. "I want to help, but Grandpa has asked me not to interfere. He insists he can handle Shane and his accusations that Grandpa hired a hit man."

"Stubborn old coot," Rosy said, then reached across the table to take my hand. "Barney didn't tell you, did he? He and Shane have reason to hate each other."

4

"So Grandpa does know Shane." I knew he had to. Otherwise Shane's accusations didn't make any sense. My anxiety pumped up. What was Grandpa and Shane's story? Why hadn't he told me?

Rosy nodded. I glanced at Nikki. She had her chin resting on her hand and looked exhausted. Turning back to Rosy, I said, "Is Grandpa in danger?"

"I don't know. But Nikki and I both think that it's Barney who drew Shane here. Why else would he bring his show to Lake Elsinore?"

I didn't like this.

Nikki added, "I understand that you don't want to upset Barney, but I need you to take this case, Sam. You have a background in magic. You have a better idea what to look for. Barney will understand that once he thinks about it."

Maybe. But in any case, Grandpa appeared to be in more trouble than he'd admitted to me, so all agreements were off. And I wanted to help Nikki and Rosy. I nodded. "Okay, I'll do it, if Gabe agrees. But Rosy, you have to tell me how Grandpa knows Shane."

Rosy met my gaze, then said, "That's fair." She turned to Nikki. "Why don't you go to my house and get some sleep?"

Nikki agreed. "Thanks, Sam." She got up and left.

I watched her go and hoped I could help by finding out whose show Shane would spoil this weekend.

Rosy said, "I told her to meet us here at McDonald's. That's why I wanted to meet here."

That made sense, but I was more worried about Grandpa. I looked at Rosy and waited.

She drank some of her coffee, then started. "More than twenty years ago, Barney mentored Shane Masters. Shane was a hoodlum, a street thug. He had a mother somewhere, but she had better things to do than worry about him. Barney was doing a two-week gig out in Irvine, and on a break, he spotted Shane. He was pickpocketing some dumb businessman who'd been flashing his cash."

I smiled a little. "Grandpa caught him?"

She smiled back. "Barney made Shane return the money. Then he offered to show him a skill he could use with his fast hands. He took Shane under his wing, used him in his shows for a while as he taught him the craft of magic."

It was all starting to make sense. "That's why Grandpa is taking Shane's coming to town so personally. He shared his love of magic with Shane." I looked down at the white lid of my coffee cup. "My mom was never interested. I loved watching Grandpa perform and had fun helping him sometimes, but I didn't love it like he does, you know?" I knew I had wandered off the subject. Grandpa had mentored a lot of magicians over decades, probably because he had no one in his own family to whom he could pass down his magic. He never pushed me toward magic, but I knew he wanted me to have the same passion he had. I just didn't. But this wasn't about me, it was about Grandpa. I looked up at Rosy. "So what happened?"

She lifted her chin off her hands and folded them over her chest. Her face turned tough-teacher hard. "Shane betrayed him. First Shane started doing small shows, doing opening acts, stuff like that. He was doing well, starting to build. Barney sponsored him into the Triple M." She stopped.

"And to Grandpa, the Triple M is more than just a trade organization. It's a brotherhood." It sounded silly on the surface, but Grandpa loved magic. And he loved magicians. They all worked together to protect the secrets of magic. They trusted one another to keep the secrets and protect their livelihoods, their ability to make a living and take care of their families. Not so silly after all.

"Exactly. Then Shane bragged that he had a Las Vegas show. Barney was thrilled. He and your grandmother, Beth, went to Vegas to see his opening, as did many other magicians." She took a deep breath, then her shoulders sagged. "And that was when they discovered that Shane was doing spoiler shows."

"Oh no," I whispered, and sat back in my chair. I didn't have to try to imagine Grandpa's horror and embarrassment. His anger. His . . .

Hurt.

It hurt me just to imagine it. He'd taught Shane the secrets of magic himself. He had treated him as he would have his own son or daughter or grandchild, had any one of us shown the passion and interest. Then Grandpa sponsored him into the fold of magicians, gave him a family. And Shane had thrown it all back at him. I looked at Rosy. "What did Grandpa do?"

"He confronted Shane. And Shane laughed at him,

called Barney a stupid party clown and boasted that he would make it big." Rosy sighed with the memory, then went on. "Barney did his best to correct his mistake. He had Shane removed from the Triple M. Shane was furious, because that cut off much of his access to information about magic and shows and what was going on in the magic community. From then on Barney refused to talk about Shane Masters."

I understood why. Grandpa considered Shane his failure. And he probably thought that he unleashed Shane's spoiler shows on the magic community. Looking at Rosy, I could see her anger and her worry, both for Grandpa and for Nikki. "And now you think Shane is in town to somehow pay back Grandpa?"

"I wish I knew, but it wouldn't surprise me. And Sam, it wouldn't take much for Shane to figure out that Barney had a hand in Nikki's career."

I felt a shiver run up my spine. "He didn't exactly mentor Nikki, but he did introduce her to magic and he sponsored her into the Triple M. But that had to be years after he had Shane thrown out."

Rosy said gently, "You saw Barney's reaction to Shane's coming to town. Do you really think that Shane's resentment has dimmed any more than Barney's?"

She had a point. "I'll start looking into this as soon as I talk to Gabe."

Heart Mates was only a couple minutes away from McDonald's. As I pulled into the cramped, one-lane parking lot, I thought about what I had learned.

Assuming Gabe agreed that I could take the case, I was going to be walking a fine line with Grandpa. But now that I knew the story of Shane and Grandpa, I agreed with Rosy. What were the chances that Shane would choose

Lake Elsinore to put on his spoiler show that will be televised by MTV? We were a town of under 40,000 with a mostly blue-collar income and a bit of an image problem. So why Elsinore? Unless Grandpa was the reason.

I had to hunt for a parking space, and as I headed into Heart Mates, I wondered if all the guys helping Blaine and Gabe were taking up too much parking. As soon as I got inside, I saw the reason for the parking problem.

The boxy reception area on the Heart Mates side had several women milling around drinking coffee from Styrofoam cups. Were they here to sign up? I looked around for Blaine—

Then spotted the reason for the women.

Gabe and his brother, Cal. Both of them had their shirts off and were tackling the wall. I stared at them. Gabe had broad shoulders roped with muscles. His back rippled as he moved. He had his tool belt slug around his trim hips to show off his tight ass in his jeans. Gabe's whole *package* screamed, *I'm a bad boy, why don't you try to tame me?*

I glanced over at Cal. He had much the same build as Gabe, but his hair was shorter and his look slightly less threatening. Add to that his cut lip and black eye, he seemed to suggest to any breathing female, *Come take care of me, I'm worth the effort.*

"Hi."

I jumped and looked at Blaine. "Uh, I, uh . . ."

"Yeah, we're getting a lot of that right now." Blaine grinned and looked around the office at the women. "It all started when one of these ladies came by to ask about our dating packages. Then she got an eyeful and started calling friends. They seem to think that we are advertising the merchandise today."

I was torn between an ugly urge to throw them all out

and glee at the idea of new clients. They could stare at Cal all day for all I cared, but Gabe—

Hell, I had to pay my half of the construction costs, so my businesswoman side won out. I met Blaine's amused gaze. "Any chance of herding them into the interview room?" And why should I blame them for enjoying the view? I certainly did.

"Sure, Boss. Nice of Gabe's brother to help out."

I turned back to Gabe and his brother. Now that I was past the initial smack of lust at seeing Gabe without his shirt, I noticed the tight line of his neck and shoulders. There was definite tension between him and Cal. "Yeah," I agreed.

"Heard you already met him."

Hearing the snicker in his voice, I turned to Blaine. "It was a mistake! I thought someone was attacking Gabe!"

"Sure. Could happen to anyone. Of course, it always happens to you." He flashed a full grin. Blaine had the look of a no-neck bouncer, but his grin made him appear more playful than threatening. His brown hair was feathered in the front with the length tied back into a ponytail reminiscent of the 1970s. His blue button-down shirt was a holdover from his days as a mechanic. I had talked Blaine into leaving the garage he worked for to come work for me when I bought Heart Mates. It was one of my best business decisions, but I paid for it daily with Blaine's teasing and attitude.

I tried to assume a businesswoman expression. "Don't you have work to do? I need to talk to Gabe for a second. I'll be in to interview the new clients shortly." I stalked over to Gabe, and then had to duck a hammer swing from his brother.

"Christ, Sam, I didn't see you," Cal said. He looked tired and hot.

"Cal, should you be working like this? You're hurt."

He smiled. It was a softer smile than Gabe's. "I'm fine. Besides, Gabe'll screw it up if I leave him alone. Then I'll have twice as much work to do to fix it."

I shook my head. I didn't get it. They were pissed at one another about something, but they were working together and trading insults. Was this how normal families resolved problems? I didn't have brothers or sisters, so I didn't really know.

"Don't feel sorry for him, Sam," Gabe said from behind me.

I turned around. Gabe's jaw was tight enough to crack walnuts. The mood between Gabe and Cal started to get on my nerves. Maybe this wasn't the best time to spring the new case on him, but I had to tell him. "Gabe, can I talk to you for a minute? In my office?"

He nodded, set the sledgehammer down, then unbuckled the tool belt and put it on the ground next to the sledgehammer.

I saw that Blaine was trying to get the women into the interview room while they craned their necks to catch a glimpse of Gabe stripping off the tool belt. *Hussies.* But they would be busy for a few minutes filling out the information and security release forms, so I could talk to Gabe. I hadn't planned to see clients this week, but here I had both new Heart Mates clients and a private investigating client. I went into my office and Gabe followed, shutting the door behind us.

I sat on the edge of my desk. Gabe walked over and looked down at me. I had to make myself ignore his bare muscular chest and look up. "I had a phone call from Rosy Malone. I stopped at McDonald's to see her."

His dark eyes rested on my face. "Blaine mentioned you'd called and said you had another stop to make."

I blurted it out. "Rosy wants to hire me."

Gabe lifted a single eyebrow. "Probably not to find her a date."

I shook my head. "She and her granddaughter, Nikki, are hiring me." I went on to explain that Nikki had showed up at McDonald's too and what they both wanted me to do, and I summed up what she'd told me. "I want to take the case."

Gabe ran his hand through his hair, then sighed and sat in the chair facing my desk. "We decided to take the week off to get the construction done."

I noticed that his shoulders were raised with tension. "I know, but you won't let me do any of the work. And I can't help that all those women came in. They were all staring at you and your brother working half-naked." Hmm, did that sound like jealousy?

Half his mouth quirked up in a grin for a second, then flattened. "I don't care about your signing on Heart Mates clients, Sam. But you need me to help with investigating. I don't have the time. As it is, I may have to go to LA, and I have a few clients I'm juggling at the same time."

Damn. I saw his point. But I had to do this. "Rosy is right, Gabe. I do know more than most about magic, and I might be able to figure out what Shane's up to."

"Or you might end up hurt or dead."

He was in a testy mood. I took a breath and added the last and most important point. "Rosy told me that Grandpa knows Shane. Apparently he mentored Shane, then Shane started doing spoiler shows. Grandpa's the one who had him removed from the Triple M. She thinks Shane's being in Lake Elsinore is tied to Grandpa." I looked up. His face was tight and grim. I could almost feel him pulling away from me. He seemed to have his own problems. "We can work this out. I know you're busy. Why do you have to go to LA?"

He didn't say anything for a few seconds. "Check into something."

Gabe was from LA and his family still lived there. "Something to do with Cal?"

He stood up. "Take the case. I'll do the background check on Shane first chance I get. If you want to do a little checking around with people you know, try to see if you can find someone working on the set up at Storm Stadium where Shane will do his show, things like that. But you need to be careful."

I frowned at him. He had changed the subject from Cal. On the other hand, Gabe was like that sometimes. He thought things out for a while before he talked about them. Whatever's going on with his brother, maybe he's still thinking. I realized he was almost to my office door. "Gabe."

He turned back. "What?"

"Is everything okay?" I wasn't sure what I was asking.

"Just stay out of trouble and everything will be fine." He turned and went out to the reception area.

A couple hours later, I was in my office with the door closed to shut out the noise and dust of the construction. I had completed the interviews with the new clients, and I was attempting to put their information into the computer. Once I got that done, then I was going to try and figure out how to run the program that cross-matched the candidates with our eligible men.

This was normally Blaine's end of things. I did the original interviews, then turned all the forms over to him. Once he had the matches, that's where my skills came in. I went over all the computer-generated matches and looked for chemistry based on my interviews with the clients and my gut.

Years of reading romance novels actually made me pretty good at this. And it was the personal touch that made Heart Mates special.

I opened a new file and started typing in the fields: name, birth date, address, phone number—the usual personal information.

A half hour later I was still struggling with inputting the information, but I was getting there. And so far, I hadn't destroyed anything on the computer. In fact, I was getting excited. One of the ladies, Olivia, was in her late thirties, divorced, and longing for a family. I had a feeling about her and a man we signed a couple weeks ago. He'd dated a couple gals, but no sparks. His name was Thom, and he had changed his life. He quit his executive job, moved out to Lake Elsinore, and now taught at the community college. He decided that he wanted a life, not just a career. I thought that Thom and Olivia might hit it off; they had the same life and love goals, as well as both having an interest in golf.

I didn't get golf. Chasing that little white ball around a course seemed kind of tiring, but to each his own.

The ringing of the phone startled me. It was my cell phone. I yanked open the desk drawer and reached into my purse to get my phone out. The caller ID told me it was Rosy.

What now? I hadn't even gotten started on the case yet.

I put the phone to my ear. "Hi, Rosy."

"Barney is going over to see Shane Masters."

Crap. "Are you sure? When? How do you know?"

"Because Hank just left your house. He went by to get the scoop from Barney about being hauled into the police station. He called me because he said Barney decided to confront Shane Masters himself."

Hank was another of the coffee club seniors that hung out at Jack in the Box. A bad feeling wrapped around my gut, and I clutched the phone tightly. "Where's Shane staying? At a motel in town?"

"Humph." Rosy made a disgusted sound. "Nikki told me that Shane has a huge custom-made motor home that he usually travels in."

Wow, ruining other magicians obviously paid well. So where would Shane park the motor home? At the stadium? But they probably didn't have all the hookups he would need. But I knew another place that would. "The campground! That must be where he's staying."

"Probably. Sam, you should go over there. See what you can find out and keep Barney out of trouble. Hank said he took his switchblade."

Oh hell. "I'm on my way!" I hung up, grabbed my purse, and hurried out of the office.

The reception area smelled like pizza and dust. A couple empty, flat boxes sat on the floor. My stomach rumbled and reminded me I hadn't had lunch. I didn't have time to see if there was any pizza left. Dang.

"Going home?"

I looked over at Gabe. They had made progress on the wall. My new office had really closed up the reception area, but when the wall came down completely it would be open and airy. "Actually, I'm going to run an errand." Why didn't I tell him? I glanced over at Cal and knew why. I had already made a colossal fool of myself in front of Cal today. I didn't want Gabe lecturing me in front of him.

Besides, Grandpa had his switchblade—I didn't have time to argue with Gabe. I had to catch up with Grandpa.

Gabe just nodded and turned back to the wall.

What happened to good-bye kisses? But we were at

work. I realized that I was being oversensitive and hurried out. I hoped I could catch Grandpa before he confronted Shane.

I made it to the campground in fifteen minutes. I estimated that Grandpa was five minutes closer from our house.

But I drove faster.

I turned left into the campground. It was early June, still cool at night, but the campground was about a quarter full. There was a scattering of trees and rows of campsites for tents and trailers. Past those was a beach that led to the lake. On the left side of the campground, closest to the Jack in the Box, there was a row of small, boxy cabins. They looked a little too rustic for my taste. I like air conditioning and room service.

I drove slowly, looking for a fancy motor home and Grandpa's black Jeep. I finally found the Jeep creeping along the last row on the far side of the campground.

I watched as Grandpa pulled up to a huge gray and cream colored motor home that had some burgundy striping. It clearly belonged to Shane since the side of the RV had a large picture of Shane Masters airbrushed on it. Wow, talk about a gigantic ego. I parked my T-bird next to the Jeep, turned off the car, and got out.

Grandpa met me at the front of the two cars. "Sam, what are you doing here?" His craggy face was still with disapproval.

I reached for his arm. "Hank told Rosy you were going to confront Shane."

He narrowed his milky blue eyes. "Rosy, that old snoop. She called you."

Even though part of me understood, I was hurt that Grandpa hadn't confided in me about Shane. And that he hadn't asked me to help him. "Grandpa, this might not be a good idea. Vance has already connected you with Shane. Don't make it worse."

He looked at the motor home. "Sam, there are things you don't understand. It's better if you leave."

My hurt was turning to anger. Gabe was cutting me out of his problems and now Grandpa was too. But no matter what, I was not going to let Grandpa confront Shane alone. "No. I'm here to talk to Shane for a client of mine."

"Who?"

"A client." I was being stubborn, and I lifted my chin to prove it.

A new voice called out, "How long are you two going to stand there and argue?"

We both looked over to the motor home. Swear to God, it looked like Mr. Clean from the commercials stood in the doorway, flanked by two sleek Dobermans. He had a bald head, muscled arms, and a tough-guy stance. I didn't think Mr. Clean wore the big diamond pebbles in his ears that Shane did though. Shane was dressed in expensive Italian black pants and a silk short-sleeved button-down shirt opened at the throat. A thick gold chain around his neck caught the sunlight. His voice was colored with sarcastic amusement. He looked like a cross between a well-dressed mafia thug and a pirate. But there was something compelling about him. He had what Grandpa called stage presence.

He looked out of place at the Lake Elsinore campground. I could only assume he stayed there to use the hookups for things like water for his motor home.

Or maybe he liked to lord his stardom over the little people. Who knew?

I tore my gaze away and looked at Grandpa.

He squared his shoulders and said under his breath, "Leave, Sam."

I shook my head, gritting my teeth.

"Come on in, Barney. I've been expecting you." Shane turned to look at me. "You're a surprise, Samantha."

"You know me?" In my experience, that was never a good thing.

"The granddaughter who didn't have the passion for magic. Of course I know who you are."

That hit me hard, sucking the air from my lungs. Had I disappointed Grandpa so much that he had told Shane about me? But then I felt Grandpa's hand curl protectively around my elbow. "She's just leaving, Shane."

I reached around my body to put my hand over his. "I am not leaving. I won't leave you alone with him." I didn't care how mad he got at me. I was scared. I glanced over and saw that both the dogs framing Shane had perked up their cropped ears and were watching us intently.

The guard dogs Vance mentioned.

It probably hadn't been a good idea to come here without some protection. Like Gabe and his gun. Or Ali. I wanted to smack myself in the forehead for not thinking ahead. This was exactly the kind of thing Gabe meant about staying out of trouble.

Shane appeared to be running out of patience. "If you're finished with your little family dispute, perhaps you could come in and we could take care of business?"

He was seriously starting to annoy me. I let go of Grandpa's hand that was still clasped on my elbow. "Let's go do this." I walked toward the trailer with my head held high.

Grandpa followed me.

Shane watched us with his gray eyes.

When I got to the pull-down steps of the motor home, I decided I needed to act confident. Men like Shane would zero in on any sign of weakness. I met his gaze and lifted my foot to the first step.

Both dogs stood instantly, drew back their lips, and growled like crazed beasts. I was close enough to see their huge gleaming teeth and the row of angry hair that rose in a stiff line down their backs. Instinctively, I jumped back, smacking the back of my hand on the door frame and scratching it. Stunned, I stood on the dirt and looked down at the back of my hand. A line of blood welled up in thick bubbles. Then I looked up at Shane.

He smiled. "Afraid of my dogs, Samantha?"

Hell yes. And worse, I thought Shane had known what the dogs would do. Had he given them some command? Or had I crossed some invisible line that set the dogs off?

"We're leaving," Grandpa said.

I glanced at Grandpa and saw that he had his switchblade out. His face had firmed up to pure rage.

I looked back at Shane. His eerie smile froze as he shifted his gray eyes to Grandpa. "Do that and I'll see that you're arrested for attempted murder by the end of the day."

5

I stared at Shane framed in the doorway of his motor home with a dog on either side of him. He threatened Grandpa to keep him from leaving, but he never even acknowledged the switchblade. Shane had no way of knowing if Grandpa had the skill to throw it right at his heart. I didn't think he cared. What pissed him off was the idea of Grandpa leaving.

He wanted Grandpa's attention. What for?

It wasn't good, whatever it was. I tried to assess the situation and decide what to do.

Shane stepped back, and both dogs moved with him. "Come in. Let's get this show on the road."

I hesitated, but Grandpa put away his switchblade, stepped up onto the built-in ladder, and went inside.

The two Dobermans watched him with interest.

Then they turned to look at me.

I had visions of them weighing and measuring in their doggy brains and deciding that I had more meat than Grandpa. Plus I was already bleeding; did they smell blood? Some deep dread had me press the thin cut on the back of my hand into my skirt to staunch the flow of blood.

Repressing a shiver, I had no choice but to follow Grandpa into the motor home. I wasn't going to leave him alone with Shane and the dogs.

It was incredible. There was a bedroom/bath through an opened door in the back. The front was the cab. In the center was a combination kitchen and living space, complete with a microwave and a big-screen TV. There was a video game frozen on the huge screen.

Sheesh, whatever happened to camping in a tent and watching the stars at night?

"Sit down." Shane indicated the cream-colored leather couch. He took a leather captain's chair. He made a move with his hand, and both dogs lay down at his feet.

I turned back to look at Shane. "What do you want with Grandpa?"

"To have a little chat. Why don't you sit down?"

I looked at the dogs again. Would Shane stop us from trying to leave? Very slowly, I lowered to the leather couch and realized that we were in a situation that I couldn't control. Gabe would have a lot to say about that.

If we ever got out of here, and if I ever chose to tell him.

"Now, here's the deal." Shane dismissed me to look at Grandpa. "Someone has sent a hit man after me. You are going to use your access to the Triple M network to find out who that is and you're going to get the hit called off. Then you are going to tell me the name of the magician who thought he could have me killed."

Grandpa shifted on the couch and said, "Why would I help you?"

Shane didn't move a muscle. "You will."

Both dogs picked up their heads and watched us.

The silence was painful and laced with uneasiness. I looked at Grandpa next to me. He studied Shane for long seconds, then his shoulders came down a fraction of an inch. He seemed to have accepted something I couldn't grasp, then said, "Why do you think a magician sent a hit man after you?"

Shane's face hardened, his gray eyes narrowing. "It's very simple—once I set the dogs on the hit man, he screamed out, 'Damn magician never said anything about dogs!' And the only threats I've gotten have all come from magicians. Your little e-mail was nothing compared to some of the threats I've had. I'd find the bastard myself, but you cut off my access to the Triple M when you tossed me out."

My first thought was that Rosy was right—Shane did have a long memory. Then I realized that Vance had held back information from us. He'd never said that the supposed hit man had said something about magicians. I looked down to see my hand was still bleeding and pulled a ruffle of my jean skirt over it to apply more pressure. Vance and I were going to have a talk. He was endangering my grandfather by not telling us everything.

Of course, Grandpa hadn't told him everything either.

Grandpa's next words brought me back to the present.

"You brought that on yourself, Shane. You betrayed all of us."

"And you are a sentimental and foolish old man. I figured out how to turn a simple skill, basically party tricks, into a fortune. And someone in your beloved *brotherhood* of magicians is trying to have me murdered. Either you find out who it is or I will give that detective all the proof he needs to destroy you."

I clenched my muscles to jump to my feet until I remembered the dogs. But even my terror of their sharp teeth and powerful jaws didn't dim the anger in my voice. "You can't do that! Grandpa hasn't done anything."

Shane smiled, revealing small perfect teeth. I almost expected two long fangs to slide down from the eyeteeth.

His smile chilled his face. "I'm a magician, Samantha. I can create enough of an illusion of his guilt to destroy his pathetic little existence."

Hot anger rushed my brain. Everyone who knew Grandpa respected him. And Shane was threatening to take that away from him. I fought to take in a breath and calm myself down enough to speak. "That's not magic, that's blackmail."

"Ah, a few of those brain cells actually work behind all those fake blond streaks and that very attractive saline rack." His gaze fell to my chest.

Pepper spray. One day, when I got Shane away from the killer dogs, I was going to reduce him to a crying mass of mucus. But for now, I had to know what we were up against. "Grandpa isn't going to be blackmailed."

"Hush, Sam."

I turned in surprise. "Grandpa, don't give into this!" But his face was set into wrinkled stone. His right hand was clenched into a fist tight enough to whiten his knuckles. I caught a glint of silver and knew the closed switchblade was tucked into that fist. He had taken severe exception to Shane's comment about my intelligence and enhanced bustline.

Grandpa looked back at me. "I don't care about Shane and his threats. But I do care about the Triple M." He turned away from me. "I'll see what I can find out."

The charm and illusion of civility dropped away in layers. "You do that, old man. And bring me the name of the prick screwing with my life."

My chest froze. I'd seen Gabe shed his dangerous-man-under-control veneer to see tough ex-cop beneath. Gabe was dangerous and lethal, living by a code of his own, a code that had to do with his strong sense of justice. But

Shane . . . the layers stripping away revealed a depth of rage that scared me to my core.

Grandpa shifted. "I'm not doing this for you. I'm not bringing you anything."

Shane's tented hands folded into two individual fists. Then slowly he turned his gaze to me. "I think you will, old man."

Then I got it—why Shane was so sure that Grandpa would help him. Damn it, now it made perfect sense why Grandpa had been trying to keep me out of this with Shane.

With a single look, Shane threatened me to get Grandpa's cooperation.

I took a breath. We had to get out of here. Calmly, I said, "Tell us about the attack and as much as you can about the hit man." I struggled to keep my voice low and reasonable.

"Very wise, Samantha."

He obviously thought I was afraid of him. Okay, I was afraid of him. But I was going to get us out of here, and then I was going to figure out what to do next.

Shane went on. "Last night I was asleep around 9:30 when I heard the scrape of the lock in the motor home door. Not the cab doors, but the one you both came in. I told both dogs to stay down and quiet. I wanted to see who it was. He was dressed in dark clothes and a black pullover cap. He had picked the lock and was armed with a gun and silencer. Seeing that, I immediately set the dogs on him.

"He sprayed Blackstone in the eyes with pepper spray and ran. Houdini got a good chunk out of his gun hand before he kicked the dog and got loose. That's when he screamed out the line, 'Damn magician never said anything about dogs!', then dropped the gun and ran off. The police have the gun."

I listened carefully, then asked, "Why didn't you shoot him? He dropped his gun; why didn't you pick it up and shoot him?" I made a mental note to ask Gabe if he could find out from his police source if there were any prints on the gun.

Shane leaned forward, reaching down to pet both his dogs, but his nostrils flared and his mouth went white with rage. "He sprayed Blackstone with pepper spray and kicked Houdini. Blackstone was writhing on the ground in pain and Houdini tried to chase him, but I couldn't let that bastard get another chance to hurt my dogs. I chose to see to my dogs and get the hit man later."

He cared about his dogs. That surprised me. I'd had the feeling that his dogs were just a tool, but as I watched him stroke both dogs' heads, I realized he really cared about them.

But he used people. Or seemed to by the way he was blackmailing Grandpa and the way he revealed the acts of magicians. I wanted to understand Shane and what we were up against. And since Rosy and Nikki had hired me to do a job, I threw out the question, "What about Nikki Eden?"

Shane stopped petting the dogs and looked right at me. Then he smirked, "What about her?"

Grandpa turned to look at me. "Sam, what's this about?"

I reached over and put my hand on Grandpa's forearm. I wanted to see if maybe I could trip him up into admitting he was using Nikki's act in his spoiler show. To Shane I said, "You broke up with her, right?"

He lifted one side of his mouth in a smirk. "I was done with her. Why do you care? Are you applying for the position?"

I squeezed Grandpa's forearm to keep him from saying or doing something. "How many women have you used and dumped like Nikki?"

He laughed. "How many dumb women are there? Nikki thought she could outsmart me. She was one of many who thought that. I let her think it while I got what I wanted from her—sex and her act. When I was finished with her, I got rid of her."

It was becoming increasingly clear to me why so many people wanted to kill Shane Masters. But while I had him in the arrogant, bragging mood, I said, "So are you exposing Nikki's act this weekend?" I was so tight with anger and disgust that my thigh muscles cramped.

"Watch the show and find out." He let out a small laugh. "In case you are thinking Nikki sent the hit man, think again. She's learned her lesson."

I sort of wished I had a gun. I really wanted to shoot that smug look off his face.

Grandpa stood up. "Nikki is a real magician."

The smug expression on Shane's face melted into bitterness. "Come on Saturday night, old man. Anyone can do the by-the-numbers tricks. I've elevated magic to a spectacular show. The world loves me. They don't care about your little awards and magic houses, they just love seeing that I can do any magic and then show them how it's done."

The dogs stood up at attention.

Grandpa had hit a nerve with Shane. Every group had their professional honors, including magicians. But since Shane had broken the code, no matter how much wealth or fame he attained, he'd never be professionally recognized by his peers.

And he knew it.

I filed that information away and rose. "I think we'll

pass on the show. Let's go, Grandpa." I prayed that Shane would let us go. And that the dogs weren't hungry.

Shane unfolded from his seat and stared at Grandpa. "You find out who sent the hit man after me."

Grandpa met his glare. "I'll find out if you've destroyed any more lives by driving a magician to try to kill you."

I grabbed Grandpa and tugged him around the dogs and out of that motor home. Shane made no move to stop us.

Once we were outside, I was shaking with anger and frustration. Stopping at our cars, I looked back at the motor home. The door was closed. Shane was done with us. Turning to Grandpa, I said, "Do you really think another magician hired a hit man to kill Shane?"

Grandpa met my gaze. "You met him. What do you think?"

Damn. "I think it's a wonder someone hasn't killed him before now."

"Yeah. But if it is a magician, then I have to find out who it is and stop him. Something like this could destroy the Triple M." He reached out and took hold of my hand. "Let me see that cut."

I looked down at my hand cradled in his. "It's fine, just a scratch." It had stopped bleeding. I had the feeling Shane had wanted me to fall, or get hurt, just as a little show of his power. His ability. My hand was fine, but I was scared of him.

"Put some medicine on that scratch," Grandpa said, and let go of my hand.

"I will," I said to assure him. Then I turned to more serious matters. "Do you think Shane could really frame you somehow?"

Grandpa's blue eyes were wide with anger. "I'm more worried about him going after you."

"I'm sorry, Grandpa. But if you had told me why you wanted to keep me out of this, I would have figured out another way. But I didn't know, and besides, he's not going to touch me." Not if I could help it. "Are you going to look for the magician that hired the hit man?" I already knew the answer.

He nodded slowly. "I have to, Sam."

"I know." I had a job to do too. I hoped he was going to understand that.

Grandpa shook his head, his shoulders slumping and appearing thinner beneath his shirt. "I didn't know about Nikki."

I put my hand on his arm, understanding now that he believed that he was responsible for Shane and what he did to all magicians, including hurting Nikki through an affair. "It's not your fault."

He took a breath, controlling his anger with a little glint of amusement. "I'll bet Rosy hired you to find out which magician's act Shane plans to spoil Saturday."

I nodded. "Rosy and Nikki. She just got into town."

"Then she's worried. So I guess we both have work to do." He leaned over and kissed my cheek. "Be very careful, Sammy."

I squeezed his arm. "Where are you going?"

"Home. I'm going to get started trying to figure out this mess. Maybe talk to a few people I trust in the Triple M."

Relieved, I said, "Okay, but don't come back here. Promise me."

"I won't for now." He turned and went to his Jeep.

I had to be content with that.

I got into my car, locked the doors, and debated calling Gabe while watching Grandpa drive off. It was after one, I was starved, and I had to pick up Joel from school in a little over an hour and a half.

Or should I forget eating and go right back to the office to talk to Gabe?

My phone rang before I could decide. I pulled it out of my purse and didn't recognize the number. "Hello?"

"Shaw, it's Detective Vance. We need to talk."

Vance. Hmm. "We do?" I stared at Shane's motor home. Was he in there watching me? "You didn't seem to feel we needed to talk before publicly embarrassing my grandfather in front of all his gossipy friends and dragging him down to the police station."

"He didn't seem embarrassed to me, and I didn't drag him. I asked him to go to the station." I heard him take a breath, then he added. "It's my job, Shaw."

"Yeah, yeah. So where do you want to meet? Or am I being summoned to the police station? Are handcuffs in my future?" I did a mental head-smack as soon as I mentioned handcuffs.

Silence.

"Vance?"

"You're a piece of work. How about Cocoa's? Is that far enough away from the police station for you? If you really want handcuffs, we could go to my house."

This time I dropped my forehead to the steering wheel. *Stupid!* I deserved that for my idiotic handcuff comment. Lifting my head, I tried for a calm, cooperative voice. "Cocoa's will be fine. I can be there in fifteen minutes."

"I'll be waiting for you." He hung up.

With or without handcuffs, I wondered as I stashed my cell phone and started the car.

Vance and I sat across from one another at a four-top booth. The lunch crowd had thinned out. Once we ordered, Vance looked at me. "Is the cut on the back of your right hand the reason you have blood on your skirt?"

Detectives. It was hard to get anything past them. His gold-flecked brown eyes didn't miss much. And I had seen him do a once-over when I walked in. I had taken him in too, noting how good he looked in his light gray suit that appeared to be custom made for his athletic shoulders. He looked much more relaxed than he had this morning, which probably meant he was up to something. Vance and I were not above using our chemistry, for lack of a better word, to get what we wanted from each other. To answer his question, I said, "Yes."

"How did you scratch your hand?"

I sipped some Diet Coke and answered, "On a door."

Vance grinned, revealing his deep dimples. "Nice and vague. Looks as if Pulizzi is teaching you a few things."

The waitress brought our lunches. I had Cobb salad with extra blue cheese dressing. Vance had a turkey and avocado sandwich with tomatoes and cottage cheese on the side. I wondered how my thighs were going to look as I dumped all the blue cheese dressing over my salad. I should exercise. Or something. I picked up my fork, then said, "Why so suspicious over a cut?"

He lifted up his sandwich. "I get paid to be suspicious." Then he took a bite.

We could do this all day. I speared a nice chunk of egg and lettuce drowned in blue cheese dressing and tried to think of what I needed to know.

And what I had to trade.

I wanted to see where Vance was on this case first. "Are you actively working the Shane Masters case?"

He set down his sandwich. "I am now."

I blinked. "Meaning?"

"This morning I set it aside for actual murder cases, but the city council got wind of Shane's trouble. The idea of a famous magician who is going to be on TV this weekend being threatened, and a hit man in town, makes them nervous."

"Ah." He was getting political pressure. Interesting. And how could I use that to my advantage? "Just how do you investigate something like this?"

"I ask questions." He took another bite and set down his sandwich.

"Of me? What would I know?" I loved avocado and speared a huge chuck, added some salt and pepper, then ate it.

"You always know more than you tell me. And I think it's time to call a truce. Work together."

Wow, Vance must be getting a hell of a lot of political pressure. "Really? So that means you'll tell me everything? Like the fact that the hit man said something about a magician sending him after Shane's dog bit him?"

Vance sighed. "Pulizzi?"

I knew he was implying that Gabe had tapped his sources and gotten that information. Proudly, I said, "Nope. Me. I found out."

"From?"

I shook my head and worked on eating my salad. I wasn't going to give anything to Vance without getting something in return. And I was debating what to tell him. I doubted anyone that knew about Shane and Grandpa's history would tell Vance. But Vance wasn't stupid, so he had to know that there was a connection between them. One that would either drive Grandpa to hire a hit man or drive Shane to accuse him of hiring a hit man.

"Tell me why a magician would want to kill Shane Masters."

I sipped some more Diet Coke, then said, "And you'll tell me what?"

His face hardened. "How much trouble your grandfather is in, for one thing."

I could work with that for now. I didn't actually know the right questions to ask Vance anyway. Besides, he was asking for general information. "Shane is what is called a spoiler magician."

"Like that masked magician from a few years ago? The one who showed how illusions were done on TV?"

I nodded. "But Shane takes it one step further. He targets a magician who is gaining national fame and exposes much of his or her act. He shows how the illusions are done. Sales often fall off, and that magician loses the valuable momentum that was his one-time shot at making it big." I dug for more egg and avocado with my fork and thought about what I was telling Vance. Would he connect it back to Grandpa?

"So the magician he targets would be upset?"

I found some egg and looked up. "Yes, but most magicians hate what Shane does. Magic is a trade and an art. Magicians have kept the secrets of magic for centuries. To become really good, most magicians have to love the craft, to really have the passion to practice and learn and imagine. . . . It's incredible how hard the really good magicians work. And these guys, these spoilers, they are selling out in the biggest way."

Vance sat back in the booth. "You sound pissed, Shaw."

I nodded. "I've been around magic all my life. I know what it takes to be that good."

He regarded me for a few seconds, then asked, "Did you ever want to be that good?"

I dropped my gaze and shook my head. "No. Like I said, I know what it takes, and I don't have that passion for magic. Not like I do for romance novels, my dating service, my boys, and now doing some PI work." He knew I was going to train with Gabe. He didn't much like it because Vance thought of me as an amateur. Which I was. At least with Gabe, he had solid police training and experience.

Quietly, Vance said, "And Pulizzi?"

I looked up at him. "What?"

He met my gaze dead on. "The list of things you have passion for."

"That wasn't my point. I was talking about what it takes to be a damn good magician." His question made me mad. I'm not sure why. Maybe because I always got the feeling that Vance didn't believe Gabe and I had the real thing. And maybe that's just a tad too close to my own doubts.

He picked up the last of his sandwich. "So you're saying that any magician might hate Shane enough to try and kill him."

"Not Grandpa." I was still mad.

Vance pushed his plate away and picked up his iced tea. "And yet Barney is the one that Shane accused of hiring the hit man. So why do you think he did that?"

I knew exactly why he did that. But I wasn't going to share the reason with Vance. Shane was blackmailing Grandpa, and Vance might use that as another reason Grandpa would try to kill him. "Why don't you tell me how much trouble Grandpa is in. And what you need to clear him."

Vance flashed a small, dimpleless smile. "Okay, we have the e-mails that could look like threats and verification that he was getting his friends to send the same e-mails. Near as we can tell so far, none of those friends are magicians. Why is that, do you suppose?"

I stated the obvious reason. "If I were a magician, I would not want to call Shane's attention to myself."

Vance nodded. "Because then he might decide to do his reveal-all show on your act."

"You're a fast learner." And smart. Vance was being really smart. I didn't think he knew much about magic or magicians, so he decided to pick my brain to learn. He knew Grandpa wasn't cooperating with him, so I was the second-best thing. I started to ask him if he believed Grandpa had hired a hit man when I thought of an even better question. "Do you believe there was an actual hit man?" I was trying to learn to work with real facts.

He watched me for a minute. "The scene supports it. We found the gun with a silencer and some other things."

He had told me that already. And the dog bite. "What doesn't support a hit man?"

"A pro would have known about the dogs."

I pushed my salad plate away and considered that. "A professional hit man would have spied on Shane first?"

Vance nodded.

I was confused. "So did someone try to kill Shane Masters?" Shane seemed to think so.

"I'm just following the facts, Shaw. One of those dogs bit someone, that much was evident from the blood. And someone used some tools to get into the motor home."

Someone *had* tried to kill Shane. "So maybe the hit man wasn't a pro? Or for some reason, he was a pro but skipped his usual surveillance?"

Vance rubbed his eyes with his thumb and forefinger. "Look, here's the truth. People are stupid. They go to a bar and try to hire someone to kill for them. And the people they solicit are usually just as dumb, in which case they lie and brag and tell the idiot what hard-ass killers they are. Or they turn out to be cops setting up the idiots. Hit men do not advertise in the back of *Magicians Are Us Magazine*."

I had to smile at that. "I don't think that's a real magazine."

"That's what I like about you, Shaw. You're quick."

I began to see his problem. "This hit man could be any yokel from anyplace."

"And if he actually grew a brain, he's gone."

I could see that Vance was frustrated. He was getting political pressure about a crime that didn't make sense. And Grandpa and I had Shane breathing down our necks to solve the same crime. What did I tell Vance? I needed to talk to Gabe and see what he thought. I wanted to help Vance, and he might be able to help us, but I needed some guidance.

I needed Gabe.

Exactly as he had said I would. And he had told me that he already had a full plate. I looked up at Vance. "You don't really think that Grandpa hired the hit man, do you?"

Once more, he assumed the blank-with-a-hard-edge cop expression. "He needs to cooperate and tell me where he was Monday night."

Silently, I agreed. "I'm sure he will."

Vance kept the hard expression. "There's a stronger connection between Shane and your grandfather than either of them are admitting. If I were you, I'd keep that in mind."

"A warning?" I wasn't sure.

"I've done murder investigations for a while. Most people can be driven to murder, Shaw."

I dug in my purse for my wallet. I was going to throw

money on the table and leave. "Grandpa did not hire a hit man."

Vance leaned across the table and grabbed my wrist. "Did you go see Shane Masters?"

His grip was firm, not painful. He dropped his gaze to the back of my hand. "Tell me how you got this."

I stared at Vance's fingers around my wrist. "It's a scratch." Something changed between us. Even after knowing Vance more than a year, I was still surprised at the sudden chemical reaction between us.

He lifted his gaze to mine. "Did you go see Shane Masters?"

I stared back at him.

The gold points in Vance's eyes gleamed. "Of course you did. You love your grandfather and you are too impulsive. Shane Masters is dangerous. He has a record. Don't go near him again."

I didn't know what to say. It was true that I loved Grandpa and I have been accused of being impulsive, although this time it had been hearing that Grandpa was going to see Shane that got me there. But I would have gotten around to it eventually. I also saw that Vance had done some research on Shane, including that he had a record. I asked him, "Are you giving me a warning as a friend?"

His face shifted in more frustration. "Hell no. You and I can't be friends."

Well that was insulting. "Why not?"

His gaze dropped from my eyes to my mouth. Then to my breasts in my red top. And finally, he looked at my face again. "The sexual attraction between us is too strong."

Ignoring his grip on my wrist, I leaned forward and said, "It is not."

He grinned. "Then why did you lean forward instead of backward? Body language, Shaw. It tells me exactly what I want to know." He slid out of the booth, stood up, and took out his wallet.

I glared up at him. "And that is?"

He pulled out a twenty and a five, dropped them on the table, then leaned down close to me. "Multiple orgasms." He stood up and added, "I'll be in touch."

6

I didn't have time to go by the office, so I called Gabe while on my way to pick up Joel from school.

"Sam, where are you?" He sounded a little concerned.

"I'm in my car on my way to pick up Joel." I turned left on Railroad Canyon and then stopped for the red light at Mission Trail. "I found out a couple things, but I don't want you to be mad."

"So I'm going to be mad?"

Probably. "Rosy called and told me Grandpa was going to see Shane."

Gabe asked softly, "Your errand?"

I knew that soft voice. I was in trouble. "Yes. I didn't want him to confront Shane alone." I hurried on. "And we found out that Vance was holding out. The hit man specifically mentioned that a magician sent him when the dogs attacked him."

"Sam—"

He was pissed. "This might be easier if I just tell you everything at once, and then you yell at me."

"Fine."

That single clipped word didn't make me feel any better. But I needed Gabe's advice. The light turned green, and I made a right onto Mission Trail and summed up my meeting with Shane and with Vance. By the time I was finished explaining, I had woven through Main Street and was passing the lake on Lake Street.

There was silence on the phone.

"Gabe?"

"Are you finished?"

My stomach cramped. "Yes."

"You took a damned stupid risk."

I tried not to wince.

"I'm tied up at the moment with stuff here at the office. Once I get a chance, I'll run a check on Shane when I do the background on the women you signed up today. And I'll call my sources to see if I can add anything to what you got from Vance." He stopped talking.

That was it? "Aren't you going to yell at me?"

"No time."

I passed the Stater Bros on my right and said, "Look, I know you said I couldn't do this without your help and that you were busy, but I'm worried about Grandpa and Nikki, Rosy's granddaughter. I have to do something. And I couldn't let Grandpa confront Shane alone."

"You could have told me you were going there."

"But you had just told me you didn't have time to help me. He's my grandfather." Anger bubbled under my breastbone. I was caught in the middle. And now that I had met Shane, I was even more worried. "Grandpa went home to start trying to figure out who sent the hit man. He is devastated that someone in his group could have done that."

Gabe's voice softened. "I know. But you don't have the training to leap into situations."

"Gabe, I'm always going to leap. It's who I am." He once told me to take the leap and he'd be there to catch me.

Was he feeling the burden of that now? The idea of moving our businesses side by side and my training for my PI license had seemed romantic, but was the reality something different?

"I need to go, Sam. I'll call you when I have the information for you."

"Gabe." What did I say?

"What?"

Or maybe I was jumping to conclusions and Gabe was just tired. "Come to dinner tonight. You and Cal. You're both going to be tired; at least come over and have dinner. Bo makes a great jambalaya." It was the best I could do for now.

"All right. Later." He hung up.

"So when are you going to tell us your news?" Joel asked for the fifteenth time. He'd been following Bo around ever since I picked him up from school. When we got home, Bo had been cooking in the kitchen and singing in his rich voice. Grandpa was unusually quiet as he worked on his computer.

Bo stuck the pan of bread in the broiler and laughed. "Not yet."

Joel took the huge bowl of salad that Bo handed him and set it on the table. "Did you bring your capes with you?"

"Sorry, dude. I don't usually cook in my capes." He winked at me as I sat out bowls and plates. "Cooking is a different kind of magic."

TJ finished setting up the six-foot folding table end to end with the picnic table on the patio. He came in the opened sliding glass door and stepped over Ali, who was sleeping. "How come you like cooking?"

I looked at TJ in surprise. Joel was everyone's instant

friend. And since Bo was a magician, that made them best buddies. But TJ, he was more suspicious and standoffish. They both had met Bo, but it had been a couple years since they had seen him.

Bo glanced over at him. He seemed to judge TJ for a second, then said, "Life on the road is full of motels and no kitchens. I'm at the mercy of fast food and greasy diners. When I'm not on the road, I enjoy the process of cooking. It sort of makes me feel like home, I guess."

I smiled at Bo. He's been teasing with Joel, but he got that TJ asked a serious question. I think Bo understood TJ was trying to get his measure and figure out if he should trust him.

TJ looked at me, then flashed a grin. "Mom tries to get out of cooking."

I made a face and tossed a tablecloth at him. "Put that on the table, smart guy."

TJ caught it and headed toward the slider, then he stopped. "Mom, how come Ali's sleeping?

I looked over and frowned. "She's pouting. Bo doesn't love her."

"Typical female," Bo said unapologetically. "I'll probably have to buy her flowers."

"Try beer," Joel suggested.

Bo set down his glass of iced tea. "No foolin'?"

"She's a lush," Joel said. "But she's the best dog in the world."

Bo shrugged. "Okay, I'll take your word for it."

"Mom, when is Gabe getting here?" Joel asked. "What's his brother like?"

"He's like Gabe, I guess. He's a fireman." On a time-out, whatever that meant.

TJ walked in from the patio. "So if Grandpa and Fletch start something on fire, he can save us?"

I mock groaned. "Fletch is coming? Where are the fire extinguishers?"

That finally got Grandpa's attention. He got up from the computer and said, "Sammy, it's all an act with Fletch. You should remember that."

I instantly felt bad. Grandpa had come face to face with what he believed was his failure in Shane today. I had to lay off teasing Fletch. "I know, Grandpa. I've seen his shows. I know how talented Fletch is."

"He has big news too!" Joel said, turning back to Bo. "Fletch is performing at the House of Cards. We all have tickets."

Bo nodded. "That is very big news." He went to the oven to get the bread out. "I love the part of his act where he keeps vanishing all his assistants by accident. It cracks me up every time."

I went to help Bo put the bread in a towel-covered basket. "He does have the comic flair," I said.

Ali barked and got up from her place by the sliding glass window and ran joyfully to the front door.

"Gabe's here!" Joel announced, and raced to the door.

Bo looked at me. "How does he know who is at the door?"

I wiped my hands on a towel. "Ali. She knows Gabe's truck, and that's her Gabe-bark."

Bo made an impressed face. "Animals aren't my thing, but that's cool."

"Finally met a female you didn't want to charm? Who knew?" I grinned, then added, "I'll be right back." I turned and headed to the front door, then laughed at the scene. "Joel, you and Ali need to let Gabe and Cal in." Ali had jumped up to put her front paws on Gabe's shoulders to greet him while Gabe held a bakery box out of her reach. In the meantime, Joel was talking a mile a minute to Cal, who had a grocery bag in his hand. They were still on the porch. Cal looked relaxed and appeared to be answering Joel. I hurried over and put my hand on Joel's shoulder. A small part of my heart worried that Joel had been scarred by his rotten dad and was therefore desperate for male attention. But most of my heart knew that was just Joel. He was outgoing and thought every minute was a new adventure.

Joel was still talking. ". . . so Ali is special because she was trained as a police dog."

Cal turned and looked at Gabe scratching Ali's ears. "I can see that. She looks like she's very smart."

I used my hand on Joel's shoulder to guide him back from the door. "Hi Cal, come on in. We're just about ready to eat. Cal looked freshly showered and had on clean jeans and a button-down shirt. His lip had scabbed again. I hoped he could eat the jambalaya. He stepped in, then leaned down and kissed me on the cheek.

"Thanks for inviting me. I'm starved." He held up the bag and added, "I brought wine. I'll find the kitchen." He headed off in the right direction.

I turned back to look at Gabe. Ali had gotten down and trotted over to follow Cal into the kitchen. Gabe came in and closed the door. He had on a green shirt and black jeans. "Are you hungry?" I asked him.

He did his wicked grin. "Oh yeah."

My stomach somersaulted. It was official, I was a hussy. "Good. Bo cooked a lot of jambalaya."

He laughed, then reached out to wrap an arm around my waist and pull me to him. To his mouth. Then he looked at me. "That'll hold me until later."

"Right. Later." God he was hot.

"I started some searches and should have the information by tonight. After everyone leaves, I'll get my laptop and we'll see what we got. Cal drove his truck so he can get home on his own."

I nodded. Work. Could we work in my room naked? I glanced at my sons chatting with Cal as they walked with him into the kitchen and had a moment of shameful regret. The boys needed a mom not a sex addict.

"We're ready!" Bo announced.

I was ready. But Bo meant dinner, not sizzling sex with Gabe. I turned out of Gabe's arm and headed to the kitchen. The food was all laid out on the table so we could fix our plates and take them to the backyard. I looked at TJ and Joel. "Don't feed Ali any of this stuff. It's not good for her."

They both rolled their eyes.

"We know, Mom," TJ said in teenage exasperation.

Bo looked up from where he was serving bowls of jambalaya. "Feed my masterpiece to a dog?"

I laughed at the outraged look on his face. "Go eat, Bo. I'll finish dishing this up." I elbowed him out of the way.

"Come on, TJ and Joel. You can taste my food and tell me how gifted I am. Then I'll do some magic for you."

"Awesome!" Joel took his plate and bowl, then bounced alongside Bo. "I can do the cups and balls trick. I'm pretty good. Grandpa says so. . . ." His voice faded.

I looked up at Grandpa. "He loves magic."

He nodded. "He's got passion for it. But he loves a lot of stuff, Sammy."

Warmth and love for this man washed up the back of my throat. I knew he wanted Joel to love magic like he did, but more than that, he wanted Joel to be Joel. "Either way, he's lucky to have you." I handed him his bowl of jambalaya. "Now go watch and make sure he doesn't keep Bo from eating." I grinned at him just as the front door flew open.

Fletch limped into the house, stopping to pet Ali. "You would not believe my day!"

I stared at him. Now he looked like Tobey Maguire after he'd been run over by a weed whacker. His brown hair sprung up here and there, his shirt was untucked, and his right pant leg was torn. "Fletch." I moved out from the back of the table toward him. "What happened to you?"

He stopped petting Ali and looked up at me with a slightly off-center grin. "I was looking at a dirt bike I wanted to rent. Somehow it fell and hit my leg.

"Ouch," I winced. That had to hurt.

Fletch looked around the house, then back to me. "I didn't exactly notice how much it hurt right then 'cause I fell backward."

"Oh. Did you hit anything?" I forced real concern in my voice to cover up my first thought, which was that I had finally found a bigger klutz than me.

"A row of those little dirt bikes. They went down like dominoes with me on the very top."

I heard two male snorts and turned around.

Gabe and Cal stood there, both with straight faces. "Stop that," I hissed. Their innocent faces didn't fool me.

Gabe moved past me and stuck his hand out. "I'm Gabe, and this is my brother, Cal."

Fletch shook their hands. "Hi, I'm Fletch. So you are Sam's boyfriend. I've heard a lot about you."

Grandpa called out from the table. "Fletch, come on in and get some dinner. Bo cooked."

I looked over my shoulder at him. "Grandpa, can you serve Fletch dinner and I'll get some ice for his leg?" I turned and headed around the corner of the kitchen and went to the freezer. I was grateful now that Grandpa had stayed home to do his Internet sleuthing and hadn't gone with Fletch to the motorcycle shop. No telling what trouble the two of them would have gotten into. I filled a zip-lock bag with ice, then realized that Grandpa had served Fletch and taken him outside. That left Gabe and Cal to help themselves. They stood at the table with their backs to me, arguing.

"Damn it, Cal," Gabe said in a low voice, "let me contact a couple of my buddies from the department—"

"No." Cal threw a piece of bread on his plate, and then fixed a rock-hard glare on Gabe. "Stay out of it." He turned and went out the sliding glass door.

I saw Gabe's shoulders tighten and rise. Still holding the ice, I moved up next to him. "Anything I can do?"

He looked down at me and forced the corners of his mouth upward. "Not unless you want to hit him again." He left too.

I stood there alone in the house with the rich, spicy smells and a simmering anger. After setting the bag of ice down on the table, I poured myself a glass of wine and drank half of it.

I did not like being cut out of Gabe's life.

I set the glass down, made a plate of food, and retrieved my glass and the ice bag. I started toward the door, then went back into the kitchen and snagged the wine bottle, managing to tuck it safely beneath my arm while juggling everything else.

If I didn't drink it, it would come in handy to hit the next male that kept a secret from me.

As soon as I sat down across from Grandpa and next to Gabe, I handed Fletch the ice bag. Once I was settled, Bo lifted his wine glass. "I'd like to make a toast."

"Can we have wine so we can make the toast?" Joel asked.

I looked past Gabe to Joel. "No."

"Bummer." Joel lifted his glass of soda.

Bo winked at TJ and Joel, then said, "To Fletch Knight and his well-deserved invitation to perform at the House of Cards."

Everyone cheered and drank. Ali thought all the noise was an invitation to play and ran around the two tables barking.

Joel slipped Ali a crust of bread, then tried to keep me from noticing by saying, "Hey, Bo, when you do close-up magic, do you have to special order your stuff like the fake fingers to match your skin color?"

I choked on my wine.

Bo looked up and covered an amused expression. "Pass me the saltshaker."

I set my wine down and watched him. He took the salt-shaker and unscrewed the lid. Then he folded one hand to create a hole at the top of his thumb and fingers. He lifted the salt and poured into the hole. He looked around the table, then tapped down the salt and opened his hands.

The salt was gone.

"Cool!" Joel said. "Bring it back."

Bo entertained all of us by dramatically making the salt reappear. Joel ran in the house to get his prop and did the same trick. Then he and Bo huddled and decided that there was very little difference in the color of their props.

Basically, Bo was very light skinned, and when he performed a salt trick, people were trying to find where the salt went to and didn't notice something like the end of his thumb being a little lighter or darker. Bo went on to explain that his goal was to keep the audience focused on the part of the illusion he wanted them to see.

Fletch said, "Hey TJ, why don't you show us your skill at counting cards."

Fletch was on the end of the table with his right leg propped up on a chair and the bag of ice on his calf. The lump was already turning vivid colors. I was really impressed that he thought to bring TJ into the conversation. That was nice of him.

TJ shook his head. "Nah. That's not magic."

Bo said, "You can count cards?"

TJ shrugged.

I knew he was pleased though, because I saw him glance up at Grandpa. And Grandpa smiled back.

"He's got a huge math brain," Joel said, and looked at his brother. "Want me to get some cards?"

"Later," TJ said. Then he looked at Bo. "What is your good news?"

That was TJ. He was happy just to have a little attention, but then he was even happier to turn the attention off himself.

Bo glanced at me. I guessed that he was asking if he should let it drop about TJ counting cards. I nodded at him to go ahead with his news. He slipped his fake thumb into his pants pocket, took a sip of his wine, and announced in his deep velvety voice, "I'll be signing a contract for a cartoon character based on my magic show. It'll be called Magic Bo."

"Wow!" I was impressed. "Bo, that is fantastic!"

Everyone else joined in.

Bo's face flooded with pleasure. "I don't have all the details yet, but it's been pretty exciting."

Grandpa raised his wineglass. "To Bo. You made it just like your dad and I knew you would!"

We all drank to Bo. I thought about how good it was for Grandpa to have both Bo and Fletch here, two of his success stories to offset his guilt and anger over Shane.

"Oh crap."

I heard the shatter of glass and looked over at Fletch.

"Sorry." He looked up and blushed. "My ice bag was

falling. I grabbed for it and dropped the wineglass." He took his leg off the chair. "Don't get up. I'll take care of it."

I stood. "No, sit down. I'll get it. You just keep the ice on your leg." I went into the kitchen and pulled a long length of paper towels off the roll, then got out the trash can. I went out and wiped up the broken glass and little bit of wine that had been left in the glass.

"I'm really sorry, Sam." Fletch watched me, looking dejected and miserable.

He probably thought he ruined Bo's big moment. "It's not a big deal, Fletch. Do you want some more wine?"

He relaxed. "Maybe coffee would be better."

I laughed. "I'll make some and serve the dessert that Gabe brought."

Gabe got up. "I'll help you." He followed me into the kitchen.

I put the trash can away and washed my hands. Gabe got started on brewing the coffee. He was silent and seemed tired. I'm sure tearing down a wall and fighting with his brother wore him out.

I glanced out the window over the sink, then I said quietly, "You don't have to stay to help me with the investigation tonight. Maybe you and Cal should talk."

He poured in the water, set the carafe under the drip, then turned on the machine. Then he settled his dark gaze on me. "You already have all the help you need, is that it?"

I had the feeling he was looking for a fight. "No." I took a deep breath and tried to keep my temper under control. "I thought that maybe you were tired and maybe you needed to work something out with your brother." What *help* was he talking about? "So far, no one has been any help, and no one knows what the hell Shane Masters is up to."

Fletch limped into the kitchen. "Sam, Barney and I are looking into Shane. Don't worry, it'll be okay."

I looked at Fletch as he carried the dripping ice bag. He walked around Gabe and came to where I stood to dump the melting ice in the sink. "Grandpa told you?"

He looked up. "Yes. After you left this morning, he told me about Shane's accusation. Then I came by this afternoon to see if he wanted to go look at dirt bikes, and he told me you two went to see Shane. Barney needs my help. The two of us will find out what's going on." Fletch drew his eyebrows together. "Don't look so upset. Barney is worried because Shane threatened you. Shane doesn't even know I'm in town. He probably doesn't even know I exist. I'll help Barney."

The sausage in the jambalaya burned in my stomach. Grandpa hadn't told me anything until he'd had to. He still hadn't told me about mentoring Shane, though he must realize that Rosy told me. But he told Fletch about Shane. What else did Grandpa tell him and not me? "Did he tell you where he was last night?" He'd told me he went to see a friend. I hadn't had the chance to press him for more information yet. I knew he hadn't gone to see Shane, but who had he gone to see?

Fletch shook his head. "I didn't ask him. Do you want me to?"

The anger washed the taste of acid up the back of my throat. I went to the pantry and pulled out a stack of paper plates, some napkins, and a box of plastic forks. I set them on the counter and glanced at Fletch. "Sure, if you think of it, ask him."

"Umm." Fletch glanced at me, then Gabe who stood silently by the coffeemaker, then added, "Okay, but is something wrong, Sam?"

I lifted the lid of the dessert Gabe had brought.

Chocolate cake.

And I didn't want it due to the lump of misery in my stomach. "Everything is fine." I got a cake knife out of the drawer and started slicing the dessert. I handed Fletch a couple plates of cake. "Go take this outside."

After he left, Gabe moved up beside me. "You didn't tell me Shane threatened you."

I stopped cutting and looked up. "It was implied, and that was the reason Grandpa had been trying to keep me out of this thing with Shane. You and I haven't had time to sit down and go over this."

"You found time to have lunch with Vance."

He was mad about that. Vance and Gabe worked together sometimes, but they didn't like each other. "He called me. He wanted information about magicians and spoilers."

"Right. He needed an ex–soccer mom's expertise."

God he was edgy tonight. And I was getting tired of defending myself. I turned back to the cake and cut a few more slices, slapped them on some plates, and picked them up. "At least he needed me." I turned and went outside.

7

After dessert, Joel had impressed everyone with his cups and balls trick. At Grandpa's urging, TJ had shown everyone his amazing ability to count cards. Bo dealt out half the deck, and TJ told him exactly how many aces and nines were in the remaining half. TJ may not have passion for magic, but he had his own talents.

Finally, Bo and Fletch both left. Grandpa and I walked them out, then came back into the kitchen, where Gabe was helping the boys finished up the dishes. Cal was eating more cake. His cut lip didn't appear to slow him down a bit.

"I'll finish up," I told TJ and Joel. "You can go watch TV or whatever."

"I have homework," TJ said.

I looked at Joel.

"Man . . ." He stomped off after his brother into their bedroom to do their homework.

"Great kids, Sam," Cal said as he tossed his empty paper plate in the trash.

I started to thank him, but a cell phone made all four of us stop and look around.

"It's mine," Cal said, and pulled his phone out of his pocket. He looked at the display window, frowned, and answered, "Hello."

"Gabe, would you mind taking this trash out?" I pulled the plastic bag out and tied it with a twisty. "Gabe?" I looked up.

He was watching Cal.

"Are you sure? Did you look out the window?" Cal said, his face drawn into a hard scowl.

Grandpa said, "I'll get the trash, Sam. Then I'm going to bed." He took the bag from my hand and headed out back.

Cal said, "Hang up and call the police." He closed his phone and looked at us. "I have to take off. Thanks for dinner, Sam." He turned and headed for the front door at a fast pace.

"Fuck," Gabe snarled and went after him.

I stood there with the box of trash bags in my hand for a couple seconds, then I tossed the box on the counter and ran after them.

Gabe left the front door open. I couldn't see them in the dark, but I could hear them.

"There's a restraining order on you! You can't go to Melanie's if he's there! Don't be stupid!"

"Get out of my way, Gabe," Cal answered in a deadly soft voice.

I ran down the porch steps.

Gabe dropped his voice. "You're throwing your life away for her."

I went up to where Gabe and Cal stood at the front left headlight of Cal's red truck. Gabe must have gotten in front of Cal to block him. They glared at each other, and neither one looked reasonable. "Gabe, Cal, what's going on?" I touched Gabe's arm.

"I'm just leaving," Cal said. He stormed around us, yanked open his truck door, and got in. The truck engine roared to life, then he backed up and took off.

Gabe headed for his truck.

I had had it. "Gabe!"

"I'll call you." He kept going.

I chased after him and grabbed his arm. "Stop it and tell me what is going on."

He halted and looked down. "Cal is on forced leave of absence from the fire department while being investigated for attacking another fireman. He could be terminated, and he won't let me help him save his job."

I took that in. I'd only met Cal today, but he didn't strike me as a hothead. If he'd been a hothead, he'd have gotten up off the floor after I smacked him with the picture frame and come after me. I gently squeezed the rock that passed for Gabe's forearm and asked, "So what happened?"

"Cal was on a 911 call. When he arrived he found a woman he used to know, Melanie. She had been badly beaten up by her husband." He took a breath and added, "Melanie is an ex-girlfriend of Cal's. She had wanted to get married, he hesitated and she left him. She married Dirk. Cal always regretted losing her, even though she's the one that broke his heart. She's the one that—"

"Gabe?"

He was furious. I could see it in the bulge of his jaw even in the dark. He blamed Melanie for hurting his brother.

"Cal's a damned idiot." Gabe shifted his weight and looked in the direction that Cal had driven off. "That night after he got off work, he went to the hospital to see Melanie. She told him where Dirk hung out. Instead of passing the info on to the police who were looking for him, Cal tracked

Dirk down, then broke his jaw and cracked a rib. Now he could be arrested for assault and lose his job."

"And how does that relate to his job?"

"Dirk claims that Cal went into the bar and attacked him without provocation, that he has anger management issues and that he's been stalking Melanie and Dirk. Cal was put on leave while the department conducts an investigation. In the meantime, he won't let me investigate and build a defense for him to save his job. His whole fucking career."

I studied Gabe in the faint light from the house. I saw that he was angry and upset, but I said gently, "Maybe his job isn't as important as Melanie. Maybe he needs your understanding and support."

Gabe shifted his weight, then stared down at me. "So I should just let my brother lose his job and possibly go to jail? That's your idea of family support?" He turned, stalked to the truck, and yanked open the door. "You don't have brothers and sisters, Sam. In my family, we stand up to each other when one of us is screwing up." He got in the truck and roared off.

That felt like a slap that cut right through to my inadequacies. My biological father cut out long before I was born, my mother went through men like most women go through purses, and my own marriage was a failure. But all this time, I thought Gabe believed in me anyway.

My alarm went off and yanked me out of my three hours of sleep. I slammed the off button and blamed Gabe Pulizzi. That got my blood going enough to drag myself through a shower and dress in a black skirt and sleeveless turquoise sweater. I added my strappy turquoise shoes and followed the scent of coffee to the kitchen.

I went directly to the coffeepot and poured out a steaming cup. Then I turned, expecting to see Grandpa.

Gabe sat at the table watching me while petting Ali.

I glared at my dog. "Some guard dog you are."

She ignored me and let Gabe scratch her ears.

"Where's Grandpa?" He was always up before the boys and me. I went to the table and sat down.

"Barney had some work to do in his bedroom."

I rolled my eyes. "He always takes your side."

Gabe grinned.

Damn. He wore a green tank top that left his arms and most of his shoulders bare. I could smell the scent of his soap. "So I assume Cal is not in jail?"

He shook his head. "A friend of Cal's called him and told him that Melanie was fine. He turned around and went back to my house."

I narrowed my eyes at Gabe. Sure it was early and my brain was only half-awake, but I was pretty sure that hadn't been a coincidence. "How did his friend get that information?"

"A cop friend of mine passed it on. Melanie called the police, and they went out to check her house and see if Dirk violated the restraining order. He had left by then."

"Ah. You were a busy ex-cop last night, I see." Gabe had lots of friends in the Los Angeles Police Department. I could easily see how he got the information, then engineered getting it passed on to a friend of Cal's—probably all from his cell phone. I moved on. "So Melanie has a restraining order against her husband, Dirk?"

Gabe nodded.

"And Dirk has a restraining order against Cal?" It was like a soap opera.

Another nod.

"Any chance Dirk will not press charges against Cal?"

Gabe's eyes darkened to nearly black-colored determination. "Possibly, if he has the right motivation."

I didn't like the sound of that. "Gabe, what are you up to?"

"Solving problems. Cal's running off to Melanie's was a problem and I solved it."

I remembered what he'd said to me last night about not understanding family. "Fine, do it your way. Why are you here?"

"To give you the information we didn't get to last night."

Wasn't that nice of him? "Great." I got up and went to Grandpa's desk right behind where Gabe sat. I got out a yellow tablet, then turned.

Gabe reached for me, catching me around my waist and pulling me down on his lap. "Nice outfit. I like the shoes."

I blinked in surprise. "Uh, thanks."

"Sam, I know you're mad. I had to leave. He's my brother."

"I know." God knows I put my two sons before Gabe. And he knew it. I wasn't upset about that. But we had bigger problems than the fact that I wasn't living up to Gabe's standards in understanding families. "I'm worried about Grandpa, and I need to find out what I can about Shane. I would like to help Nikki by figuring out whose show Shane is spoiling." I stood up.

Gabe let me go, watching with his dark eyes. "Shane is a street thug. Like Vance told you, he has a record for assault. It was a little harder for me to find out about it because Shane was a juvenile at the time. I had to go to a few more sources until I talked to a friend of my mom's who is a retired parole officer. She remembers Shane. Two arrests, no jail time. But she said he had a mean streak."

I sat down in my chair. Gabe had done some extensive work on this for me. "Oh." I started making a few notes.

"Shane has never been married, no apparent kids. He does a few major spoiler shows a year now and is commanding huge audiences and TV spots. He's been interviewed on most of the TV magazine shows but gives little away about his personal life. He has an excellent security team to protect his shows and his property, but I can't find any evidence of personal security."

I was fascinated. Gabe had done a thorough background. "Like a bodyguard?"

He got up and refilled his coffee cup. "Right. So what we have here is a man who thinks he can take care of himself."

I shook my head as Gabe came back and sat down. "It's his two dogs. He loves those dogs, and they are scary. They are all the security he needs." I sipped some coffee and added, "They ran off the hit man."

Gabe nodded. "Good point. And according to my police source, it's like Vance told you, the hit man doesn't look like a pro. A pro would have done research and learned about the dogs."

"So what do you think happened?"

Gabe sighed. "I think a dumb-ass magician hired some two-bit thug off the street. That guy read a book, or an article off the Internet, and thought he could make a quick ten grand." He made a face. "For some reason, it's always ten thousand. It's like they hear that number on a TV show and assume that's the going rate for a kill."

I stared at Gabe. He was tired—I could see it in the slight hunch to his wide shoulders and the fatigue around his eyes. But he was also street smart. It was the kind of street knowledge that experience bred into a person at a young age. It's not something that could be learned later in life. "What is the going rate for a hit like that?"

He glanced at me with a small smile. "There's not exactly a union wage, Sam."

I couldn't help it; I laughed. "But where does that leave us?"

"I already talked to Barney. I told him that if he suspects anyone, we can try to get a look at their financials to see if there are some big, unexplained withdrawals from their checking or savings accounts, or an advance on their credit cards, that kind of thing. But the smarter thing to do is to give Vance the info and let him do it."

I liked that idea. I didn't want Grandpa involved in this. "Did Grandpa listen?"

"Barney always listens. Then he does what he wants to anyway."

"True." So I was back to worrying about him. And Nikki. "Did you find anything about Shane's show this Saturday?"

He shook his head. "No."

"All right. Well, thanks. What are you going to do today?"

He leaned forward. "I'd like to spend the day helping you. But I have to run down some other stuff I'm working on. And I need to get to the office. Cal is already there with Blaine and the other men Blaine has helping. The wall is down, and we're doing clean up and patching the adjacent walls for painting tomorrow. The electrician will be in soon. I might need to run to LA—" His face tightened, and he took a drink of coffee.

"For Cal?" Was I ever going to learn? He wanted me to stay out of it.

Gabe thumped his mug down on the glass-topped table. "He doesn't seem to care if he loses his job."

I watched Gabe. "Maybe he doesn't care."

He shook his head. "Sam, all Cal ever wanted to be was

a fireman. He worked his ass off, and he's moved up the ranks. He loves his job."

Their dad had been a fireman and he'd been killed when Gabe and his siblings were young. I wasn't exactly clear on the details of it, but something like that left a mark on kids, the kind of mark that might make Cal want to be a fireman just like the dad that he lost. And Gabe—he became a cop. I knew it had to do with the hero streak that ran deep inside of Gabe—a hero streak that I suspected woke up the day his father was murdered. Back to the subject, I said softly, "Maybe you should tell Melanie that about Cal." If she cared for Cal, she wouldn't want Cal to throw his career away.

"Cal doesn't want me talking to her. She wouldn't take my calls anyway."

I stared down into my coffee and said, "Maybe she'd talk to me."

Gabe shoved his chair back and lunged to his feet. "Are you out of your mind? You aren't going anywhere near her. Do not get involved in this, Sam."

I looked up at him and struggled not to let the hurt show on my face. "Whatever you want. I have my own work to do. I'll see you later at the office." I stood up.

Gabe closed the distance between us. "I don't want you going near Melanie, because it's possible that her husband will show up. Then you'd be in danger. A man who knocks around a woman he supposedly loves isn't going to think twice about going through you to get to her."

That was a little better than banishing me from his family problems because he thought I didn't understand. "Okay."

He leaned down and kissed me. "Sam, we need to get away. Just the two of us. We've never done that."

He looked like he needed it. "Gabe, the boys . . . I can't leave them." I was not going to be the kind of mom who ran off for weekends with my boyfriends. When the boys were grown, that would be different. But they had already lost their dad, and I meant to be there for them.

He didn't miss a beat, just pressed his forehead against mine and said, "Okay, just the four of us." He took a breath then added, "But you're sleeping with me."

"But—"

He kissed me and I shut up.

We heard Grandpa coming down the hallway and broke apart. I realized Gabe was right. We were dealing with all the details of life, but we hadn't had any time together to relax.

"I've got to go." He looked down at me. "There's not much you can do at the office today. Just stop by and see how it's looking when you get time."

"I'm going to go through my phone tree and see if I can find someone who might have a clue about Shane's upcoming show."

Gabe shrugged. "Can't hurt. Just be careful." He kissed me, then turned and left.

I sat back down at the table, and Grandpa joined me with a steaming cup of coffee for himself. We had about fifteen minutes before the boys exploded out of their rooms. "Was Gabe here when you got up?" I asked Grandpa as he sat down.

He shook his head. "Showed up just when I was making coffee." He winked at me. "Guess he was too late to sneak into your room before I saw him."

I tried not to blush. He was my grandfather! I figured since Grandpa's bedroom faced the front of the house, he'd probably heard our discussion last night. I changed the subject. "Grandpa, why didn't you just tell me about Shane?"

He reached out and took hold of my hand. "I knew

Shane would use you or the boys to get to me. That's the reason I didn't tell you about him, Sam. And my pride. Shane was a huge mistake that I regret." He sighed, his gaze shifting from mine to look out the sliding glass door. "Your grandmother said I was trying to mentor young people because I thought I failed your mom. She was probably right. Beth was usually right."

I was stunned. "Grandpa, you didn't fail Mom."

He looked back to me. "I did, Sammy. She left Elsinore and wanted nothing to do with us. When she came back, she was different, bitter, and she refused to talk about your father. She was four months pregnant. I was furious. I can't explain the fury of knowing my daughter was hurting and I couldn't fix it. She wouldn't let me fix it."

"Like Gabe won't let me help him fix his problems," I said, thinking that I could talk to Melanie and see where she stood on the mess. But then I shook that off. "But Mom doesn't think you failed her."

He looked at me sadly. "Your mom thinks I should have given up magic and gotten a real job. A nine-to-five job where I wore a suit and had a title."

"But you're a magician!" I knew my mother. Grandpa was right in a way, but I could never understand it. I had the coolest grandpa ever while growing up. It made up for not having a dad.

"It wasn't easy for your mom. We struggled more when she was little, Sam. And your grandma, she was the best assistant ever, but she gave it up to raise your mom. Katy knows that and somehow felt that it was unfair, that I got my cake and ate it too while her mom sacrificed."

I had seen pictures of my grandma on stage, but it didn't really seem like the cookie-making woman I remember. Grandma was the woman who introduced me to romance novels. We could talk for hours about books, characters, authors . . . but it had never once occurred to me that she had regrets. "Did Grandma regret giving up magic?"

Grandpa nodded. "She did sometimes. And there were times when your mom was young that we fought about it. It was right when your mom started school. Before that, it was simple to take her on the road with us, and Beth got to do some work. But once your mom started school, all that stopped. It was an adjustment for all of us."

"I never knew." I thought of my mom realizing that her mom had given up a dream for her and maybe was a little unhappy for it. It made her quest to find a successful man for herself while I was growing up understandable. Since my husband had a nine-to-five job and wore a suit, in my mom's eyes, that meant security for me.

Gabe, with his unconventional job and slightly dangerous aura, meant heartache.

"How had I been so oblivious?"

Grandpa looked back at me and smiled. "Because Beth and I had worked all that out years ago, Sammy. You saw us in a different phase of our lives. But what I'm telling you is that every relationship goes through adjustment periods. Like you and Gabe right now. And maybe Gabe and his brother."

I squeezed his hand. He was giving me hope, making me believe that Gabe and I could hang in there and work it out. "Thanks, Grandpa. In the meantime, you and I need to talk. Fletch said he's helping you look for the magician who hired the hit man. Do you think that's a good idea?"

Grandpa let go of my hand and sipped his coffee. "Afraid he might blow up the Internet?"

I grinned in spite of myself. "Is that possible? I would have thought you'd tell Bo rather than Fletch."

Grandpa shook his head and grinned. "I think the

Internet is safe, Sam." Then he sobered. "I didn't want to tell Bo. He has a bit of a temper, and I don't want him doing something impulsive. And he's just gotten his big break; he's here to celebrate, not worry about a spoiler magician."

I studied Grandpa for a minute, then smiled. "You fraud. The difference between Fletch and Bo is that you can control Fletch. Bo's a lot more opinionated and stubborn. Fletch wants to please you like an overgrown puppy. He'll let you do dangerous things instead of protecting you the way Bo would."

Grandpa lifted his chin and looked down his nose at me. "Hmph. Bo gets it into his fool head that I'm an old man. Fletch knows better."

"Bo does not think you're an old man." If I laughed, Grandpa might smack me. He was an old man, but he was as sharp and crafty as any thirty-year-old. Bo did not think he was feeble. Bo was just a protective man by nature. "I don't think Bo came to Elsinore to tell an old man his good news."

"Bah." He waved his hand in the air, dismissing the subject. "Fletch is helping me put together a list of magicians whose shows Shane has exposed. We're starting there. And we've been asking around a little to see if any magician has a particular grudge against Shane."

My stomach clenched. "What if the magician finds out you are doing this? I know Gabe said you can look for large withdrawals, but I don't want you taking risks and getting caught by the killer." If a magician was desperate enough to hire a hit man to kill Shane, wouldn't he consider Grandpa nosing around a threat? If Grandpa broke into a magician's financial records, could the magician find out?

He shook his head. "Sammy, I'm being careful and so is

Fletch. Stop fretting. I'm not going to break into any financial records unless I need to."

I didn't like that. "What are you going to do if you do find the magician?"

Grandpa stared at me. "The right thing. I'll tell Vance, not Shane."

I felt better then. And I would find a way to protect my grandfather from Shane's wrath. Since I was finally getting answers, I asked, "Who did you go see Monday night?" Vance wanted to know, and he was going to press Grandpa soon.

"A friend. And I'll tell Vance the name if I have to. But until then, I'm going to keep that to myself. I have my reasons."

8

Grandpa took the kids to school, and I sat down with some coffee and my Rolodex phone tree. I caught Linda Simpkins, the PTA president, at home. After we did the usual greetings and gossip, I asked, "So have you heard anything about Shane Masters, the magician?"

"Nope, and we have tried. We hoped he'd consider signing a few posters of the upcoming show for the PTA to auction off as a fund-raiser. But we can't get anywhere."

I grinned in spite of the fact that Shane was a spoiler magician. He was still famous, and that meant Linda Simpkins would hone in on him to raise money for the schools. On the other hand, if Linda hadn't found out any information with her vast gossip vine, that meant Shane had a solid lid on things. "Too bad, Linda, those posters would have sold well." Even though I broke out in hives at the very mention of PTA and soccer, I did understand fund-raising. "I know a couple magicians that might donate something. They aren't as famous as Shane, but they are getting pretty well known."

"That'd be fantastic," Linda said.

A loud knock at the door interrupted my thoughts.

"Someone's at the door. I'll let you know about the magicians." I hung up the cordless phone as I walked to the door. Ali beat me there and gave me a canine look that suggested I was a little slow. I pulled open the door. "Fletch. Hi. Uh, what's up?" The sun caught the reddish gold highlights in his brown hair.

"Barney and I are supposed to get an early start."

"Oh. Come in. Grandpa took the boys to school. He usually goes to Jack in the Box, but if he knows your coming over, he'll come right home."

"He was going to stop by Jack in the Box to see if anyone heard any gossip."

I shut the door. "Help yourself to some coffee." I sat down to look up the next phone number in my Rolodex. "Hey, Fletch, the local PTA is planning an auction soon. Do you have any programs or things that you can sign and donate?"

He poured some coffee, fished a doggie cookie out of the pantry for my shameless hussy of a dog, and came to the table. "I'm sure I can find some stuff, Sam." He gave Ali the cookie, then looked at me. "What are you doing?"

"Making some calls to see if anyone has an in with Shane's show over at the stadium. I'm trying to find out whose show Shane will spoil Saturday night." I dialed but got an answering machine.

"Shane's usually got that locked down tight, I hear." Fletch sipped his coffee. "Are you helping Barney with this?"

I shook my head. "Another client. But of course, if I come across information that helps Grandpa, that's even better."

Fletch reached over and put his hand over my fingers on the Rolodex. "Sam, I wish you wouldn't do this."

Startled, I looked up. "Why?"

With his back to the sliding glass door, he was backlit by the morning sunshine. But I could see his serious expression. "Shane threatened you. I'm worried. Listen, the guy is bad news, always was bad news from what I hear. You know how much I love Barney; I'll do anything to help him. But you getting hurt, that would kill him."

Fletch really did love Grandpa. "I know. But this is just a list of my contacts from my days as a soccer mom and on the PTA. Nothing dangerous here, I promise."

"I'd just feel better if you didn't poke around. Shane's unpredictable. Barney was really upset that he threatened you. I'm not sure you understand—" He held up a hand. "Don't look at me like that. I mean, that Shane's the magician who went bad. I'm the one who is succeeding. I understand a little better how Shane thinks and how Shane's betrayal is a black mark on Barney's stellar career."

"It's not Grandpa's fault that Shane is what he is." I picked up the phone to dial the next number.

"Convince Barney of that, Sam."

I met Fletch's blue eyes and felt my shoulders sag. "I know. But I'm going to help, both my client and Grandpa."

Fletch took his hand off mine and nodded. "I know I can't talk you out of it. Just be careful. I don't want anything to happen to you." He turned on his silly grin. "As soon as you are done with your PI, I'm going to ask you to marry me."

I rolled my eyes. "You just want to marry me so you can claim Grandpa." The phone rang in my hand before I could dial. "Hello?"

The icy voice of my mother crackled through the phone line. "Samantha, I just had breakfast with some of the city leaders. Your grandfather is an embarrassment, and it's going to stop right now. I'll be there in fifteen minutes." She hung up.

Oh boy, I had to make a run for it before my mom showed up. I stood, grabbed my Rolodex, and looked at Fletch. "Got to get to the office. Emergency." In the form of my mother. She was on a tear. She had obviously heard that Grandpa was questioned in connection with the attempt on Shane's life. I hurried down the hallway to grab my purse off my bed and came back out. I looked at Fletch sitting at the table. Should I warn him about my mom? And what about Grandpa?

Nah, they were both magicians and masters at misdirection. They could handle my mom. I left.

When I got to Heart Mates, I barely had time to take in the big opening between the two suites. Gabe and Cal were patching the adjacent walls, and Blaine was talking to a man whom I presumed to be the electrician. Forcing cheerfulness to cover my desperation to avoid my mother, I said, "Hi, no time to chat. If my mom shows up or calls, I'm not here!" I hurried into my office and closed the door.

I spent the next hour going through several more names on my phone tree. My first glimmer of hope was Molly. She and her husband owned Frank's Flowers, which was located right across from the campground where Shane was staying. Molly said her younger brother, Louis, worked on the maintenance crew that took care of the grounds of Storm Stadium. He would be there today doing some work. I hung up and decided to go chat with Louis. And while I was there, maybe I'd get a chance to look around.

I hadn't heard a word from my mother. I really doubted Blaine, Cal, and Gabe could have stopped her if she decided to check my office. I doubted that anyone could stop my mom. She probably got sidetracked with showing a property or closing a deal. And now if she did show up at the office, I would be gone.

With a sigh of relief, I went to the door and pulled it open. All the men were busy. Blaine, Gabe, and Cal were all talking with the electrician. It appeared they were talking about the electrical outlets and phone lines that we wanted in the floor where Blaine's circular desk would go. They had already cut some holes.

I walked over to let them know I was running out for a while when the door on my side of the office opened. I looked up.

Oh.

The men stopped talking.

The woman who walked in was spectacular—a dark-haired beauty with shiny red lips and dangerous curves packed into a black knit dress. My first thought was, why the hell did she need a dating service? I shook off my shock and started toward the woman.

She passed by me in a delicate cloud of luscious-smelling perfume. I turned.

The men were all frozen, staring at her.

She bypassed Gabe, Cal, and the electrician. She slid to a stop directly in front of Blaine.

Umm, so maybe Blaine met her and suggested Heart Mates?

"Hello, Blaine. I'm home." Her voice was Britney Spears breathy, her dark eyes huge and pleading as she looked at Blaine. She licked her red lips, and then added, "I've come home to be a proper wife to you."

Huh?

Blaine's normally placid face iced over into something I'd never seen on him before. He stood up straighter, his wide shoulders spreading in a stance of raw anger. His jaw hardened as color darkened his face and turned the tips of his ears tomato red. "Too late, Lola." Then he turned and walked over to Gabe's side of the office and disappeared around the corner.

I was frozen to my spot. Lola? Was married to Blaine? My Blaine? Blaine was married? To a woman who looked like a sex siren?

Had I fallen asleep and this was a dream?

Lola broke the spell when she turned around and headed toward me. "You must be Samantha Shaw. I'm Lola Jimenez Newport, and I'd like to sign up for your dating service." She stopped two feet from me. "What do I need to do?"

Newport was Blaine's last name, but all I could do was stare at her. She had skin as smooth as cocoa butter. She was ridiculously sexy, and I wasn't sure she was even trying. This had to be a joke.

Blaine was a beer-and-nachos-while-watching-NASCAR kind of guy. He didn't have a hard body—well, actually he wasn't flabby. He was big, like a wrestler with no neck. This woman belonged to a Latin singing sensation.

Not my Blaine.

If Blaine were married, his wife would look like a character actress that played the lead's plump, good-natured best friend.

I glanced over at Gabe, his brother, and the electrician. They were still caught in a brain freeze. Finally, I snapped out of it and held out my hand. "I'm Sam. It's nice to meet you. But if you are married, I'm not sure that Heart Mates is the right place for you." *Married to Blaine.* I couldn't get my brain to comprehend that fact.

"Apparently, I'm not married. Just on paper. I don't really think that counts, do you?"

My brain was starting to thaw. "Lola, Blaine works for

me. If you signed up for Heart Mates, that might cause problems." Huge problems judging by Blaine's reaction. I'd never seen a jealous streak in Blaine before, but then, I'd never seen him date. Probably because he had a wife I hadn't known about.

She shrugged. "He doesn't care. He's made no effort to contact me. I'd really like to sign up with your service. I won't be any trouble. I just want to . . ." For the first time, her breathy voice wobbled. "Please."

My female instincts kicked in. I really wanted to know the story behind Blaine and Lola. I reached out and took her arm. "Let's go talk in my interview room." I looked back at Gabe and the others. "Maybe you could get back to work now?"

Gabe grinned and waved his hand.

Hell, I couldn't even be mad. I had been staring at Lola too. She was stunning and sexy.

But Blaine's wife?

I got Lola settled into the interview room where no one could hear us. "Would you like some coffee?" We'd been keeping the coffee in the interview room where it was out of the path of construction dust and debris. I stared down at the coffee setup on a TV tray in the corner of the room. I didn't quite know where to start. I really couldn't let Lola sign on as a client, but I was dying to know the story behind her and Blaine.

Blaine was married?

Wait, Lola was talking.

"I usually take cream and sugar, but I should drink it black."

I looked over at her. Yep, still gorgeous and sexy. "Umm, why? We have powdered cream and plenty of sugar."

Lola's huge brown eyes filled with tears. "My boss is firing me because I'm too fat."

"Fat?" That would make me a card-carrying cow. I ran a critical eye over Lola. The knit dress clung to her curves. Big breasts were bestowed on her by God, not a surgeon as mine had been. She had a nice curve to her waist. Sure, there was a little poof to her belly, but that went nicely with her rounded hips. Fat? More like dangerous. Gabe and Cal had both been stunned stupid by her sexiness. I don't think either one of them would call her fat. "Lola, that's ridiculous. Besides, that's discrimination. Your boss can't fire you for your weight."

She sniffled and recovered. "My boss can. But I'll take some coffee with that fake sweetener if you have it."

I reached for the packet of sweetener. "So what's the story with you and Blaine? He's worked for me for almost two years and I had no idea he was married." I took the coffee to her and sat down.

"Thanks." She sipped some of the coffee, then said, "He never divorced me. I really don't know why. He should have."

This was crazy. "Did you leave him?"

She nodded, her face shadowing. Suddenly she looked closer to human than sex goddess. "I just thought there was more. Blaine and I met my last year of high school. I fell hard for him. He treated me like a princess. My family was poor and my father mean. Blaine was like a dream. We married, and for a couple years it was fine. But then I began to realize that I wanted more. Everyone told me I was beautiful. . . ." She stopped and looked straight at me. "You must think I'm horrible."

"I'm not sure what to think." I told her the truth. "This is all a bit of a shock to me. But I would like to hear more. Just so you know, Blaine is my friend. I care about him."

She nodded. "I understand. Blaine is exactly what you see. A good man, a hard-working blue-collar guy. He loved me, and I threw that away for some white-collar fairy tale."

I think I was getting it. "Like a white-collar prince in the big city?"

Some kind of emotion, maybe guilt or regret, darkened her luminous eyes. "And maybe a career in acting. I wanted to be a game show hostess."

She had the look for it. But beneath her words, I heard a bucket full of disillusionment and regret. "And now?"

She looked down at her coffee. "I just want what I had."

"With Blaine?"

She nodded, her hair falling forward in a dark curtain of gentle waves.

"And you think signing on at Heart Mates will get him back?" I knew the parts of Blaine that he allowed me to know. Somehow, I didn't think her idea was going to work.

"It's all I can think of. When I got to town, I went to the garage he used to work for and found out that he's working here. I found out other stuff too." She lifted her head, her face tight with some emotion. "Things have been bad for him."

I knew that Blaine had a problem with cocaine, but it looked like that was news to Lola. But I wasn't going to discuss that with her. That was Blaine's business. He'd gotten clean and, as far as I knew, only had an occasional beer. But I wondered if losing Lola had done something to him—something painful enough to lead him to drugs. Blaine was such a strong-willed person that I'd always wondered how he'd gotten into drugs.

All of us have our breaking points.

Lola said, "Is he dating?"

I shrugged. "I don't know. I suppose he goes out, but I

don't think he's serious about anyone. Except my car, he loves my car." I smiled.

"Is that white T-bird in the parking lot yours?" Lola asked.

I nodded. "That's it. Blaine takes care of it for me."

Her smile opened up like a flower. "He would love that car. He loves the classic muscle cars. Blaine has a magic with cars. I didn't understand that back then. I wanted to move up and on."

I took a chance. "You didn't want to be married to a man like your father?"

She blinked in surprise. "It took me years to figure that out. My father worked in construction—when there was work. And I guess I figured Blaine being a mechanic was too similar. But Blaine, he was never mean like my father. He was just flat-out a better man. I don't know why I couldn't understand what I had."

I liked her. I was surprised by that, but there it was. I liked a woman who could own up to her mistakes and try to rectify them. "Lola, what if Blaine doesn't want you back? Ever?"

She took another sip of coffee and then sighed deeply. "I have to try. And it's not going to happen overnight. I just want him to start seeing who I am now. I want to sign on to your dating service so that I can come to your mixers and social events. I don't want to date. I plan to stay here in Elsinore now."

"What about your job?"

"I have to get a new one. Shane has made it very clear that my job is over after this weekend."

Stunned, I dropped both my hands to the table. "Shane? As in Shane Masters? He's your boss?"

She nodded. "I'm a magician's assistant. I just took the job to pay the bills until I got discovered. But now I just want to settle down and stay in one place. Find a job at an office or something. Or I could be a teacher's assistant. I'm good with kids."

My head was spinning. How could this be a coincidence? I tried to think this out. Her motives for trying to get back with Blaine might not be as clear cut as I first thought. She could be desperate and looking for him to take care of her. She could be acting. "Lola, how long have you known Shane wanted to fire you?"

Her face hardened. "He's threatened for two months. But Monday night he told me this was my last gig. And he threatened me to keep my mouth shut." She shuddered. "I don't want to cross him."

I was desperately trying to catch up. I thought of Nikki, of all the magicians who were anxiously waiting to find out whose show Shane would be exposing. "I understand," I said soothingly. "But you could help some magicians, Lola, and Shane would never have to know it was you. Do you know whose show Shane is featuring in his spoiler this weekend?"

She vehemently shook her head. "I signed an agreement. And even if I hadn't signed one, you don't know him. He'd know it was me and he'd . . . get even." She shivered a little, then added, "I really don't know. We all rehearse our parts, and that's it until the final run-through on Thursday and Friday."

She was really afraid. It hit me that I might have not only a potential client for Heart Mates in front of me but a suspect in the failed murder-for-hire plot against Shane Masters. I did the only thing I could think of. I signed her up for Heart Mates and had her sign the background check release. At least Gabe would have someplace to start to investigate her.

And her permission to do it.

I walked Lola out of the interview room. Blaine wasn't there. Gabe and Cal were repairing and spackling the walls. Painting would be next. Once Lola left, I turned around. "Gabe, where's Blaine?"

He set down the trowel thing and came over to me. "He went to get lunch." Dropping his gaze to the papers in my hand, he added, "You didn't sign her on, did you?" A frown gathered between his winged brows over his dark eyes.

"I did. But I did it because she works for Shane Masters. And she has reason to be pissed at him." I told him that Shane was planning to fire her for being too fat. "So I figured this way we'd have all the information, plus her permission, to do a background check and see what pops on her."

The frown melted into sheer incredulousness. "Shane Masters thinks she's fat?"

Damn. I'd kind of hoped he'd be impressed with my quick thinking. Of course, his male brain was still on Lola's luscious curves. I was losing patience. "Apparently, he likes the leaner look. Now try to pay attention, stud. First off, Lola was not interested in you. So you can just keep your shirt on." Umm, did that sound jealous?

Cal snickered.

I turned around. "Did you say something?"

His shoulders stopped shaking. "No. Just clearing my throat."

I ignored him and focused on Gabe. "The point is that we can run a background check on Lola. Find out if there's any reason we might suspect her of hiring a hit man." I waved the papers in front of him. "You do remember how to run background checks, right?"

Gabe grinned. "I think I can manage."

Men. "Fine. I'm going over to the stadium. My friend's

brother works on the maintenance crew there, so I'm going to talk to him."

Gabe took a step toward me. "Not alone." Then his gaze rose from my face to behind me.

The hairs on the back of my neck stood up. Who was behind me?

"Samantha, that was rude of you to leave Fletch alone at the house and run off."

My mother!

Gabe's mouth twitched. Swear to God, if he laughed I was going to take off my shoe and whack him one. My shoulders tensed, and I turned around. "Mother, I have a business to run." My mom was dressed to sell. She had on cream slacks with a pale green sweater accentuated with a silk scarf and an expensive-looking broach. Her tasteful jewelry, flawless make-up, and wedge-cut hairstyle supported her successful businesswoman image. She carried a slim purse. I knew she had an expensive leather briefcase in her car.

She tilted her head, smoothing out the slight wrinkles in her neck, and glared at me. "This?" She ran her gaze around her room. "This is more important than your grand-father?"

"I didn't say that." I suddenly felt about thirteen. An invisible band formed and tightened around my forehead. I took a slow breath. "Mom, Grandpa is fine. He simply answered some questions for the police."

"Samantha, Fletch told me that you are in danger. I want you to stop all this nonsense immediately." She looked me over from head to foot. "And put a black blazer on, dear. Those shoes are not appropriate for office wear. Black pumps and stockings are the thing."

Gabe leaned down and whispered, "I like your shoes."

"Shut up."

"Samantha!" My mother's tone had frosted to dry ice.

"I meant Gabe, Mom." Gabe thought this was funny. He was so dead. "Mom, I am not in danger; I am doing my job."

She wrinkled her nose. "This isn't a job. For heaven's sake, you don't even have professionals doing your renovations." Her gaze went to Cal.

"That's Gabe's brother, Cal. He took time off from his job as a firefighter to help us." I turned to Cal. "This is my mother, Kathryn."

Cal nodded. "Nice to meet you. You have a lovely daughter."

My mom nodded. "Thank you." Then she turned back to me. "You can't possibly afford all this."

My stomach cramped, and the band around my head squeezed until I wanted to scream, *That's why I'm taking the job to find out which magician's show Shane is spoiling!* But instead, I said, "Mom, I have to go run an errand. I'll call you later."

"Sam . . ." Gabe warned.

I turned around. "Back off, Pulizzi. I know what I'm doing." He wasn't the only one feeling stressed and tired.

"Exactly what are you doing?" my mom asked.

Gabe answered, "She's going to talk to a groundskeeper at Storm Stadium about Shane Masters. Sam has a client who wants to know whose show Shane is spoiling on Saturday night."

My mother turned her stare back to me. "A groundskeeper? Really Samantha, is that the best you can do? I know lots of important people. Come along, dear. I'm sure I can find out more than you could with your little groundskeeper." She turned and strolled out with her Queen Mother walk.

I whirled around.

"Now Sam," Gabe held up both his hands, "I was just trying to help."

"Think you're funny, don't you?"

His face hardened. "I don't want you going there alone. At least with your mom, I know you'll be safe."

"Safe? Are you nuts? Have you met my mother?" With all the buzzing fury in my head, it was hard to tell whether I was shrieking or not. "Or is this just your way of getting me off your hands? Is that it, Pulizzi? You thought you were going to have to do the job of babysitting me, but my mom came in and saved you?" When I stopped for a breath, I noticed Cal had disappeared. I'm sure he was on the phone now, explaining to his family that Gabe was dating a lunatic.

"Don't insult me, Sam."

I opened my mouth, but a loud horn sounded. I looked out the window to see my mother idling her car in front of the door. I turned and stalked out of the office. I was going to get even with Gabe for this. I would find a way.

9

I couldn't believe Gabe had manipulated me into going with my mom—my mom!—to the stadium to talk to Louis about Shane Masters. But since we were in my mom's car and pulling into the dirt lot across from the stadium, I had no choice but to deal with it.

And get even with Gabe later.

We got out of the car and crossed the street to find the grounds maintenance crew working on the front of the stadium. It didn't take me long to find Louis. He wore a long-sleeved tan shirt with his name in blue sewn on the pocket. His wheat-colored hair was plastered to his head beneath a straw hat. "Louis, I'm Sam Shaw, a friend of your sister, Molly."

He looked at me with blatant curiously. "Yeah?"

"Molly thought you could help me. I'm doing some research on Shane Masters. Have you been working here every day while his crew is setting up?"

He shook his head. "No. Just today. Wednesday is our regular day. And they are being real pains about it too."

My mother shifted on her classic pumps and said, "Samantha, we should move along."

I ignored her. "What do you mean, Louis?"

"His security is watching every move, questioning every-where we go. They won't let us in the gates to do our work." He shook his head. "Guess they had some trouble last night, but why would I care about a bunch of magician stuff?"

"Trouble?" My adrenaline kicked up. "What kind of trouble?"

He shrugged. "I guess someone tried to break into one of those trailers over in the main parking lot." He waved toward the blacktop parking lot that led up to the ticket booths.

What did I ask? "Did you hear anything else?"

"Just that crazy magician screaming at the security guys. And they all stood there and took it from him. I'd have told him to shove it up his ass." He blushed. "Sorry."

Shane had to be the crazy magician. I patted his arm. "I know what you mean, Louis. Do you know what's in those trailers? Did you hear the magician say anything specific?"

He shook his head. "He called them incompetent and worse kinds of insults. I didn't hear nothin' else." He glanced around and said, "Here comes another security dude. I gotta get back to work."

I saw a large man dressed in a suit bearing down on us. I tried to think of a story. The man was large, built like a barrel with a heavy but solid-looking middle. His suit was rumpled, and his scowl looked like it had a lot of use today.

"Hi." I walked up to greet him and held out my hand. "I'm Samantha Shaw."

He ignored my hand. "What are you doing here?"

My mom moved up next to me and held out her card. "I'm Kathryn, a real estate agent, and I'm taking a look at the stadium for my clients. They are considering putting a bid into the city to purchase the property. We won't be in your way."

Dang, my mom was good. The lie flowed out of her mouth effortlessly. And the city was trying to sell the stadium, so it was a somewhat plausible lie.

The man frowned at the business card, then handed it back to us with a warning glare. "Come back next week."

"I don't think so, Mr. . . . what is your name? My client is a wealthy corporation. They don't wait."

"I don't give a rat's ass who your client is. You need to leave or I'll have you escorted off the property. We have a contract on this property for the week. Get lost."

My mom stood her ground. "I'd like to have a word with your boss."

The goon pulled out his walkie-talkie. "I need some muscle to escort two broads off the property."

"Two broads?" My mom turned to look at me. "Did he just call us broads?"

Her eyes glittered brown rage. "I believe he did." I looked up to see two more goons heading our way. One was talking into a walkie-talkie, and the other was drinking a carton of milk. To my mom, I added, "They want to throw us off the property."

My mom looked around. "Samantha, come here." She turned and walked toward the sidewalk surrounding the property. I saw her open up her chic little bag and take something out. She stopped on the sidewalk and turned around.

I shrugged, went to stand next to her, and got out my own small canister of pepper spray. Not under the pain of death would I ever admit to Gabe that I thought he'd had a good idea in sending my mom with me. He had been right about one thing—my mom knew how to take care of herself. And she might be able to criticize me, but she'd never allow anyone else to. I watched the first goon approach us, followed by two more sub-goons. The sub-goons were coatless and had their sleeves rolled up. They all wore matching scowls. Were scowls a job requirement?

The boss goon stopped in front of us, then turned to his flunkies. "Escort them to their car and get them the hell out of here. I don't want Masters to see unauthorized people around here."

Both goons moved forward.

I kind of felt sorry for them. "You might want to think about it, guys. Umm, we're standing on the sidewalk now." I glanced down to make sure my snazzy turquoise shoes were on the sidewalk. Yep. I looked up. "It's a public area. Now think real hard—"

"Shut up, blondie," the smaller goon with the carton of milk snarled, and grabbed my arm.

Sheesh, you try to warn a guy.

I heard the second goon roar out, "Shit! What . . . arrrg!"

"Let go," I suggested to my milk-drinking goon.

He dropped my arm and turned to see his buddy on the ground, clawing at his eyes. He stood there frozen for a second as if he couldn't quite process what he saw.

Then he lifted his head to look at my mom. Unfreezing, he let out a roar. "You bitch!" He lunged at her, still clutching his carton of milk. He got his left hand around her arm and tried to shake her like a rug.

A red haze of fury swarmed in front of my eyes. No one attacked my mom! My vision narrowed down to the man who had a hold of my mom's arm, whipping her back and forth while holding his carton of milk out of the way. I took a big step and kicked the back of his knee as hard as I could. "Get your hands off my mother!"

"Ouch!" he yelled, and let go of my mom. His right

knee buckled from the impact of my kick. He caught his balance while still holding his carton of milk like it was a fragile vase. "You kicked me!" he screamed, and started to turn toward me.

My mom raised her hand, and the stream of pepper spray splashed directly into his eyes before he could turn.

"Ahhh! My eyes!" He fell backward.

I saw the threat and tried to moved. But before I could get out of the way, one hundred and seventy pounds of goon landed on me. I slammed hard onto the concrete. My butt hit first, then my head landed in a pile of leaves and cracked through to the cement below. A ringing sound peeled in my brain while I lay stunned on the ground.

The man writhed around and managed to roll off me. Having sprayed myself once, I knew he was experiencing searing pain in his eyes. I ignored him and stared up at the sky, willing the ringing in my head to stop.

"Samantha, get up. Your underwear is showing."

I shifted my gaze right to see my mother standing over me. She didn't even look winded.

"Lady, are you okay?"

The grounds maintenance guy, Louis, stood on my left. "I think so." At least the ringing in my head was fading away.

He reached down and helped me to my feet.

I smoothed my skirt down over my black lace panties and then brushed the leaves and sticks out of my hair. I tried to look dignified, but I think I probably achieved comical. I forced a smile and said, "Thank you."

Louis smiled back. "That was the best thing I've seen all week. Those guys are assholes. I should thank you." He looked to my right.

My mom was giving the boss goon in the coat an earful.

He had streams of sweat pouring down his face. He huffed in frustration and said, "Listen lady, we ran off a guy last night who was trying to break into one of Mr. Masters's trailers. We're a little edgy. It's our job to protect all that stuff!"

My mom asked calmly, "Did this burglar get into the trailers?"

Boss goon shook his head. "We have those trailers wired. Our silent alarm went off. We almost caught him, but he got away. The trailers are safe. But that magician, he's insane about the near break-in."

My mother sighed and shook her head. "Was all this really worth risking going to jail for assaulting my daughter and me?"

"It's that . . . uh . . . Mr. Masters. He has us all a little jumpy. Look lady, just go away. Please. Don't call the cops."

My mom turned to look at me. Then she turned back to the goon. "You'll pay for my daughter's skirt, of course."

His hand shook when he reached inside his coat and pulled out a business card. "Sure, sure. Just leave. Call my office and I'll write you a check."

What was wrong with my skirt? I looked down and saw a big blob of wet spreading on the front of my skirt. "Ewww! What is that?"

Louis bent over, picked up the carton off the ground, and held it up. "Milk."

"Oh." I stopped squirming. "I was kind of afraid that goon had peed on me." I'd had milk spilt on me lots of times by the boys.

Louis burst out laughing.

"Oh, for heaven's sake, Samantha," my mother said. "That's disgusting. Now let's go."

I waved at Louis. "Thanks for everything."

He grinned, leaned forward, and said, "Nice underwear." Then he turned and tossed the empty milk carton in the pile of leaves.

I caught up to my mom at her car. "God, Mom, you are scary," I said as I slid into the leather seat and pulled the door closed. I turned and looked at her. "But if you ever tell Gabe how much help you were to me, I swear I'll dress in my leather miniskirt and halter top and show up at your office when you have an important client."

"That's a little extreme, dear." My mom pulled the car out onto the road. "And I can't imagine why I'd be talking to Gabe in any case."

"True." I leaned my head back against the headrest. "But we did find out someone was trying to break into one of the trailers."

"The hit man?" my mom suggested.

I couldn't imagine why. "I doubt it. Besides, Vance and Gabe both think that guy was an amateur." Only one scenario made sense to me. "It's someone trying to find out whose show Shane is exposing this weekend."

"Could be the same magician that tried to have Shane killed." My mom looked over at me. "Who is your client?"

"Rosy Malone and her granddaughter."

"Nikki? She's in town?"

"Yes."

My mom drove in silence for a little while, then said, "You've been talking to Detective Vance? You said he didn't think the hit man was a pro."

"We had lunch yesterday."

"Really? He's a nice-looking man. And career cops have pensions and health insurance. They don't have great hours, but he's a detective. That's something."

I rolled my head toward her on the headrest. "Mom!"

She sucked in her lips until there was just a thin coral slash. "Don't *Mom* me. You're going to outgrow Gabe. You need a stable man, a businessman who can provide for you and the boys. And you have to get out of that dreadful private investigating."

"I like it."

"It's not safe, Samantha."

We rode in silence. We were just never going to see eye to eye. But after talking to Grandpa this morning, I understood a little more of the fear that drove my mom. She wasn't afraid of three goons, but she was afraid of men like Gabe.

It made me wonder about my father.

"Mom, are we ever going to talk about my father?"

Her hands tightened on the steering wheel. "We've talked about him dozens of times."

My head throbbed. She'd told me dozens of stories. Maybe one of them was true, maybe not. And maybe my mom had a horrible experience and I was wrong to force her to tell me. "No, we haven't. I'm not a child anymore. I just want the truth. I'd just like to know."

She turned into Heart Mates and slid her car to a stop behind my T-bird. "Go home and change before the milk on your skirt sours and starts to smell."

I lifted my head off the headrest and studied her face. It was tight with tension. Softly, I said, "I just want to know."

"I'm late for a showing, Samantha."

I got out and watched her pull away. I thought about going into Heart Mates just to yell at Gabe, but the milk had soaked through and my thighs were starting to chafe. I decided to run home and think about what I knew so far about Shane Masters, his show this Saturday, and the hit man.

Plus I had to plan my revenge on Gabe.

I still hadn't come up with a really good revenge plan by the time I turned into the dirt lot in front of my house.

Sometimes, I thought that Gabe brought out my evil side. But the truth was that Gabe brought out the strength in me. He never settled for less than my best ability. Even when he was pissed and trying to keep me out of his business, he never expected me to pull back on mine. Gabe didn't try to stop me from taking this case and he didn't try to stop me from going to the stadium where Shane might be. Instead, he sent my mom along to make sure I had protection.

And God, she had been something to watch. I couldn't help but smile at the memory. Too bad I couldn't ask my mom's advice on getting back at Gabe. That might be something to see . . .

My thought died away as I slid to a stop and noticed the black SUV parked on the other side of Grandpa's Jeep.

I had a bad feeling that wasn't from the stiffly drying milk on my skirt. I got out of the T-bird and heard yelling. I looked up to see Grandpa in the middle of the porch, nose to chin with Shane Masters.

I hurried to the steps and raced up them. I spotted Ali at the front window inside the house, growling and barking for all she was worth. I could see the stiff line of hair standing straight up along her back. She had her lips pulled back, exposing her powerful teeth.

At the top of the porch steps, I stopped a few feet from the men and used my stop-it-this-instant Mom voice. "What is going on here?"

Shane turned his gaze on me. "I want answers and I want them now."

Uh-oh, this probably had to do with the break-in attempt on one of his prop trailers at the stadium. I looked at Grandpa. His face was beet red, and his thin chest was rising and falling like he'd just run around the block. He didn't look like he was hurt, just angry. I had to find out what Shane wanted. "Answers about what?"

"Someone tried to break into one of my prop trailers." A vein on the side of Shane's head bulged. He reached into his pocket and pulled something out. "He dropped this."

I stared at the flesh-colored item. Bigger than a thimble, it was a hollow thumb that magicians used for their close-up magic. Oh God. I just saw that thumb last night— Bo Kelly had used it to do a close-up magic trick.

Shane went on. "He's here. The magician that sent the hit man is here." He turned back to Grandpa. "I want a name, Webb. I want it now!"

"You'll get your answers when I have them," Grandpa said.

Shane's bald head darkened even more. "I'm done waiting, old man. You know who sent that hit man. You know who this thumb belongs to. Either you tell me or I'll start with Samantha."

Start what? I almost stepped back, then thought better of it. I'd just seen my mom handle three goons. I could handle Shane—I hoped. I took a deep breath and fished my pepper spray out of my purse. I uncapped it, then said to Shane, "Get off our property."

Shane shifted his gaze back to me. He flicked his ice blue eyes over the can of spray, then back to my eyes. "Think you are fast enough? I doubt it."

Shivers of damp fear broke out on my skin. I believed him. He scared the crap out of me. I just wanted him gone. Away from all of us. Far away. It took every sense of self-preservation I had to hold my ground. "I didn't ask your opinion. Just leave."

He turned toward me and made a show of returning

the fake thumb to his pants pocket. Then he said, "I don't like being ordered around or threatened. I'm giving the orders here."

The shivers prickled up my spine. "Stop threatening my grandpa and leave right now." I prayed that sounded confident and not like a scared female plea. "I will not tolerate spoiled little boys having temper tantrums."

He took one long step and used his left hand to knock the spray out of my right hand.

I was stunned.

Then he slapped me, snapping my head hard to the right. The breath whooshed from my body as pain exploded into a fiery heat on the left side of my face.

"You bastard!" Grandpa bellowed.

"Shit!" Shane screamed out a string of curses.

I didn't know why he was screaming. My left eye watered too much to see anything. I turned my head and was able to look out of my right eye. Grandpa held a pen in his hand. It had to be the fake pen filled with pepper spray that Grandpa had ordered off the Internet. Obviously, he'd sprayed Shane with pepper spray from the pen. I caught sight of Grandpa running to the door, probably to let Ali out or to call the police.

But I didn't wait to find out. I turned so I could see Shane from my right eye. He had his hands over his eyes and was still spewing curses and threats. Rage and the need to protect my grandfather bubbled up into a full-blown geyser. I rushed him with both arms straight out in front of me. I caught his belly with both hands. We both flew off the porch. He landed with a loud thud. I hit the dirt, then skidded past him, stirring up a cloud of dust. Ugh. I scrambled to my feet.

Ali exploded out of the house and raced down the steps.

I ran up the steps to Grandpa and grabbed his arm, dragging him toward the house.

When I looked back, Shane was on his hands and knees and getting to his feet.

Ali skidded to a stop and clamped her jaws down on the right cheek of his ass.

"Goddamnit, I'll kill this fucking dog!"

"Ali, come!" I didn't know if he had a gun or a knife. I was pissed and panicked; my brain whirled so fast that my body was obeying my brain's commands before I even realized I had thought them. I pushed Grandpa ahead of me. "Get in the house!" I followed him in.

Ali ran in after us.

I slammed the door and locked it.

God, my face hurt. But we were all okay.

And Shane Masters was a raving, dangerous lunatic.

10

"You are going to have a black eye and a bruise on your cheekbone. I think we should call the police." Grandpa pushed the bag of frozen peas back on my face. On the kitchen table was a plate of cheese, apple slices, and crackers that Grandpa set out for us to eat. He was taking care of me; he had always taken care of me.

I sipped some hot coffee to offset the cold on my face and started to shake my head, then thought better of it. Man, getting slapped hurt. Especially by Mr. Clean. He could have pulled his punch or something. Sheesh. Besides, Grandpa was right—it was time to tell Vance what was going on. "You're going to have to tell Vance the truth. All of it," I told him.

Grandpa sat back and studied me. "Maybe we should call Gabe instead."

"No!" Ali lifted her head up off my lap at the sound of my voice. I forced myself to calm down and petted her head to reassure her. "No, he'll kill Shane." It took a lot to make Gabe lose his temper, but Shane's hitting me might do it.

"You're right, I should do it myself." He stood up.

I jumped to my feet. "Grandpa, stop!" I grabbed his arm as he tried to pass me.

Ali sat on her haunches and whined.

"It's okay, Ali," I said to her, then looked up into Grandpa's face. "You already took care of Shane. You nailed him with the pepper spray. And Ali bit him in the ass." I could feel the rage tremble through his arm. "You already saved me. Please, Grandpa, sit down."

He stared hard at me, glimmers of a younger man pushing through his craggy face.

"I mean it. If you try to go after Shane, I'll call Vance and have you arrested. I'm not letting you go after him. He's crazy." Tears welled up in my eyes, and my throat tightened painfully.

"Sammy, he hit you." His voice shook.

I nodded, trying to imagine what I would have done if Shane had hit Grandpa. I understood his anger. "Let's figure this out, and then we'll call Vance, okay? I'm going to have to tell Gabe too, I will. I just want to keep him from doing something stupid."

"Protecting you is not stupid."

His love for me made everything okay. Didn't he know that? "I'm fine, Grandpa. You made sure I'm fine. Gabe will be fine once he realizes that you took care of me."

Finally, the mask of determination on his face relaxed. "You are patronizing me, but I like it." He reached over and picked up the bag of frozen peas. "Put this back on your eye."

We sat down, and I inhaled a breath of relief.

Ali sat between us. I reached over and scratched her ears. "Good bite, Ali."

She put her head back in my lap. I realized then how really scared I was. Shane could have killed Grandpa. I don't know that he would have, but I think he would kill if he was backed in a corner. At least he didn't bring his dogs. That was something.

"Fletch and I have a list of about eight names of magicians who had their acts spoiled by Shane's show. We're trying to contact them. Two have sent e-mails that they have nothing to say to us. Nothing else yet. Magicians are afraid to talk about Shane."

They didn't want to draw his attention and end up one of his show victims. I put my hand over Grandpa's. "You saw that fake thumb."

His shoulders bowed. "Bo. But why would Bo break into one of Shane's trailers?"

He knew the answer, but I said it anyway. "To see if Shane was targeting his show. He was looking for capes and other props."

"The cartoon venture. He's afraid Shane will reveal the magic that goes into his show and that will affect his cartoon venture, I guess." Grandpa took a sip of his coffee, then asked, "Do you think he had a tip or something?"

I thought about it. "How does Shane decide what show to spoil? Does he warn the magician? How does he learn about the magician's illusions? If it is Bo's show Shane's spoiling, maybe Shane did some kind of research that tipped Bo off?" My head throbbed both from being smacked and from the stress of trying to fit the puzzle pieces together. It didn't quite add up.

"I've never heard whether Shane warns a magician. It's another thing they would probably keep secret—trying to keep the damage that Shane does to their show at a minimum. They wouldn't advertise that he's going to reveal their illusions." He took a second to rub his eyes with the finger and thumb of his right hand. "And it'd be easy to find out the content of a magician's show, Sam. Anyone can describe the act, and Shane could reproduce it. He doesn't even have to be accurate in the exact method of how the magician does the trick. The audience he's showing doesn't know."

That was true. "We don't even know if it was Bo that tried to break into the trailer. A lot of magicians have a fake thumb. . . ."

Grandpa looked grim. "They don't tend to carry them around. Before you arrived, Shane told me it wasn't his fake thumb. He keeps his props very tightly controlled so nosy people won't get a clue to his shows. He found the thumb right outside the trailer. Someone was trying to pick the lock."

Bo understood locking mechanisms—he did some escapes in his act. "Mom and I found out that the trailers are all wired for security. Shane has very tough security." My mind was flitting all over the place. "Mom heard about Shane, and your involvement, from city leaders this morning, then came by the house, and I guess Fletch told her a lot more before you got home." I looked up at Grandpa. "You should have seen her, Grandpa. She went with me to the stadium to nose around, and when we were hassled, she sprayed two of the security guys and told off the boss security goon. He even agreed to pay for my skirt." I looked down. The milk had dried to a white cakelike substance and was now covered in dirt. My turquoise shirt was stretched and dirty, and I think there was a smear of blood from my left arm where I slid in the dirt. I sighed. Every case ruined more clothes and cost me some skin.

Grandpa grinned. "That's my Katy. Tough as they come. Fletch was here for a while this morning, then left to go get ready for his skydiving adventure." His grin melted away. "I have to talk to Bo. Find out if it was him and what makes him think he might be a target."

I closed my eyes, feeling a wash of nausea at my next

thought. "Could he be desperate enough to hire a hit man?"

Grandpa was silent.

I opened my eyes and saw his sad expression.

"I hope not."

I had to fix this. "But if he did, nothing happened. Shane is okay. We can still make this right, get Bo some help—he doesn't have to lose everything."

"Sam."

I sighed, acknowledging that attempted murder was not something a magician or ex–soccer mom could fix. "Let's call Vance. We'll set up a meeting. In the meantime we can try to talk to Bo."

Grandpa handed me the phone. I dug out Vance's business card and dialed while Grandpa went to the sink and wet a couple paper towels. I got Vance's voice mail and left a message. "Vance, it's me, Sam. I want to set up a meeting with you. Grandpa and I just had a little run-in with Shane Masters." I hung up.

Grandpa returned to the table. "Let me see your arm."

I handed him the phone and said, "You call Bo at the motel. I'll do that." I took the damp paper towel from him. While he called Bo, I bent my arm at the elbow and saw a long scrape on the backside of my forearm. It hadn't bled much, and I wiped it clean. What I needed to do was take a shower and change clothes.

"He's not there."

I looked into Grandpa's worried gaze. "We'll find him." I stood up. "I'm going to clean up and change—" The phone rang and cut me off. I grabbed it. "Hello?"

"Is it true?" Blaine snarled in my ear.

Oh crap. "Is what true?" I stalled for time.

"Did you take on Lola as a client of Heart Mates?"

Cripes, I really should have talked to Blaine and explained this. "Yes, but I only did it to—"

"Your client is in the office. Either get down here and deal with her or I'm kicking her butt to the curb. Again." He hung up.

"Oh boy." I clicked the phone off. I have never heard Blaine that mad. That—

Hurt.

And he had a right to be hurt. I'd had good reason to sign up Lola, but Blaine deserved to know from me right away why I did it. I was dead wrong, and it felt worse than my throbbing face. I looked at Grandpa. "I have to go to the office. You're coming with me." No way did I trust him. He'd probably go after Shane.

Or worse, he'd call Fletch and they'd cook up a dumb and dangerous scheme.

I hurried into my room, stripped off the skirt and panties, grabbed a clear pair of underwear, and yanked them on. Then I pulled out a pair of boot-cut black jeans and did a little dance to get them up and snapped. I left on the shoes and shirt, collected Grandpa, and rushed to the office.

Grandpa was agreeable about going to the office with me. I chalked that up to wanting to keep me safe and got us to Heart Mates as fast as I could. We both rushed inside.

Only Cal and Lola were in the front. Cal was finishing taping up some drywall patches and spackling over them. Lola had changed into a pair of capri pants and a halter top, and she handed stuff to Cal.

That would have been okay.

But she managed to rub up against him, touch his arm,

and laugh breathlessly while flipping her hair. She was in High Flirting Mode, and she looked damned good at it.

Where were Gabe and Blaine?

Lola said to Cal in a breathy voice, "You look hot and thirsty. Why don't we go get something to drink when you're done here?" She looked up at him with her huge dark eyes.

Cal swept his gaze over me and Grandpa, clearly having heard us come in, then looked down to Lola. "What'd you have in mind?"

She flashed him a killer smile. "Ice cold beer at my place?"

Blaine roared out of Gabe's office. "You are not bringing a man you just met to your place! He could be a serial killer for all you know! When did you get this stupid?"

The throbbing fury in Blaine's voice increased my bitchslapped headache. I hurried over to block Blaine before he got to Lola. He had an I'm-gonna-strangle-you look in his eyes.

"What's your problem, Blaine?" Lola said over my shoulder. "You told me I'm too late, so I'm moving on. Stay out of my life!"

Blaine's brown eyes iced to frozen root beer. His face pulled tight and hard. He glared at me. "Get her out of here, Sam."

"Blaine." I put my hand on his arm and felt his muscles contracting into concrete. "I'm sorry. This is my fault. I should have told you. I'll take care of it."

I turned to Lola. "Why don't we go into my office and talk? With all the construction going on here, this isn't the time to drop in. It could be dangerous." Not from the construction but from my furious office manager.

"But I'm helping Cal. I like helping Cal. He's nice. And he doesn't think I'm stupid."

"That's because he doesn't know you!" Blaine yelled past my throbbing head.

"All right, stop it!" I bellowed, and regretted it immediately. I turned so that I could see both Blaine and Lola. Lowering my voice, I said, "I want both of you to act like adults."

At that second, Gabe came storming out from his office. His shoulders were back, his face set in hard anger, and his eyes zeroed in on me.

On my face to be exact.

Grandpa shuffled out behind him.

That rat! While I had been dealing with Cal, Lola, and Blaine, Grandpa had gone and told Gabe that Shane had smacked me. That was when I realized he'd agreed to come with me way too easily. *The sneaky tattletale.*

Gabe smoothly went around Blaine and stopped in front of me. I could smell his anger. Quickly, I said, "I'm fine. It's not that bad."

He blinked once. "Shane Masters hit you? How many times, Sam?"

Cal handed the spackle tool to Lola and moved up to stand by Gabe and study my face. Then he whistled. "That's gotta hurt."

I glared at him. "You're not helping. Besides, look at you! You're more beat up than I am."

He shrugged. "Not the same thing."

Lola moved up by Cal, put her hand on his bicep, and said to him, "Should we get her some ice?"

I tried to roll my eyes but that hurt too much.

"Answer me," Gabe suggested in a voice so cold I didn't think I'd need ice.

"Just once. It's not a big deal." Really, I was more scared of Gabe's fury than getting hit by Shane. Gabe operated by his own code.

He stepped in closer so that I had to look up. "Why didn't you call me?"

That was easy. "I knew you would get mad. And Grandpa and I took care of Shane. We sprayed him with pepper spray and pushed him off the porch, and Ali bit him. So there's nothing for you to do." Did I think for a second Gabe was going to buy that?

He lowered his face so that his mouth was an inch from mine. "Wrong. No one hits you. Ever. You stay here with Cal, Blaine, and Barney. Do not leave this office."

He kissed me softly, but I could feel the rage coursing through him.

Then he pulled back. "And put some ice on that bruise." He turned and stormed out.

"Gabe! Where are you going?" I knew it was a stupid question. Gabe didn't pause or look back, he just kept going.

I turned back around and glared at Cal. "Well?"

Cal spread his hands open wide. "What?"

I tried to give him a hard look, but I think my blackening eye might have ruined it. "Don't pull that innocent crap on me. Go stop your brother!"

He shook his head. "Can't do that, Sam."

Were men put on earth just to annoy women? "Why not?"

"Because, I don't want Gabe interfering in my decisions and I won't interfere in his. And this Shane Masters apparently needs someone to beat the shit out of him. Gabe's on it."

I fought to keep from screaming. Putting my hands on my hips, I glared at Cal out of my good eye. "How is beating Shane up going to help? Explain that to me. And what if Gabe ends up arrested? Will that help? Or maybe Gabe will end up seriously hurt or dead. That's a big help, right?"

Blaine picked that moment to butt in. "Gabe can handle himself, Boss. And Cal's right, Gabe's taking care of business."

I turned and did the one-eye glare at Grandpa. "Do you see what you did?"

His blue eyes weren't the least bit remorseful. "Now Sammy, Gabe had a right to know."

I was done being reasonable. I whirled back around and advanced on Cal. "You are going to go after your brother right now and stop him."

"I am?"

He had the same amused twist to his mouth that Gabe often wore. That just made me angrier. He thought I was some helpless little woman. "Yes, you are." I poked him in the chest with my right index finger. "Because if you don't, then I will. And when I get there, I'm going to go into Gabe's truck and get his gun out. The thing is, I don't know anything about guns, but I promise you, I will shoot someone." God, I was mad.

For the first time, Cal looked concerned. "You shouldn't handle guns if you don't know anything about them."

I blew out an aggravated breath. "Do I look like I'm in the mood for a lecture on weapons, Cal? Now either you go after your brother or I will. Which is it going to be?"

"I don't want Cal getting hurt!" Lola put her hand on his forearm and pouted.

I grabbed Lola's left arm and yanked her off Cal and over to stand by me. "You," I said to the sex siren, "stand here and be quiet."

She sighed but didn't say another word.

I turned back to Cal. "Well?"

"I'm going." He headed to the door.

Grandpa hurried after him. "I'll tell you how to get there."

I swallowed a groan. "Don't you go with him, Grandpa! You stay here!"

"Damn, she's bossy," Cal muttered as he and Grandpa walked out.

I turned back to Blaine and Lola. I still had a hold on Lola's arm. "As for you two, just stay away from each other." I cut my gaze to Lola. "You stop trying to make Blaine jealous and stay off Gabe's brother. He's got enough problems."

Lola looked down at her four-inch wedge sandals.

I shifted to Blaine. "And you, stop acting like a big, mad bear. I'm sorry I didn't tell you I signed Lola on as a client. We'll talk about it later."

Blaine lifted his lip in a sneer. "What's to talk about? I don't care what she does." He turned and stomped off to Gabe's side of the office, probably to cut some phone line he could use to strangle me.

Lord this was turning into a bad day. And where the hell was Grandpa? If he went with Cal, I was going to—

"Sam?"

I blinked and looked at Lola. "What?"

"Can you let go of my arm now?"

I realized I was practically digging my fingers into her arm. I let go instantly. "Oh Lola, I'm so sorry!"

She grinned, making her appear impossibly young, carefree, and sexy. "It's men. They make us nuts."

"Sam," Grandpa came back in. "Vance is here."

I ran to the front window. Yep, that was Vance's unmarked green Ford Taurus pulling into a parking spot. I watched as Vance unfolded himself from the car, shut the door, and looked this way.

"He's one fine-looking man."

I looked over at Lola. "Are you ovulating or something?"

She grinned. "A girl's gonna notice."

She looked so cute and sexy at the same time, I really wanted to hate her. So naturally, I liked her.

Vance walked through the door, looked around, then settled his stare on Lola.

"Detective Vance, this is Lola. She's . . . uhh . . . a client."

He slid forward to take her hand in his. "Hello." His voice was as smooth as his butt probably was. "Why would a lovely woman like you sign up at a dating service?"

Lola flashed him a killer smile. "I like my men to be pre-screened."

"Smart," Vance conceded.

I stood behind Vance and cleared my throat. "Any chance you are here because you got my phone message?"

He turned around. "You said you wanted to talk about—" Vance broke off and reached out to take hold of my chin. "What happened?"

I pulled my face from his hand and took control. "Let's go in my office—"

Vance stepped closer. "Who hit you, Shaw? Tell me now."

"Shane Masters hit her," Grandpa said.

Vance managed to back me up to the wall. His expression darkened. "Didn't I tell you to stay away from him? How bad are you hurt? Where's the blood smear on your shirt from?"

His voice had slid from anger to something softer. "Just my arm. I'm fine. And I didn't go to Shane, he came to us." Vance towered over me. I could smell his sun and coconut scent, although right now he didn't resemble a sun god; he looked more like a pissed-off warrior. Was he mad at me? "This isn't my fault! Someone tried to break into one of Shane's prop trailers, and Shane thinks Grandpa knows who did it. He was threatening Grandpa right on our front porch. What was I supposed to do?"

"Call me."

I threw up my hands in frustration. "I did call you—that's why you're here now!"

His jaw bulged. "I'm here now because a dead body turned up with a dog bite on his hand."

Oh God. Things were spiraling out of control. "The hit man? Was he murdered?"

His face was stony. "We're talking about you. Let me be clear. Shane Masters went to your house, threatened your grandfather, then hit you?"

I nodded cautiously. "I pulled out my pepper spray and told him to leave. He didn't like that. He knocked it out of my hand and smacked me."

He looked down and took hold of my arm. "How did you get this?" His fingers were warm as he gently bent my arm up.

"I tackled him and knocked him off the porch. Unfortunately I flew off the porch with him. It's just a scrape. Vance, what about the body? Was it the hit man? Was he murdered?" We had to tell him where Grandpa was Monday night. And what did this have to do with the attempt to break into Shane's prop trailer?

"You tackled him after he hit you?"

Huh? Oh, Shane. "And after Grandpa sprayed him with his pepper spray pen."

Vance's jaw throbbed. "Stay here. I'll be back." He dropped my arm and headed out the door.

"Vance! Where are you going?" Frustration clawed through my stomach.

He stopped and turned around, his entire body tight

with tension. "I don't care how famous Shane Masters is. No one comes to my town and starts smacking around women that I c . . ." He sucked in a breath. "Any woman." He stormed off.

I stood there stunned. "Are all men insane? Is it a full moon?" Vance had had a violent look in his eye.

Lola put her hand on my shoulder. "He cares about you."

I looked at her. "He thinks I'm a bimbo pain in the butt." I just could not believe this day. "And I think he's a stuck-up, by-the-book, pain in my butt." Which is what made this really weird. Vance came here for a reason, and obviously the reason had been the dead body that might be the hit man who attempted to kill Shane. And Vance just abandoned that reason to run off after Shane. Maybe Vance was having a breakdown.

Lola nodded. "So you care about him too."

Now that was just insulting. "I do not." I lifted my chin and wished for some Tylenol. "Vance and I have an agreement to dislike each other. Just yesterday he told me we could never be friends."

"Men," Lola said.

Blaine walked out holding a bottle of water. He swept Lola with his glare before settling it on me. "Why is she still here?" He held out the water and a couple pills in his hand.

"What are those?" Given his anger, I was a tad suspicious.

"Advil." He dumped them into my hand.

I tossed the Advil in my mouth and washed them down while thinking. Vance had a dead body, and judging by what he'd said, it could be the hit man. I looked over to see Grandpa and Blaine standing on one side of the newly opened-up space between the two suites and watching me, and Lola was on the other side. I looked at Grandpa. "You have to tell Vance where you were Monday night. And we have to tell him . . . the other stuff." Like Bo. And that I had a client. I looked over at Lola. Maybe about her too. As it was, there were three people who might have reason to want Shane dead. Bo Kelly, if he thought Shane would spoil his show and ruin his chance for his Magic Bo cartoon. Nikki Eden for breaking her heart and maybe using her to get information to spoil her show. And Lola, whom Shane was firing for being fat. I should have told Vance yesterday.

I walked across the empty reception area. "If Gabe were here, he would know what to do," I muttered. But Gabe was at Shane's possibly committing a crime, and Vance was on his way there right now to witness the crime. I made a decision. "Let's go."

Blaine stepped in front of me. "Where are you going? What about her?" He jerked his thumb toward Lola.

I gritted my teeth to keep from screaming. But that hurt my bruised cheek. Sheesh. I took a breath and said in a perfectly reasonable boss voice, "I'm going to track down all the insane men who don't think I can take care of myself before they do something more stupid than usual. And I'm taking Grandpa with me, as he's going to tell Vance exactly where he was Monday night once we find those stupid, stupid men."

Blaine crossed his arms over his chest. "Take her too. Don't leave her here with me."

Sure, why not? It'll be a party when we get to Shane's expensive, fancy trailer. I had never seen Blaine this passionate and emotional about anything that didn't have an engine and consume motor oil. But I didn't have time to think about that; I had to chase down two of the most unreasonable men in Lake Elsinore.

"Fine." I stomped out with Grandpa and Lola. Both of them took one look at my bruised and furious face and wisely chose to follow without complaining.

We got to the campground just in time to see several cop cars with flashing lights and sirens racing up to Shane's trailer.

Something bad had happened.

11

The police were setting up a barricade to keep everyone back from Shane Masters's motor home. I parked the Jeep a few campsites away, then Grandpa, Lola, and I got out and made our way toward the taped-off motor home.

"Shane must have been murdered," Grandpa said. "I didn't stop it."

I looked over at him as he walked between Lola and me. His shoulders were hunched, and his face looked clammy in the afternoon sunlight. I saw Lola put her hand on his arm, which told me that she was as caring as she was sexy. I put my hand on his right arm. "Whatever happened, it's not your fault."

An animal control van drove past us through the police barricade toward Shane's motor home. That was weird.

"Shaw."

I had been watching the van and didn't see Vance approach. He caught us just before we reached where the police were setting up the barricade. "Vance, what happened? Where's Gabe?" I saw his truck, and Cal's truck. Where were they?

Vance stopped and looked down at me. "What time did Shane leave your house?"

"Uhh," It was a little after three now. "I guess it was about one o'clock?" I turned to look at Grandpa.

He nodded.

Vance had his small notebook out and made a note. Then he looked up. "Where were you?"

"Me?" Oh God, Shane had to be dead. "Vance, what is going on?"

He tightened his face into a hard expression. "Answer the question."

"Grandpa and I went in the house until Blaine called me to tell me that I was ... uh ... needed at the office."

"Time?"

I shrugged. "I'm not sure."

Lola answered. "I was at the office. I heard Blaine call Sam around 1:45 and I think she got there in less than a half hour."

Vance looked at Lola, only this time his expression was suspicious. "I'll get your information later." He turned to Grandpa. "What time did Shane arrive at the house and what did he want?"

Grandpa straightened his back. "He arrived no more than ten minutes before Sam got home, so that would be around ten to one. He demanded that I tell him the magician trying to kill him. I told him I didn't know. He didn't believe me, and he pulled out a fake thumb that he said he found right outside a prop trailer that someone tried to break into. It was Shane's theory that the magician who sent the hit man had now come to Elsinore to kill him in person."

A muscle along Vance's jaw twitched. "Someone has killed Shane Masters. Do you know who it is?"

I blurted out, "Shane's been killed?"

Vance ignored me. "Mr. Webb?" he said to Grandpa.

"No, I don't know."

Vance came right back with, "But you were trying to find out for Masters?"

Grandpa shook his head. "Sam and I saw Shane yesterday, and he was trying to blackmail me into using my connections to find out if a magician had put a hit out on him. I was trying, but not for Shane. I just needed to know."

I slid my hand down Grandpa's arm and took his hand in mine.

Vance cut his gaze to me and then down to the thin scab on the back of my hand. "Guess you forgot to mention that little detail yesterday."

My stomach flipped over.

He turned back to Grandpa. "Did the fake thumb Masters showed you today mean anything?"

Grandpa's hand tightened on mine. "I'm not sure, Detective, because it's a common prop most magicians have. However, last night at my house Bo Kelly was doing some close-up magic with one just like it. When Bo left, it was in his pocket."

"Who is Bo Kelly?"

I let Grandpa answer that while I looked around. Where were Gabe and Cal? Could Vance have had them taken down to the police station? Had Gabe found Shane murdered? Why was the animal control unit there? Vance was writing something down and I said, "Where are Shane's dogs? Were they hurt?"

Vance zeroed in on my face. "Why do you ask?"

I'd hit on something. I could see it from Vance's carefully schooled face. But I had no idea what I'd hit on. "Well, the animal control van is here, and they let the van through the police barricade. I can't hear the dogs. . . ."

I trailed off, realizing the dogs could have been killed too.

I wasn't a big fan of those dogs, but I didn't want them dead. Where was Gabe?

Vance sighed. "The dogs are alive, but it looks like they have been tranquilized or poisoned. They are both out cold."

"Oh." I didn't know what to make of that.

Vance turned back to Grandpa. "Where were you Monday night?"

That got my attention. Was this about the hit man he found dead?

Grandpa said, "I was with a friend."

Lola jumped in. "He was with me. He was helping me figure out where to get a job."

"With you?" I was stunned. But then I started thinking. How had Grandpa known where Shane was staying when he went to see him Tuesday? Lola had told him. And now it made sense why he wouldn't tell Vance where he was Monday night—he was protecting Lola. She had already told me that Shane had them all sign contracts to keep his shows a secret. Besides, Lola had seemed really afraid of Shane. Grandpa was exactly the kind of man who would protect her.

Vance studied Lola. "How long have you lived in Lake Elsinore? What is the nature of your relationship with Mr. Webb?"

Lola brushed her long wavy hair back. "I'm one of Shane's assistants. He wasn't planning to keep me on after the show on Saturday. I decided to stay here in Elsinore because I grew up here. And Barney is just being a friend. He didn't tell you about me because if Shane found out, he would have fired me instantly instead of after the Saturday show."

"How did you and Mr. Webb meet exactly? Did you know him when you lived here?"

She shook her head. "I met him on the Internet. Magicians' assistants have an e-mail loop where we chat and stuff. Barney was a guest one night for a chat. We started privately e-mailing after that."

Vance wrote down some notes. After he was finished, he lifted his head to look at me speculatively, then looked back at Lola. "And it was just a coincidence that you happened to go to Heart Mates and sign up?"

For the first time, Lola looked uncomfortable. "Not exactly."

"Explain."

I jumped a couple inches at Vance's sharp voice. He was getting really mad.

Lola swallowed and said, "I left my husband a few years back and I wanted to reconcile with him. Since he works at Heart Mates, it seemed like a good idea . . . ." She trailed off and looked at me.

I was in enough trouble. For once, I kept my mouth shut.

"Who is your husband?" Vance asked in a perfectly reasonable voice.

"Blaine Newport."

Vance turned his gaze on me, and this time his stare stuck.

I was instantly defensive. "I only found out this morning!"

Vance turned and waved a uniform over. Once the cop trotted over, Vance gestured toward Grandpa and Lola. "Escort these two over to where the two witnesses are sitting. Make sure they don't talk."

The policeman was young and very courteous. "If you'll come with me please," he said, and walked with them toward the police barricade. I heard him say, "I can get you some water or coffee."

I watched them walk away and tried not to acknowledge Vance staring at me. But finally I had to turn and meet his flat brown eyes. "The other witnesses—are they Gabe and Cal?"

He scissored his jaw for about ten seconds, then said, "Yes. Pulizzi found Shane. He called it in, and the call was patched through to me in my car."

I lifted my chin. "I want to see Gabe." Was he okay?

"I called you yesterday for help, Shaw. Now Shane Masters has been murdered in my town. Any idea how much heat is going to come down on me?"

My throat tightened. "I didn't know. . . . I had a client, I was just trying to—"

He took a step closer. "You are not a professional. You are a soccer mom! When are you going to understand that you can trust me?" His voice dropped.

"I'm sorry. But damn it, Vance, you suspected my grandfather. How did I know I could trust you? Shane threatened to set him up! He swore he could make him look guilty of hiring a hit man. I just wanted to talk to Gabe, then I was going to tell you everything I knew. And it wasn't much!"

He leaned in. "Who are you working for now? This client that you have, who is it?"

I didn't hesitate. "Nikki Eden and her grandmother, Rosy Malone." I took a breath. "Nikki is a rising magician who currently has a show in Las Vegas. She came into town yesterday. She had an affair with Shane that ended badly, and she was afraid he was going to spoil her show this weekend. She hired me to try and find out."

"Did you find out if it was her show?"

I shook my head. "I went to the stadium today to see if I could talk to a few people, maybe spot some props. See, Nikki does high-concept, or sometimes called high-cost, illusions like riding onto the stage on a motorcycle, then vanishing the bike while riding it. Her illusions have large props, so I thought maybe someone would have seen something."

Vance wrote more notes and clenched his jaw so tight I wondered if his eyes hurt. His whole body was rigid as a boulder. Finally he said, "Let's recap: A famous magician comes to my town and someone tries to kill him. And just by coincidence, Shane's employee, whom he is firing, signs on with your dating service and has secret meetings with your grandfather and a secret marriage with your office assistant. Then two magicians just happen to show up in Elsinore and have reason to see you."

He paused to suck in air to feed his tirade, and it popped into my head that three magicians had come to town, not two. But Fletch was helping Grandpa and had nothing to do with either the hit man or killing Shane. There was no reason to piss Vance off more by mentioning him. Besides, Fletch was skydiving today, so he had a rock-solid alibi.

Vance continued, "First is Bo Kelly, who has a possible contract for a cartoon character and may have attempted to break into one of Shane's prop trailers to see if Shane was spoiling his show and his chances for the cartoon. Then Shane's ex-lover, who had a bad breakup with him, hired you to see if he was going to spoil her magic show Saturday night. On top of all that, your grandfather was being blackmailed by the murdered magician. Did I get that all correct, Shaw?"

"Uh, yeah." He managed to summarize the last two days into a paragraph. Guess that's why he made detective.

But he wasn't done. "All the suspects who had reason to kill Shane Masters are hooked up with you. Which you never bothered to tell me. And," he leaned an inch closer, "the magician has now been murdered in my town!"

Uh-oh. "It wasn't like that!"

He narrowed his gaze. "You and all your cohorts can explain exactly what it was like in formal statements down at the station."

It was dark by the time Gabe and I left the police station. Grandpa, Lola, and Cal had escaped first since they had less complicated stories. Gabe and I had been kept separate, but as a guess, I assumed he was put through a bit more because he found Shane dead.

Needless to say, Vance was a little pissed off. Murdered famous people in his town ruined his day. So he made sure to ruin ours, which in retrospect seemed like a fair trade-off. Vance was really angry at me. The only thing that mollified him was that I had called him after Shane left our house. He believed Grandpa and I were going to tell him all that we knew.

And I truly hadn't known much yesterday at lunch.

Gabe took my arm as we went out of the building into the parking lot. I didn't have my car since Grandpa and I had been using his Jeep, and once Vance was finished with him, he had taken the Jeep home. As we walked to where Gabe's truck was parked, I said, "Are you all right? That had to be awful to find Shane."

He didn't miss a step and just said, "Fine."

I had so many emotions rushing through me I couldn't keep them all straight. One of them was guilt over being the reason Gabe went to Shane's and found him murdered. "If only you hadn't run off to Shane's like that."

He came to a sudden stop at the back bumper of his truck. "What?"

I looked up into his face. We stood under one of those amber-colored lights that cast a glow over the hard-edged planes of Gabe's face. His anger practically glimmered in the light. "You wouldn't listen to me. If you hadn't gone there, you wouldn't have found him and you wouldn't have had to go through all this." It wasn't a hard concept.

He asked softly, "So you think I should let a man knock you around? Is that it, Sam? Or are you mad because you had already called Vance to rescue you?"

I tried to yank my arm from his grasp, but he held on firmly. "I didn't need to be rescued! I tried to tell you that, but you were so busy being the hotshot hero, you just sprang into action." Bone-deep fatigue and raw anger mixed to a dangerous potion. "But God forbid I should try to help you. You cut me out of your family problems and refuse to tell me what's really bothering you about our new arrangement, and I'm the one that's got the problem?"

He dropped my arm. "Now you're pissed because I'm not eating bonbons and sharing my feelings? Pissed enough to go running to Vance?"

"I never ran to Vance! I called him after Shane attacked me because he's a cop. That's rational, Pulizzi. Your running off to beat the shit out of Shane is not rational." My anger and anxiety shoved out my tiredness. My deepest fears shot right up from the dark places inside of me. "I didn't ask you to go on *Dr. Phil* and split open a vein. I asked you to tell me when you have a problem. I'm supposed to be your partner, but you are shutting me out." I hated the pain wrapping around my insides, and I practically yelled, "Do you think I'm so stupid I can't see you are having regrets?"

Gabe leaned into me. "As it happens, sugar, I've been a

little busy for teatime chats. I've been working my ass off on the construction to save you money. I've had to juggle my clients, and then Cal managed to fuck up his life, really cutting into the time I usually reserve for your daily crises and the self-esteem feeding you require every three hours!"

I stepped back, feeling like I'd been God-smacked with the truth. I was a drain on him. Scalding tears burned my eyes and clogged my throat. Embarrassment, anger, and hurt roiled up, and I said, "You go take care of your family and I'll take care of mine!" Shaking with emotion I didn't want to name, I added, "And why don't you pull that old wall out from up your ass, then put it back up between our businesses. Then you won't have to worry about me or my self-esteem ever again." I turned around and stormed off toward the doors of the police station.

"Goddamn it, Sam. Get back here!" Gabe yelled at me.

I ignored him and pulled my phone out of my purse. Who did I call? My best friend Angel was out of town on a buying trip. Blaine was mad as hell at me, and he had been staying with the boys while Grandpa and I were at the police station. I had never felt so alone. I stared at my phone through my tears and called the last person I ever imagined I would. "Mom?"

"Samantha, what's wrong?"

"I'm at the police station. Can you come get me?" I waited, knowing she would launch into a lecture with a thousand questions. I kept my stare on the sidewalk at my feet.

"I'm over at Cocoa's; I can be there in five minutes." She hung up.

Shocked, I hung up. I guess she heard my tears in my voice.

Gabe touched my shoulder.

I turned around. "Don't touch me. I'm such a huge problem for you? Then I'll solve it. I'll pay you back and I'll be out of your life."

His face drained of everything. All he said was, "Don't leave this parking lot. Wait for your mom." Then he strode across the parking lot, got into his truck, and roared off.

"Don't cry over a man, Samantha. They aren't worth it." My mom pulled out of the police station. She had a white-knuckled grip on the steering wheel. "What happened to your face?"

"Shane." I was just too tired and depressed. Gabe's expression when I'd told him I'd be out of his life was imprinted on my brain. But what did he want from me?

"And now he's been murdered. Did Gabe kill him?"

"What?" I sat up. "No. Gabe didn't kill him."

She pulled her mouth tight. "He's going to hurt you. Better to be done with him now."

He'd already hurt me. "Mom, I told him it was over, okay?" But I didn't want it to be over. I wanted to fix that horrible look on his face. Had I been wrong? Was I being unfair?

Mom took a deep breath. "Then you're stronger and smarter than I ever was."

I gaped at my mom's profile in the dark. Into her fifties, she was still an attractive woman. Her neck was getting a little looser, and there were lines around her eyes and mouth, but men still looked at my mom. They always had. So what did her comment mean? "You always had boyfriends." Each one had become the center of her universe while he lasted.

She didn't look at me but concentrated on driving. "Getting them is easy. Keeping them isn't. And men call us fickle. But at least you didn't wait around for Gabe to break your heart."

It hit me so hard, I lost my breath. That was exactly what I had done. For days, the fear that Gabe didn't want me anymore had been building. And when it finally bubbled to a confrontation, when he said something that I could seize on as proof, I struck first. I hurt him, just in case he suddenly morphed into the cheating worm my dead husband had been.

Regret pressed down on me and mixed with a sick feeling of self-disgust. I didn't give Gabe a chance. I didn't let him tell me exactly what he felt. What his worries, burdens, and fears were.

"How long is your lease on the building for Heart Mates, Samantha?"

I blinked and tried to follow along. "I just signed another year."

"Okay, we can work the lease into selling the business, I think. Give me your landlord's name."

I sat up straight. We were almost to the house. "Mom, I'm not selling Heart Mates. Not now and not ever."

She pulled into the dirt lot in front of the house and stopped, leaving the car idling. "You'll work next to Gabe even if you've broken up? I'll pay to have that wall replaced, then we will—"

"No." My head throbbed, my eye ached, and I felt like the worst kind of failure. But Heart Mates was mine. I was building it step by step. And right now, we had bigger problems with Shane's murder. I knew Grandpa was not going to stop until he found the magician who killed Shane.

Even if it was Bo Kelly.

I was going to set my problems and worries aside to be

there for Grandpa and help him. I also had to talk to Nikki and Rosy. I had failed to find out what they wanted, and I'd had to tell Vance about Nikki and Shane's affair. I needed to talk to them.

"Mom, thank you for picking me up and giving me a ride home. But I have to sort things out for myself." Before she could answer, I got out of the car and slammed the door.

She watched me through the window with a tight expression, then she drove away.

My mom drove me crazy, but she had come when I'd needed her, and I loved her for it. I just wished that I could have told her that. But we weren't a huggy-feely mother and daughter.

I turned to go into the house when the sound of a truck caught my attention. My heart leaped, but when I looked, it was a small truck pulling in just as my mom left—the truck that Fletch had rented.

I went up on the porch and waited for Fletch. In the pool of amber given off by the porch light, his skin look pale, making his freckles stand out. "Hey, you okay?" I asked as I reached past him to open the door.

He flashed a toothy grin. "Yeah. I went for my parachuting lesson." We both walked in the house. The boys were eating pizza at the table with Grandpa. No sign of Blaine, so he must have gone home. I supposed he was still mad at me over Lola.

"There's plenty of pizza," Grandpa said.

Fletch groaned. "I think I'll just have some water."

I followed him into the kitchen. A little worry about him crowded in among all my other feelings. I paused to kiss TJ and Joel and pat Ali. "No pizza for her," I reminded the boys. Then I went to the fridge to pull out a beer and handed Fletch a bottle of water. Under the fluorescent light, he had an almost green tint to his skin. "Your jump didn't go well?"

He took the water, drank a small sip, then said, "I was fine until the airplane took off."

Joel snickered.

TJ announced, "Airsick," and took another piece of pizza.

Fletch laughed too. "Who knew? I never thought of getting airsick. The instructor wouldn't let me jump." He took another drink of his water and fixed his gaze on me. "What happened to you?"

Joel set his pizza down. "Grandpa told us not to ask Mom about it until she settled down. He said she's all nerved up and mad at Gabe."

Grandpa knew Gabe and I had a fight at the police station?

Fletch slammed his water down on the counter. "Gabe? Your boyfriend? He hit you?"

Here we go again, I thought tiredly. *Another outraged male.* "No. Gabe did not hit me. Gabe would never hit me. Shane Masters smacked me. Gabe and most every other available male in the city went after him, but they were too late. Shane was dead." Belatedly, I thought about the boys. I should never have said it like that. Quickly, I walked toward them. "But I'm fine."

TJ swiveled around in his chair to look at my face. "Your face doesn't look fine to me. And you shouldn't be mad at Gabe, Mom. He did the right thing."

What happened to my sweet little boys with the chubby arms and dirty hands that hugged me tight? My heart caught and swelled when I looked at my two sons. My babies were growing into men. Both of them had their dad's blue eyes. TJ had a harder cut face that was pulled tight with outrage. Joel usually had charm stamped all over his

face, but right now he frowned with anger. I could see responsible young men with a strong sense of justice and a
protective streak for me, their mom. God I was proud of
them. "You might be right, TJ," I said to my oldest son.
"But Gabe should also have listened. Your grandpa, Ali,
and I handled Shane."

Joel nodded approvingly. "Grandpa told us."

Fletch sat down heavily at the table and swallowed.
"Shane is dead? What happened?"

It would be all over Lake Elsinore and in the newspapers, so I couldn't protect the boys from the truth. With
my hand on TJ's shoulder, I said, "Someone shot him."

TJ looked up at me. "Mom, are you investigating?"

I wasn't even sure Gabe and I were working together
anymore after what I'd said to him. Or if I had a client
once I talked to Nikki and Rosy. "I'm going to talk to my
client in a little bit, TJ. We'll see from there." Grandpa did-
n't appear to be a suspect anymore. But someone killed
that hit man and Shane. And we were all afraid it was a magician.

Grandpa set down his iced tea. "I'm not stopping. I
have to find out if one of the Triple M magicians is behind
this."

I noticed he barely ate any of his slice of pizza and that
he didn't mention Bo in front of the boys. No reason to
worry them any more than they already were. They both
liked Bo. "But you are being careful, right?"

Fletch was recovering from the shock and cut in. "I'll
stay and help him tonight. We'll be careful." He glanced at
Grandpa. "We are just looking for information. No one
will know."

Fletch stared down at his hands playing with a napkin. I
felt a little sorry for him. He came to visit his mentor,
Grandpa, and was thrust into this mess. But I was more

worried about Grandpa. Someone was desperate enough to try to have Shane killed, then to probably do it himself when that failed. If that person found out that Grandpa was on his trail, he might decide to get rid of Grandpa. But I didn't want to say that in front of the boys. "Just promise me you'll stay here in the house tonight."

Grandpa said, "I'll be careful, Sam. Now stop worrying about me."

He sidestepped my question, but I decided to wait until I could talk to him without the boys around. I turned to Fletch. "Do you want some chicken soup or some toast?" He still looked greenish, and he appeared to be avoiding looking at the pizza.

He shook his head. "Nah. It'll wear off in a while and my appetite will be back."

I didn't have much of an appetite either. I was trying to figure out what to do next when the doorbell rang.

Ali raced to the door, barking loudly. I went to the front window and looked out. Then I ran to the door and yanked it open. "Cal? What's wrong? Is Gabe okay?"

12

Cal stood in the doorway and grinned at me. "Gabe's being an ass, uh I mean a bear. Can I stay here tonight?"

Huh? TJ and Joel came up behind me, which explained Cal's changing his choice of words, but why would he ask to stay here? Had Gabe told him we'd had a fight?

Of course he had, and that was why Cal was here.

I narrowed my eyes. "Gabe sent you."

Cal's face hardened. "Either I sleep on your couch or in my truck. Your choice."

I opened the door, then turned and stormed down to my bedroom where I slammed the door. I stood there in the middle of my room and felt like an idiot. Cal was just like his brother, Gabe. Just like him. And he probably hated me for what I said to Gabe. But that hero streak must run through the whole Pulizzi clan, so they couldn't leave us unprotected.

I had to pull myself together. With Cal here to watch over Grandpa and the boys, I could go talk to Nikki and hunt down Bo. I'd take my stun gun and pepper spray. Better to leave Ali here as an extra layer of protection.

Did Cal have a gun?

"Sam?"

I jumped and whirled around.

Cal walked into my bedroom and shut the door behind him. He wore a haunted and tired expression. His face looked better than yesterday though. I don't know why I was surprised that he came into my bedroom. Gabe appeared in my room whenever he damn well felt like it. I lifted my chin. "Did you come in here to yell at me?"

Cal stopped short a couple feet from me. "Christ, no."

"Then what?" Cal looked a lot like Gabe, but whenever Gabe came into my bedroom the sexual sizzle nearly burned the house down. With Cal I just felt defensive and inadequate. No sizzle. But what pissed me off more, because I didn't understand it, was that I felt safe.

He closed the distance between us. "I came in here to see if you are all right."

"Of course I am. I can take care of my own family. I told Gabe that. He doesn't have to worry about us." I tried to look strong, but regret weighed heavily on me. I knew I wasn't being fair to Gabe.

Cal looked down at me. "He wants to worry about you." He said softly, "I've never seen Gabe love anyone the way he loves you."

That statement took my breath away. "Don't say that. You don't know what I said to him. . . ." I turned away and looked out the dark window set high on the wall over my bookcases.

Cal put his hand on my shoulder. "I don't know what you said, but I've known Gabe all his life. I've said a few things to him I regret. He's never held it against me. He's said things to me—it's what families do."

I stared out that dark rectangle. "I was afraid. A coward."

Cal snorted.

I turned around, knocking his hand off my shoulder. "Why do you men snort?"

"Coward? You?" He snorted again. "You attacked a man twice your size after he hit you."

I straightened my shoulders. "That was fear. He was threatening my grandfather." Knocking Shane off the front porch had nothing to do with bravery and everything to do with fear for Grandpa's safety.

He shook his head. "Sam, you aren't a coward. And don't take all the blame for your fight. I've watched Gabe push you away. Tonight you pushed back. You are exactly the kind of woman Gabe needs."

I looked up at my ceiling. "You Pulizzis are a strange lot, you know that? I'm older than Gabe. I have teenagers! I don't want babies. And I don't want to get married. I'm not leaving my grandfather to live alone. And I'm not going to be bossed around by a stubborn, strong-willed man no matter how sexy he is!" Gabe's mom liked me, and now his brother liked me, and *oh hell*— "Tell me I didn't say that out loud."

Cal cracked a grin that probably hurt his scabbed lip. "'Fraid so."

Great. Nothing like telling Gabe's brother I find Gabe sexy. I wondered if the family collected all my embarrassing moments for the nights when there's nothing on TV? Maybe that's why they want Gabe to keep seeing me—my entertainment value. I pushed that away and said, "Why did you come to Gabe's, Cal?" I knew Gabe wanted me to stay out of Cal's problems, but he was already pissed at me.

The humor in his expression died. "I thought Gabe would understand." He turned away from me, looking toward my desk in the corner by the bathroom door. "Maybe he does. I don't know. I knew that Gabe would stand with me though, no matter how much I screwed up."

I stared at Cal's profile; it was hard and longing at the same time. "Do you love her? Your Melanie?"

"Loved. As in the past."

"Then why did you go after her husband?" I was trying to understand.

He walked to my desk and sat down in my folding chair. "Because I did love her once, and in a way, I felt like I drove her to that bastard by not marrying her when she wanted me to. But I wasn't going after him to beat him up. I was going to call the cops and tell them where he was once I verified it."

I didn't understand. I walked over and sat down on the corner of my desk. "So what happened?"

Cal picked up one of my romance novels for which I had recently finished writing a critique, and he seemed to study the book cover. "He was with a couple firefighter buddies of his who were protecting him, two men who strongly suggested that I should mind my own business and let Dirk handle his wife." Cal's face darkened. "I told them that no one gets a free walk on putting a woman in the hospital, not even a fellow fireman."

I studied his face as he stared intently at the book cover. I knew he didn't see the cover, but some internal struggle. Then I got it. "They jumped you, didn't they? And the guys are Dirk's witnesses that you attacked him."

He looked up at me with his dark eyes. "My dad was a firefighter."

Cripes. I reached over and put my hand over his holding the book. "I didn't get the chance to meet your dad, but I've met your mom and I know Gabe. I bet your dad would be much more proud of the man you are than the career you chose."

Surprise softened his face. "Maybe."

"You've put off telling Gabe this because he'll go after these other firefighters? Dig up stuff on them to support your story?" Jeopardizing his future as a firefighter. Oh sure, technically it shouldn't happen. But we didn't live in a perfect world.

"Partly. And because as a cop, Gabe was part of a brotherhood too. He still has close ties to those guys."

Jeez, Cal was afraid Gabe wouldn't understand. Quietly, I said, "Gabe was your brother long before he ever became a cop."

He nodded, accepting that as fact. "Thanks, Sam. I just need some time."

It was my turn to nod. "And I have to go find Gabe."

Cal checked his watch. "He should be heading over to the motel where Bo Kelly is staying. Gabe worked on a diagram of the murder scene, and he's been running down as much information as he can find on Bo."

I frowned. "But Bo's not at his motel, we've try calling . . . oh." Gabe was going to get into his room and take a look around. I started putting some pieces together: Grandpa knowing that I'd had a fight with Gabe at the police station, and his sidestepping my question about staying in tonight. Gabe had talked to him, probably told him we'd fought, and now Grandpa and Gabe were working together. Grandpa had avoided my question about going out because he would go out if Gabe found Bo. "Gabe called Grandpa after our fight."

Cal nodded. "He told Barney he'd work on physically tracking down Bo. And he suggested Barney try getting into Bo's bank accounts to see if he had any large withdrawals. Since Bo registered at the motel, if Barney could track down the credit card he used, that card might lead Barney to Bo's bank."

I stood up off the desk. "I'm going to find Gabe."

"The Night Haven Motel."

I nodded. "Thanks. I kind of wish I had a brother like you." I hoped he didn't think I was being too sappy.

Cal stood up and hugged me to him. "Now you do." Then he turned and left the room.

Damn.

I changed into a black tank top with a built-in panel that doubled as a flimsy bra and traded in my turquoise shoes for tennies. If I was going to do some breaking and entering with Gabe—assuming Gabe was even speaking to me—I wanted to be dressed for it. I gathered up my stun gun and pepper spray. Then I said good-bye to the boys, who were fine with me leaving once they determined I'd be with Gabe. They were happy to hang out with Cal while Fletch and Grandpa worked on the computer.

Breaking and entering into motel records and banks. I repressed a shudder and prayed Grandpa didn't get caught.

Ali met me at the door.

"No Ali, you have to stay here."

She stared harder at the closed door and barked.

"Take her, Sam," Grandpa said.

I shrugged and let her out. She ran for my car and jumped in as soon as I opened the door.

Once Ali and I got on the road, I dug my cell phone out and dialed Rosy's phone number.

"Hello?" Her voice sounded tired.

"Rosy, it's Sam. Have you heard about Shane?"

"The police have been here. Nikki's down at the station now, talking to the detective."

I winced. "Oh. Rosy, I'm sorry but with Shane being murdered, I had to tell them . . ."

"Sam, we know. Can you come by in the morning and we'll talk then? We have to find out who killed Shane. To clear Nikki."

I looked over at Ali. She was alternating between sticking her nose out the two-inch crack in the window and watching me while I drove and talked. "You still want me to work for you?"

"Yes. Tomorrow, okay?"

"I'll be there in the morning. Bye." I hung up and put the phone in my purse. It was around eight o'clock, and the traffic was light. Ali wasn't very talkative so I spent the next ten minutes thinking about Gabe and me, and Gabe and his brother. My nerves were strung tight enough to play a tune on by the time I pulled into the Night Haven Motel.

I looked around. It was Wednesday night, and there were a dozen or so cars in the parking lot. I didn't see Gabe's black truck. Fletch's truck was at my house. What had Bo driven? I know I saw it when I drove up to the house yesterday after picking Joel up from school. It had been a . . . Mustang. A green Mustang. I didn't see one here. I slowly drove the length of the parking lot facing the rooms. Then I pulled into a parking space, readying to back out and turn around, when I saw Gabe's big black truck pull into the motel.

I stayed where I was, watching the truck and dealing with a killer case of nerves.

Ali stood up on the seat and barked. She recognized the sound of Gabe's truck.

"Hush, Ali."

She sat down and whined. Gabe was her buddy.

I put my hand on her regal head and said softly, "We'll go see him, I promise. But you have to be quiet and stay with us. No running around."

Gabe drove by, then he turned around and pulled out. Ali whined again.

"He'll be back," I assured her. Sure enough, a few minutes later, I saw him walking down the sidewalk. He'd parked his truck in another spot. I sighed. "He's better at this than we are, girl."

She made a soft sound. Probably she was pointing out that I was the one who sucked at this, not her. I turned and looked at her. "We're going to get out. You stay quiet." Then I opened my door and stepped out. Ali followed me, then she ran over to Gabe. But she didn't make a sound.

I followed a little more slowly. I was pretty sure that he had spotted us already and that Cal had called him to let him know Ali and I were coming to meet him.

Gabe said something to Ali, and she sat down by his side. I could see him scratching her ears with his hand while he watched me. *Cal should see what a big coward I am now,* I thought. I forced myself to walk up to the sidewalk that ran in front of the doors, then down the length of three doors to Gabe.

As soon as I got to him, he said, "Take Ali and walk around like you are looking for a room number while I handle this." He tilted his head toward the door he stood by.

I nodded. "Come on, Ali, we have to find the room." I started walking.

My well-trained dog fell into step beside me. She sniffed the ground and nosed a wadded-up piece of paper while I made a show of looking at each room number as we passed by. When we got down to the end, I turned around to head back and saw that Gabe had the door open. "Found it, Ali," I said in what I hoped was a normal voice. Then I hurried toward Gabe.

He handed me a pair of gloves and said, "Inside."

I passed by him, noticing that he already had gloves on, right before I caught a glimpse of his blank expression. God. What if he just wanted to tell me to get lost? What if Bo came in while he was telling me to get lost? I took a breath and looked around the room. King-size bed covered in a green bedspread. Two bedside tables. Two lamps bolted to the walls. There was a round table with two chairs to my right in front of the window that, thankfully, had the drapes pulled tight. Straight ahead was a mirrored closet, a sink and dressing area, and a door to a bathroom. On my left was a dresser with a TV on top and—

Gabe.

He stood a few feet to my left, watching me.

I sucked in a breath. "Gabe, I should have—"

"Later. Right now let's see what we can find out about Bo Kelly." He went to the dresser and started opening drawers.

I stood there stunned while Ali trotted over to sniff around the dresser. Then I passed Gabe and headed to the bathroom. I found a shaving kit, deodorant, fresh towels, and everything tidy enough that I suspected the maid had been here. I found nothing unusual.

I went to the closet and opened it up. There was a small suitcase on the floor next to some shoes. There were a couple changes of clothes hanging up. "He must intend to come back tonight. His suitcase is here. And a toothbrush in the bathroom." I tried to stay focused.

"Nothing in the drawers except boxers, socks, and some shirts."

I went to the nightstand. "What are we looking for?" I thumbed through a *Newsweek* and *People* magazine when a handwritten note fell out.

"A gun, silencer, sleeping pills, lock-picking tools. Notes

on hit men. A bank slip noting a large withdrawal. A large sum of cash to pay a hit man. Directions to the abandoned house the murdered hit man was found in. Anything that tells us where Bo is now or what he was looking for at the stadium."

I picked up the note and stared at Gabe's back. He finished up the last drawer and stood.

When he saw me staring, he frowned. "What?"

"You've found out so much. It was the hit man that Vance found? How did he die?"

"Overdose of sleeping pills with booze. The severe dog bite points to him being the hit man. They are running prints to see if that will identify him. There was no ID on the body, so look for a wallet or ID that doesn't belong to Bo." Gabe started toward the other side of the bed, then dropped his gaze. "What's in your hand?"

I looked down to the piece of paper I had picked up and read it. "It's the date and time of Shane's show on Saturday. The name of the security company." I looked up at Gabe. "I remember that because my mom and I talked to them at the stadium, and my mom sprayed two of them with pepper spray."

The tense, blank look on Gabe's face splintered for a second, and he lifted an eyebrow.

"Never mind," I said, staring at the paper. "It also has the campground where Shane was staying and a couple names. One of them is Lola. I don't recognize the others. They are women, so maybe they are Shane's assistants."

"That suggests that Bo came here to find Shane," Gabe said. "Anything else on there?"

I shook my head.

"Take the paper and keep looking." Gabe headed into the bathroom to recheck. Since I hadn't known exactly what we were looking for, I didn't let that get to me.

I stuffed the paper in my pocket and looked through the nightstand drawers. It felt creepy to look through Bo's things. But it was creepier to think of him as a killer.

"Sleeping pills. Ambien." Gabe came out with a brown prescription bottle. He opened it and looked in. "There's only two left."

"How many does it take to overdose someone?" I asked, feeling a wet chill soak my body.

"I'm not sure, especially mixed with booze and maybe something else. There'll be a tox report with the autopsy."

I shuddered at the idea of Bo being the killer. I couldn't believe it. To hire a hit man, then kill the hit man when he failed, and then kill Shane, that was desperate. Really desperate. Bo didn't seem that desperate to me. He seemed like Bo. Nikki had seemed more strung out to me than Bo had. I saw that Gabe was copying down all the information from the prescription bottle. Guess he didn't plan on swiping it.

Gabe started back to the bathroom when we both heard a car door slam.

Ali lifted her head off her paws and looked at the door.

Shit. What now? I moved as quietly as I could toward the drapes. Gabe turned off the light, and I parted the drapes a sliver to see outside.

A woman walked to the door of the room next to us. Relief allowed me to drag in a large breath. "Next door," I whispered and let the drapes fall.

Gabe nodded and hurried into the bathroom, then he came out. "Let's go. We've found all we can."

I followed him out of the room after we checked that no one was looking. Gabe shut the door and took my arm, walking me to my car. "Meet me at my house."

I stopped at the door to my T-bird. "The dogs." I could

see his face clearly in the lights mounted outside the doors of the motel. "Were they poisoned? Or drugged?"

"I'll tell you later." He turned and left.

I opened the door for Ali, then got in after her. My shoulders were tight enough to bounce a nickel off of. My stomach churned. I started my car and backed out.

I got to Gabe's house first. Ali sat by me as I stared at his front door and debated using my key. I knew the alarm code too. I could wait inside and pretend we just had a little disagreement.

Or I could wait out here and acknowledge that I didn't know where we stood.

Thank God, Gabe's truck drove up before my brain exploded from the pressure of my thoughts. Ali raced off to greet him as he got out of the truck. I stuck Gabe's house key into my purse and watched Gabe and Ali come up the sidewalk. He unlocked the door, keyed the alarm code, then closed the door behind us.

I looked into his office in the fourth bedroom behind the front door. It was empty except for the box of pictures.

"I've got all my work at the table in the kitchen." Gabe walked away with Ali running ahead because she knew Gabe kept treats for her.

I had this kind of strained relationship with my mother where we didn't really talk. My relationship with my husband had deteriorated to pathetic noncommunication after I realized that the boys and I were only window dressing in his life. Gabe had never, ever let me get away with that in our relationship.

Now he was ignoring our problems.

What was I going to do about it?

I took a breath, straightened up, and hoped I had a fraction of the courage Cal thought I did. I turned down the hallway that opened into the family room and kitchen. Ali had a brand-new chewy bone and plopped down in the family room to gnaw on it.

Gabe stood by his kitchen table in the breakfast nook. I walked up to him and said, "We need to talk."

He picked up the cordless handset of his phone. "Right, but let's see what Barney has first. Maybe he's found a way into Bo's bank accounts to see if he's had large withdrawals."

I grabbed the phone and slammed it down on the table.

The right side of Gabe's jaw twitched. "Don't push me, Sam."

I heard the low threat in his voice and didn't give a rat's ass. "Why the hell not? You've been pushing me away for days."

Gabe went still, except for a slow blink of his dark eyes. "Back off, Sam. We have work to do—"

Fear sparked an adrenaline rush. "Screw work! I want the truth from you. I want to know if you regret our arrangement!" Damn it, if I cried I swear I was going to get my pepper spray out of my purse and make Gabe cry.

Gabe shoulders stiffened and I saw him clench and un-clench his fists at his sides. The nerve deep in his jaw throbbed in beat to his fury. The silence hung thickly, ex-cept for the sound of Ali chewing on her bone.

But I was not going to back down. If Gabe was going to bail out on me, I'd rather know now. And he would bail knowing the whole truth. "I hate feeling this scared, this vulnerable. I can deal with killers and liars, but I can't deal with you hating me for being a burden." *No tears.* I shut my mouth and pressed my lips together to control the urge to cry or throw up. A flash of pain from my black eye and sore cheek made me ease up. But that was a mistake, releasing the hold on my emotions. "You sent your brother to babysit me? God, you must hate that hero streak that forces you to make sure I'm safe. And look at you now." I threw up my right hand to indicate the table covered in diagrams and notes. "Forced to help me find this killer because your conscience won't let you just walk away." I glared at him.

Color flooded his granite face. His eyes burned. He started to lean into a step toward me, then caught hold of himself. "Are you finished?"

I closed my eyes, desperate not to cry. He didn't care. It swept me back to Trent. In the last years, we didn't even fight. We didn't care enough. We just sniped at one another, then stayed away. So was I finished? "Yes. I'm finished." I picked my purse up on the table. *One foot in front of the other and don't cry. Keep walking.*

Dog. God, don't forget my dog. I couldn't come back here. "Ali, come on."

"Ali, stay," Gabe said.

I stopped in the hallway, my back to the wall. Ali looked at me, then at Gabe.

I looked at Gabe. What was he doing?

Ali whined her confusion deep in her throat. She was loyal to Gabe and to me. "Don't do that to her! She doesn't understand!" I felt a tear slip and hated myself. "Fine, she can stay here." I turned and headed for the door.

Gabe caught my arm and pushed my back up to the hallway wall. His face was raw with anger, and maybe pain. "Don't cry."

I sniffled but kept my tears from falling. "Get away from me."

"Too late."

Ali stuck her nose between us.

Gabe let go of my arm and stepped back. He dropped down to his haunches and stroked Ali's head. "That's a good girl."

Her powerful shoulders relaxed and she licked Gabe's hand.

"Go lay down with your bone, Ali." He looked up at me, then back down to Ali. "She's not leaving."

13

I stood in the hallway of Gabe's house with my back to the wall and wondered who the hell Gabe thought he was ordering me and my dog around.

Ali seemed to think it was okay that he told her I wasn't leaving, and she went back to chewing on her bone in the family room.

Gabe stood from the crouched position in which he'd talked to Ali and took hold of my arm. Before I could snatch my arm back, he dragged me with him down the hallway. He hung a left into his bedroom, pulling me behind him. He let go of my arm, reached past me, and shut the door.

Mentally, I tried to catch up. I guessed he wasn't going to yell at me in front of Ali. She wouldn't like it. Why did he have to care about my dog? If he didn't care about my dog, I wouldn't have to remember his face when I'd said he didn't have to worry about me anymore, that I'd be out of his life.

That had been cruel. I had been cruel.

Gabe turned back to me. "I am not going to get away from you. It's your own damn fault. If you don't want me near you, then don't come looking for me. And don't come into my house. Don't stand in front of me with your demands and think I don't have demands of my own." He advanced.

I backed up, not afraid of him physically. "Demands?"

He reached out, taking hold of my shoulders. "I saw Shane dead, and it could have been you that had the bullet through your head. He was killed *minutes* after he left you."

His hands tightened slightly and I felt the tremor go through him, the tremor that urged him to shake me, but Gabe controlled that. But something deep and wild was testing his control. "But I'm fine. I wasn't in danger. What demands?"

"The hell you weren't! Shane smacked you around, and I call that danger. A killer found him fifteen fucking minutes after he left you. That's danger." His jaw tightened, and the cords on his neck stood out.

I could feel the battle in him. "Gabe? What demands?"

"This." He yanked me to him, bringing his mouth down on mine. He opened his mouth, sliding his tongue deep inside of me. His hands released their hold on my shoulders to caress my back. One hand slid around the curve of my hip and pulled me into him.

Into his hard erection trapped in his jeans.

The need for Gabe roared through my blood, and I stopped thinking. Stopped trying to understand. He had demands, and his mouth and hands grew insistent to meet those demands. He caught the edge of my tank top and broke the kiss to haul the top over my head.

I was breathing hard. Wanting him. Wanting a reassurance of him I hadn't known I needed. The solid weight of Gabe over me, thrusting into me.

Gabe moved up to replace cool air on my breasts with

his hot hands. I looked up to his face. "Clothes," I said, and reached for his shirt, dragging it over his head.

He pulled off his pants. I got rid of my shoes, pants, socks. Gabe caught my waist, backing me up to his huge king-size bed before I could remove my panties.

His body gleamed in the bedside light, his skin golden over hard, rippling muscles in his chest that moved as he pushed me back. His erection stood out from between his powerful thighs. I let him push me back and scooted halfway up the bed when he caught the edge of my panties, stripping me bare.

He stood there at the edge of the bed. His gaze, as dark as the fears that made us both so vulnerable, swept down my length until he reached out and parted my knees and looked his fill.

I shivered beneath his stare, seeing the heat roll over him, making his penis dance with anticipation. Warmth spread through me, creating an aching emptiness that only he could fill. "Gabe."

He met my gaze and closed his eyes for a second. "Tell me now if you want gentleness." He opened his eyes. "If I can."

"I want you." I swallowed and fought the flood of desire, need, and fear. "I love you."

He let go of my thighs, put his knee on the bed, and came down on top of me. Taking hold of my wrists, he pulled them over my head and kissed me hungrily with no gentleness but an unrelenting demand. Using one hand to hold my wrists, he dragged his free hand down my length, teasing my breasts, and then he slid his fingers between my legs.

I bucked up against him, needing him. "Now," I said into his mouth. I was beyond gentle. I wanted to possess this man, draw him into me and drive him to losing control until he gave me that part of himself he gave to no one else.

He shifted until his penis prodded against me, poised at the opening to my body. Gabe went still. Holding my hands stretched above us, he looked down into my face. Into my eyes. "Take me." His voice was soft and thick.

I arched up.

He met me, plunging deeply and taking my breath away. The dam of his control broke.

For both of us.

He brought his other arm up and linked his fingers with mine and lowered his head to ravage my mouth. The pressure that had been building for days ripped through both our bodies, forcing us to a frenzied mating. The tensions and needs ratcheted up with every thrust until Gabe lifted his mouth from mine, his breathing ragged, sweat dotting his face. "Give me everything, sweetheart." Then he pulled out and came back into me, and I shattered.

As soon as I went over into a blistering orgasm, Gabe's body went rigid and he drove deeper to gain his release.

Gabe caught his breath and rolled off me. I turned just as he reached for me, holding me. "I'm sorry I hurt you with what I said at the police station."

He grinned, his easy humor returning. "I'm pretty sure pulling that wall out of my ass would hurt too."

I winced. "I was angry and scared—"

He leaned down, kissing me. "Go to sleep."

A slice of panic cut through my languor. "I can't. I have to go home to the boys, and I have to work on this case."

He brought his hand up to touch my sore cheek. "Cal will watch over the boys and Barney with his life. He has a gun with him, one of mine, and he knows how to use it. You need to rest. If you won't sleep with me here, then we're going to your house and the two of us will cram ourselves into your bed." His touch was gentle yet possessive. "We'll fix the world later. But we're going to take a couple hours for ourselves."

I settled against him, knowing that the boys would call me if they wanted me. But I had to tell him two things. "You need to talk to Cal, Gabe." I wasn't going to tell Cal's story. They were brothers—they could work this out. "Sooner rather than later."

"I just bet you got the whole story out of him."

I ignored the sarcasm in his voice. That had been the easy part. Now came a little truth I had been avoiding even telling myself. "I love Heart Mates. It's mine. I know I sound like a child, but it's . . . mine." How did I explain it?

"Sam, I know."

His voice was thickening with drowsiness. I had to get this out. "I don't know if I can do both. The PI stuff and Heart Mates. You signed a lease. I know how much we've spent. How much you've spent. How much work you've done. Your brother is even helping. And Blaine, and the painters are coming tomorrow. . . ." I ran out of words.

Gabe's silence reached every shadowed corner of the bedroom. Then he turned on his side to face me. He was backlit by the bedside lamp, making his black hair gleam and outlining his powerful body. He leaned forward until his face touched mine. "We'll figure it out. But it doesn't change one thing."

Relief sank into me. He wasn't yelling at me. "What?"

"I love you."

I took a sip of coffee and said, "I hope it's decaf." It was midnight, and we'd gotten up to do some work before going to my house.

"Wuss. Next thing you know, you'll be adding water."

I laughed. "Now that you've had sex, you think you're

pretty hot stuff, don't you, stud?" The awful tension between us had eased. The problems were still there, but so was the belief that we'd find a way to deal with them.

Gabe picked up his diagram of the motor home and lifted an eyebrow. "Twice, babe. Want to go for three?"

I rolled my eyes at him and tried not to squirm at the pleasant thought. "Try to concentrate on something besides sex." I reached out and took the diagram from him.

It was Shane's sitting area with the captain chairs, the couch, and the big-screen TV. Gabe had drawn Shane's body where it fell a few feet from the door. "So the killer got a little ways into the motor home?"

"And shut the door," Gabe said,

I looked up.

"Blood spatter."

Ugh. Thankfully he hadn't drawn that in. I assumed he meant some of Shane's blood hit the door where it had been shut. I kept looking at the drawing. Then I realized what that told us. "Someone was in the motor home when Shane went in. That's why Shane was closest to the door and some of his blood hit the door." I shuddered at the thought. I didn't like Shane, but killing him in cold blood was wrong.

"Exactly," Gabe confirmed.

I frowned and looked the hard lines Gabe had drawn to resemble the motor home. Shane was on the floor, but something was missing. "Wait, where are the dogs?" I looked up at Gabe. "Do we know if the dogs were poisoned or drugged?" That seemed really important.

Gabe sat down with his coffee. "Drugged. Sleeping pills or something like that. And they were on Shane's bed."

I sat back in my chair and tried to get a picture in my head of how it happened. "Did they feel sick and go climb up on his bed? Or did the killer put them there?"

Gabe said, "First off, the dogs each had one of those doggie beds by Shane's bed so I doubt they got up on his bed." He tapped the picture. "If I were the killer, I'd want the dogs where Shane wouldn't see them when he walked in. Sure he'd be suspicious that they didn't come running, but if he saw them sprawled on the ground, his instincts would go on high alert."

"So the killer got inside, drugged the dogs, and maybe he put them on the bed. But couldn't he have just dragged them out of his way instead of lifting them onto the bed?" I thought about that. "And he didn't kill the dogs. He went to the trouble of tranquilizing them. He likes dogs. It might be that he knows dogs well enough to know how to get them to eat the tranquilizer."

"If that's how he administered it," Gabe pointed out.

True. "Now what about the other body Vance said was the hit man?"

Gabe said, "They found him in an abandoned house. The house was clean except for a plastic cup, and there were no prints, just the strong smell of alcohol. No bottles of alcohol or pills or even bandages. Just a sleeping bag the dead man was lying on and the cup. The theory is that the hit man met up with the person who hired him. That person brought the alcohol and pills in the guise of helping the hit man but ultimately ended up killing him."

That was cold. "But how do the police know it's not suicide?"

He sipped his coffee. "There'd be bottles of liquor, a wallet, something. The place was cleaned. Not robbed, cleaned."

I nodded. "And so maybe it was the same tranquilizer or sleeping pills used on the dogs." I thought of the sleeping pills we had found in Bo's motel room. I tried to be objective, but the dogs bothered me. "Bo doesn't like dogs. He doesn't know anything about them."

Gabe shrugged. "Doesn't take a dog lover to roll up a sleeping pill in a chunk of hamburger."

It didn't add up. "But lifting them up on the bed?"

"Getting them out of the way."

He was playing devil's advocate. "Maybe."

"But you don't think so."

I shook my head but said, "I don't know. Do we know if Bo has a gun? What kind of gun did the killer use?"

"Not yet. A small .22 pistol. Up close and personal, and not a lot of room for mistakes. A hit man would never use a .22."

That struck me. "I don't know a whole lot about guns, but going from trying to use a hit man to killing him personally with a close-up-type gun—that sounds like our killer's getting angrier or perhaps the stakes are rising. But how did the killer get into the motor home to get that close? It's back against some trees, but wouldn't someone see a person skulking around?"

Gabe sat forward. "The door had a scrape on it, probably from lock picks. I couldn't be sure if they were from the hit man who broke in on Monday night or something more recent. That's part of why I went in." His face hardened, and he cast his gaze over my cheek and eye. "Plus I saw Shane's SUV there. I knew the bastard was inside."

My heart tripped over. The message was that nothing had been going to stop Gabe from going after the man who hit me. "You have a lot in common with your brother," I muttered.

"Melanie doesn't belong to Cal. You belong to me."

I sat up straight. "You don't own me, Pulizzi." God, he irritated me with that attitude.

He grinned, slow and wicked with sensual heat simmering in his gaze.

"Caveman."

"*Man*, sugar. All man."

A smile cracked through my irritation. "I noticed. But back to this." I moved the diagram Gabe had drawn. "So if someone picked the lock in broad daylight to get inside to murder Shane, there might be a witness."

"I'll go canvass the campground tomorrow morning. You go talk to Nikki. She seemed to have a solid reason to hate Shane. Two reasons if it's her show Shane had been planning to spoil Saturday night."

"A woman scorned," I said, thinking about Nikki. "I'll talk to her. Rosy said that Vance had her in the police station this evening. So our two suspects are Bo Kelly and Nikki Eden." That made me sad for Grandpa and for me. I cast around for a better suspect. "Grandpa and Fletch are looking through the Triple M for anything they can find. Maybe they will come up with something. In the meantime, Lola was hanging around the office making Blaine nuts when Shane was murdered, so she's off the suspect list."

He nodded. "I saw her there. But Bo and Nikki had motive. We don't know where either of them were during the murder. Do you think either of them can pick open a lock?"

I had to think for a second. "Bo does different illusions based on his superhero theme. He's big on levitation among other things. He could have some lock-picking skills if he's rescuing a chained-up damsel in distress or something. And Nikki, she does some big escapist illusions, so I would bet she knows how to pick a lock." Lead settled in my stomach as I considered her. "And Nikki would have known the dogs. She could have gotten into Shane's motor home pretty easy, I would think. The dogs would know her."

"Enough to eat from her," Gabe added. He looked down at the watch on his arm. "Who is Nikki, Sam? What drives her?"

I tried to get to the core of her. "Smart, young, chip on her shoulder attitude but loves her grandma. Magic saved her, gave her a purpose and kept her out of juvie, when her parents divorced. She credits Grandpa with that. Her show is high concept, meaning big illusions that cost a hell of a lot of money."

"Love life?"

I shrugged. "My sense is that she takes men when they appeal to her but guards her heart."

"Until Shane?"

I got this. I understood this. It's why I was good at Heart Mates and at critiquing romances. "He was her soul mate, a bad boy to her bad girl. A man with a chip on his shoulder, a tough life. They shared an understanding of making it in spite of the odds against them."

Gabe added, "And he betrayed her. Would that drive her to murder?"

I didn't know and shrugged in frustration. "Would she hire me if she had killed him?"

"Sure, you'd be her inside information. Especially if she thought she was smarter than you. That's the thing about killers, they tend to really think they can get away with it. Now what about Bo?" Gabe pressed on.

I shifted my thoughts back to Bo and what drove him. "There's the cartoon character based on him. That's a powerful reason to keep Shane from spoiling his show." I thought about Bo and his career, and his wife. "He chose magic over his wife. When he realized his being on the road made her unhappy, he let her go. And he loved her."

Gabe whistled softly. "I can answer that one. He gave up a woman he loved for his career, and now he's making it to the big time and the sacrifices are paying off. I don't even have to ask if he'd kill to keep Shane from destroying that."

I set a cup of coffee in front of Grandpa.

He looked up from his computer screen. "You and Gabe got in late last night."

That felt downright weird. Gabe had left early to get to the office and help Blaine before heading over to canvass the campground for witnesses. "Uh, Gabe wanted his brother to get some sleep, so he sent Cal home and stayed here." In my bed. A tight fit, but we both slept. At least until he talked me into taking a shower with him this morning. After that, Gabe had left before the boys got up to go help Blaine get ready for the painters.

Grandpa grinned. "Do we have to talk about safe sex, Sammy?"

I dropped into a chair at the table. "Don't you dare. If you do, I'll tell Mom that you're dating a woman half your age."

His smile soured. "You're just mean in the morning." He clicked through some windows on the computer and said, "I got into one of Bo's bank account, but I haven't found any large withdrawals. This is his everyday checking account. I haven't found a savings account. I'll keep looking."

TJ straggled out, looking tired. I got up and kissed his forehead. "What time did you get to bed?" I had a stab of guilt. I should have been here to make sure he got to bed early.

"I'm always tired in the morning, Mom. We went to bed at ten. Joel and I played video games with Cal. I beat them." He grinned as he made his way to the table for cereal.

"Who cares?" Joel shuffled out. He looked more awake. "Video games are for geeks." He stopped by me. "Mom, Cal's totally awesome. He told us about some mega fires he's been in."

I smiled. "Yeah?"

Joel looked around. "I thought Cal was spending the night."

"Gabe switched places with him around midnight." I got busy searching my purse for lunch money.

Joel stared at me with huge blue eyes. "So where's Gabe?"

"Went to work." I pulled out two fives. It was all I had at the moment. I needed to go to the ATM.

"What about you? Are you working on that magician's murder?" Joel went to the table and picked up the box of cereal.

I heard the doorbell ring and saw Grandpa and Ali get up to answer it. To Joel's question I said, "Yes." I didn't tell the boys that I was having second thoughts about going after my PI license, mostly because I didn't know what I wanted. I did want to work cases, but I didn't want to lose Heart Mates.

Joel nodded.

TJ stopped eating and looked up. "Is it dangerous, Mom? I mean, Gabe thought we needed a babysitter last night."

Fletch came into the kitchen just as I poured some more coffee. I got another cup down and filled it for him. Then I took my coffee and the money to the table. I sat down, gave TJ and Joel each a five for lunch money, then said, "Gabe is always careful with us, TJ."

"Grandpa says it's 'cause he loves you," Joel said. "If you

marry him, are we gonna live at Gabe's house? Can I have my own room?"

TJ stopped eating but stared at his cereal.

Oh boy. Gabe had never said a word about marriage, and I didn't want to marry, partly because I didn't want to leave Grandpa alone. And I was scared to death of marriage. I'd spent thirteen years in a dead marriage. I never wanted to do that again. "Joel, I'm not going to marry Gabe, and he hasn't asked me to. You, your brother, and I are going to stay here with Grandpa as long as he lets us." I had no intention of leaving him alone.

Joel glanced at Grandpa sitting at his computer. Fletch had pulled up a chair next to him. Then Joel looked back at me and said, "I want to stay here."

"Me too." I smiled at him, then looked at my other son. "TJ, I'm certain that you and Joel are not in any danger. But like Gabe, I'm always going to be cautious. If that means having Gabe or his brother hang around, then that is what we'll do."

TJ rolled his eyes. "I meant is it dangerous to you. Besides your clothes."

I laughed. "Do you think I should wear old clothes today?" I had on a tangerine-colored silk sleeveless top and form-fitting black pants. "I don't think I'm in any danger at the moment, but I'll be careful."

TJ glanced at Grandpa, then me. "I think you should stay on it, Mom," he said, then got up and took his bowl to the sink.

I watched my more serious, older son. That boy was sharp. He had caught on that the one who might be in danger was Grandpa. Somehow it was all connected to Grandpa. In one way or another, all the players were connected to him: Grandpa mentored Shane, then tossed him out of the Triple M; Grandpa introduced both Nikki and Bo to magic and got them into the Triple M, and Fletch too.

Joel got up to rinse his dish and added it to the dishwasher, then both boys went into their rooms to finish getting ready for school.

Fletch's voice interrupted my thoughts. "I think we should look into Nikki's bank accounts."

I turned around. Fletch sat with his coffee on the other side of Grandpa.

Grandpa looked thoughtful. "I don't really feel right. We had a reason to look at Bo with the fake thumb and all. And Nikki is Sam's client."

Fletch set his cup down and looked at Grandpa. "But if there's nothing there we can rule her out."

Grandpa turned to me.

I was uncomfortable. Gabe and I had broken into Bo's motel room while Grandpa had broken into his bank accounts. What if he was innocent? Then what we did was wrong. And Nikki hired me to work for her. "Let me talk to her first. I'll call you after I do that and get to work to talk to Gabe."

Nikki looked like she hadn't slept at all. She wore a pair of black boxer-style shorts and a gray tank top. Her hazel eyes were puffy and her spiky hair wilted. She sat at the kitchen table in the sunny little nook staring at a mug of tea that smelled like lemon.

Rosy stood at my shoulder. "Coffee, Sam?"

"I'd like that, thanks, Rosy." I sat down and put down my yellow tablet with the list of magicians tucked in the back. "How are you, Nikki?"

She lifted her gaze. "I can hardly believe he is dead."

"Shane?" Of course she meant Shane. But I wanted her to talk. I wanted to figure out her state of mind. Judging

by the way she looked, it could be grief, horror, or remorse.

She nodded. "He was bigger than life. Even when he
dumped me, he was . . . so alive." She rubbed her eyes,
spreading black mascara residue.

Rosy set a steaming cup of coffee in front of me, then
she excused herself to go get dressed. I focused on Nikki.

She said, "I didn't kill him, Sam. I couldn't have. I
wanted revenge, but I couldn't have killed him."

I glanced down at my coffee, thinking about women in
love. We were in my territory now—romance. Nikki was
watching me when I looked up and said, "You couldn't kill
him because you loved him once." But I knew that love
could turn into hate.

She smiled, her lean face softening. "I was going to beat
him at his own game."

"The confidentiality agreement. Nikki, I need to know
what that's about." Did it matter anymore if Shane was
dead? It had to do with him, obviously.

"A network special. I was going to host a special to air
after Shane's show, showing what goes into building a
magic act and how Shane took a shortcut to fame by destroying hardworking magicians. I was going to expose the
real Shane Masters to the world, including that he was
nothing more than a street thug. It was half a 'behind the
scenes' of magicians and half a biography of Shane." She
looked into the kitchen, her eyes unfocused. "Shane didn't
know as much as he thought he did. It never occurred to
him that I would get my own TV show."

That's what Nikki had hired me for, to get her addi-
tional information for her TV special. And that's why she
approached Shane in the first place—she had been planning to do to Shane what he did to others. It all added up.
Finally. Except I had really believed she loved him. But

maybe she hadn't. Maybe she had just been using him. "So you didn't love him?"

"I fell in love with him. And I went to his show in Vegas before coming here, ready to tell him the truth and break my contract with my show, if Shane would give up his spoiler shows. We could create a magic show together, like Penn and Teller, or Siegfried and Roy, but I never got past my first two words before Shane dumped me."

"Oh." Nikki Eden had a lot of reasons to be pissed. She had been going to give up her prime-time chance at fame for Shane. And he had dumped her. "What were the two words you did get out?"

She looked back at me with her head held high, exposing her long neck. "I'm pregnant."

14

My head spun with the shocking news that Nikki was pregnant by Shane Masters. Sitting across the table, I searched her face. No tears. She looked numb. I could understand that. "Did you tell the police this?" No wonder Vance had her down at the station for so long.

"Every word. And I gave them all my documents. I don't have an alibi for the time of Shane's murder. I was here sleeping, and Grandma was off doing her reading program at the school."

I nodded, knowing she meant Rosy's volunteer tutoring of middle school kids with lagging reading skills. But I wasn't sure about the documents. "The stuff you were compiling on Shane for your TV show?"

She lifted the cup of tepid tea and took a sip. "Yes."

That meant her documents were out of my reach if Vance had them. I wished I could have seen them. "What about your TV special? Is it cancelled now?"

"My manager is in talks. He's pitching a couple ideas." She shrugged.

I got the impression that Nikki didn't really care about the TV show anymore. Numb. She just seemed numb. The shock of being pregnant, of getting dumped by Shane, Shane's murder, then what was probably a grueling police interview . . . she was numb.

Rosy came out dressed in bright pink capri pants and a loose printed T-shirt. She set a thin plastic case in front of Nikki. It appeared to be a CD case.

"Thanks, Grandma."

Rosy put her hand on Nikki's shoulder. "You didn't drink much tea."

She smiled. "I'll drink some later."

Rosy fixed herself some coffee and sat down between us. She didn't say a word.

My admiration for Rosy went up. She was supporting her granddaughter in a tough time.

Nikki slid the plastic case across the table to me. "This is a copy of everything that I gave the police that I had on Shane, Sam. I know I originally hired you to find out everything you could about Shane, but now I want you to find out who murdered him. I know what he was. . . ." She stopped talking and swallowed.

Rosy put her hand on Nikki's arm and turned to me. "She didn't kill Shane. We need you to find who did, so Nikki and her baby can have some peace."

I understood Nikki's need. She had fallen in love with the wrong man and now she was having his child. I had done that myself. But TJ and Joel were worth every second of my lifeless marriage. I would tell Nikki that another time. Right now, what she needed was for Shane's murderer to be found so she could move ahead with a life for herself and her baby. "I'll do what I can."

I drove right to work, hoping to catch Gabe before he went to canvass the campground. I parked my T-bird and spotted the painters' trucks. The front of Heart Mates looked like an office supply store had thrown up. Chairs, desks, lamps, and office equipment covered in blankets were stacked all over the sidewalk. I wove my way through the mess and caught the pungent smell of wet paint.

My stomach clenched. I'd chosen a pale rose for my side, a light pecan for Gabe's, and cream for the center where Blaine sat. I'd chosen a beautiful wood trim for the floor and ceiling, and the rose, brown, and cream carpet would bring it all together.

But what if Gabe hated it?

"Why are you standing here with that frozen look on your face?"

I turned and saw Cal grinning at me. He had paint splatters on his old jeans and white T-shirt. "Does Gabe hate it?" Damn, I'd meant to say hi and thanks for staying with the boys.

He laughed. "The painters started painting his office that pink color. He was sorted of speechless. Lola figured out the mistake pretty quick and set everyone straight."

"Bet Blaine loved that."

"Blaine was out of the office somewhere when Lola showed up. Blaine just got back about twenty minutes ago, and he's about ready to blow."

"Uh-oh. Why is Lola here, anyway?"

Cal shrugged. "Where else would she go? She doesn't have a job now, and she's at loose ends."

Blaine stormed out the door. "Get rid of her, Sam, or I quit!" He stomped off to his car and opened the trunk.

"God, I hope he doesn't have a tire iron in there," I muttered, and turned to go into Heart Mates. The paint smell was stronger. I could see through to my office. It was a sheer rose. "Beautiful."

Gabe strode across the reception area to me. "They tried to put that in my office."

I laughed. "Maybe you shouldn't have sicced my mother on me when I went to the stadium."

He leaned down and kissed me. "So that's your revenge? A pink office? 'Cause Lola already fixed that."

"Did she? Guess I'll have to think of something else." I turned and headed to Gabe's side and hung a left down the short hallway, then looked into his conference room on the right. The room was nearly done. There were two men in there rolling on the light-pecan-colored paint. Perfect. I turned to Gabe. "Did you go to the campground yet?"

He shook his head. "About ready to just now."

"Grandpa didn't find anything on Bo, and I just talked to Nikki. She swears she didn't kill Shane. She says she couldn't have."

Gabe arched a single eyebrow. "Because she loved him? Lots of women kill the men they love."

He was so cynical. "Because she's pregnant by him."

"And he dumped her when she told him?"

I nodded. "She gave me a CD with all her research on Shane." I summed up Nikki's TV show.

"So she loses the show now that Shane's dead? Would it have been worth losing that chance for national TV exposure to kill Shane?" He took a step back from me and added, "How hormonal is Nikki from her pregnancy?"

Men. "If she were that hormonal, it seems like she would have killed him when he first dumped her, not a couple weeks later."

"Had to ask," Gabe said. "We'll see what I get from the campground. What are you going to do?"

"I'm going to try to look at this CD." I glanced around the office. "Are any of the computers hooked up?"

He shook his head. "Use my laptop. I'll get it for you; it's in my truck. Be right back."

I followed him back out to the reception area, then watched him walk outside. I was admiring the view of his broad shoulders, trim waist, and tight ass when I heard Blaine swear. Then Cal strode past me, glanced over, and shrugged, flashing his sunny grin.

I heard Lola say, "It was an accident!"

I sighed and headed down the short hallway to the end where it opened into Gabe's office. His heavy desk and been moved to the center and was half-covered with a drop cloth. Lola stood by the desk with her back to me. She wore a pair of capri-length jeans that hugged her shapely Jennifer Lopez butt, a yellow T-shirt, and a pair of wedge sandals. I could see the defensive line of her spine and shoulders.

Blaine stood across the room holding a couple light switch plates and a screwdriver. Furious color crawled up his neck from the opened collar of his blue work shirt. "You spilled a whole can of grape soda on the carpet!"

I looked down. Yep, a can rested on the carpet, spreading a dark stain. I gathered that Lola was trying to cover the desk for the painters and knocked the can off. But so what? The carpet was being replaced tomorrow.

I could see Lola's long, dark ponytail swing as she waved her arm expressively. "I'm sorry! I'm just trying to help!"

Blaine yelled right back. "You're not helping, you're just in the way. Go away, Lola."

I thought about what Cal had said about Lola not really having any place to go. I felt sorry for her and walked up to stand next to her. "Blaine," I said softly, "it's okay. We're getting new carpet tomorrow."

He sucked in a huge breath, exposing a hard line in his face. "You don't get it, Sam. She's useless. Her sole job for that magician was to look pretty and distract the audience.

Where's the skill in that? She's living on her looks and doesn't have a skill in the world. She expects me to take care of her. I would have done that once, with pleasure, but no more."

"I am not useless!"

I needed earplugs. But before I could put a stop to this, Blaine shot back.

"You don't have a job. How are you going to support yourself? Your meal ticket is dead, and now you are following me around like lost puppy thinking I'll adopt you." He took two steps until he stood in front of her. "I have my own life now, and it doesn't include you. You walked." His voice dropped to the low thrum of a powerful engine idling. "Beauty only lasts so long." He stalked past her.

She whirled around, smacking me in the face with her ponytail. "I'm not useless! I'll show you! I'm going to help Sam find out who murdered Shane!"

"What?" I stared at Lola.

She turned to face me. "That's right." She lifted her chin and thrust out her chest. "I'll be your inside person. I knew Shane. I worked on the act. I can help. I. Am. Not. Useless."

She was stunning with her Noxzema-clean skin mixed with a Latin sultry face flushed to a glow. Blaine was right that she was beautiful, but he missed her eyes. In those dark eyes, I saw grim determination. Still I tried to reason with her. "Lola, thank you for the offer. I'm sure I'll have some questions for you and you'll be a big help, but—"

Her eyes filled with huge tears. "You think I'm useless too."

Sheesh. "No—"

Gabe walked in holding his laptop computer. "Hiring more people already, Sam? I thought Lola was a client."

Lola turned to look at Gabe. "I don't want to be a client. I want to be useful. I know I can help Sam."

Gabe stared at her, then said, "I'm sure Sam can use the help." He held out the laptop to Lola and flashed her—swear to God—a goofy smile.

What the hell?

Lola took the laptop. "Where do I start?" she asked Gabe, while staring at him as if he were chocolate and she were having the worst PMS day in the history of womankind.

"Start?" Gabe said.

Lola smiled. "Working. On the case."

"Right. Shane's murder. The case."

"Hello!" I said, though it might have sounded like a snarl. "I'm standing right here." I glared at Gabe, hoping to snap him out of his sexy-beauty-induced stupor.

He blinked and looked at me like I'd suddenly gone stupid on him. "No one said you weren't standing there."

He was so dead. I turned to Lola and handed her the CD case with Nikki's files on Shane. "Go find somewhere to set up that laptop and open this CD. You do know how to use a laptop, right?"

She nodded. "Thanks, Sam. You won't regret letting me help." She turned and practically skipped out.

"Nice kid," Gabe said.

I turned back to my hunky Italian Romeo. "Is your brain powering up again, stud?"

He frowned, going from besotted fool to the darker, dangerous man I knew. "Come again?"

I pointed out the events of the last few minutes. "You were flirting with Lola and you just gave her a job."

"I didn't . . ." Gabe snapped his mouth shut and turned to stare at the empty doorway. Then he lifted his hand and ran it through his straight black hair. "Humph."

"Coming back to you now?" He looked so put out that I almost laughed.

He turned his gaze back to me. And took a step. "I wasn't flirting with her."

I tried to arch one eyebrow, but it felt like a lopsided squint. "So you are hiring a replacement for me?"

Another step brought him toe to toe with me. "I'm not replacing you. I wasn't flirting with her. I just don't like women to cry."

I gave up on trying to arch an eyebrow and rolled my eyes. "Whatever. Go canvass the campground. It'll save me from having to drag in a hose and cool you off." I hated being jealous. But I refused to beg for reassurance, not after what Gabe had said at the police station about needing to feed my self-esteem every three hours. I wanted to be a strong, successful woman, not a bottomless hole of insecurity.

Gabe leaned down. "Are you planning on making me hot?"

A skitter of warm desire ran through my belly and almost made me forget my need to be strong. "Don't try to charm your way out of this."

He grinned. Not the dopey grin that Lola got out of him, but the sexy, wicked, and dangerous smile that promised decadent things. "Sure, babe, Lola is one hot girl. But she's a kid. I would watch her walk down the street, then forget about her." He lowered his face and softened his voice. "But it's you that makes me want to rip your clothes off and devour you."

Well, hell, that was reassuring.

"Sam," Cal interrupted from the doorway, "Bo's here and says he has to see you right away."

I forced myself to turn from Gabe. I had to focus. "Thanks, Cal." I went out to the reception area.

Bo was crawling on the floor in the reception area with

the plug from Gabe's laptop in his hand. The laptop itself was on a small card table that I'd bet Cal set up for Lola.

"I'm sure there's a plug somewhere," Bo said.

"Bo, get up," I sighed. I would have yelled at Lola, but she was busy opening up the laptop. Honest to God, she was used to men crawling around floors to help her. She wasn't even trying. I wondered where Blaine had stormed off to. I owed him for bringing Lola on as a client in the first place. I didn't want him to ever hear that we'd kind of hired her. I was going to talk to Lola about that as soon as I finished with Bo.

"Just a second, Sam. I need to plug this in for Lola," Bo said.

How long had Bo been here? Maybe five minutes, and he was now good friends with Lola? I needed a couple Tylenol. And a drink.

Gabe walked out with his brother and came over to me.

"I'm going to the campground. You be careful." He glanced at Bo. Then he kissed me and left. But I saw him look at Bo scuttling around on the floor and smirk.

Men.

I was done being nice. "Bo!"

"Found it." Bo got up and brushed off his hands, beaming at Lola.

"Thanks, Bo," Lola said, and pressed the power button to boot up the computer.

I went up and tapped Bo on the shoulder.

He turned. "Hi Sam." He leaned down and kissed me. His face dropped all the charm and went grim. "Barney called me early this morning and told me about Shane and that the police want to talk to me." His serious look turned angry. "What happened to your face?"

Bo had shaken off the Lola haze. "Shane didn't like me

ordering him off our property much." I explained about the argument with Grandpa and Shane smacking me. Bo already knew from Grandpa that Shane had found a fake thumb.

Bo nodded, a slight flush staining his cheeks. "That was me. I did try to break into Shane's trailer. I was desperate, Sam. My agent said that if Shane spoiled my show this weekend, there was a chance it would blow the Magic Bo cartoon deal." He glanced at Lola, who was busy at the computer. Then he looked at me. "I didn't kill him. I can prove it. I left Elsinore by noon and have a debit card receipt from Orange County around the actual time of the murder." He reached into his back pocket and took out his wallet. Once he opened it up, he fished out a receipt and handed it to me.

I studied the receipt. It was for gas at an off-ramp off the 91 Freeway at least forty miles from Elsinore. That did seem to clear Bo. I tried not to think about how Gabe and I broke into his room. "I'm sorry, Bo. We had to tell the detective everything."

He shook his head, then reached out and took my hand. "It's not your fault, it's Shane Masters's. The surprise is that someone didn't kill him sooner." He gently touched my cheek with his finger. "I might have killed him for this."

I was getting used to the overreaction of men. "Grandpa and I handled it. But I'm sorry for the trouble this might cause you."

"Barney's a good friend of mine, Sam. I came here in part to see if Shane was going to expose my show. But the other reason was that I wanted to give Barney moral support. And I'm going to stay here through the week. I'll be around once I clear this up with the police."

"Thank you, Bo. Do you want me to go with you to the police station?"

He shook his head. "No. I just wanted to check in and make sure you are okay before I talk to the police. Then I'm going to grab a shower and a couple hours sleep. I went to a party last night and met a woman. . . ." He shrugged with male smugness.

"And yet here you are flirting with Lola," I scolded him.

He laughed. "Darlin', I didn't get married. Just met her and had a good time. I'm going to head over to the police station now. I'll call you or Barney after I get some sleep."

I watched him walk out, then turned to help Lola search through the CD Nikki gave us.

Blaine came through the interview room, presumably from the storage area in the back of Heart Mates carrying some old sheets. He stopped and stared at Lola.

Then he looked up at me and said, "She's in the way. Get her out of here."

I was getting really sick of this. "Blaine, are you forgetting who is the boss here?" He stopped beside me and looked down. His brown eyes were ringed with dark half moons and topped by heavy lids. His face was tight with faint white lines around his mouth. He had been working damn hard, and I felt bad about my snotty remark.

Blaine said, "Have you forgotten we are painting this reception area once the offices are done?"

I winced and put my hand on my assistant's arm. "I'm sorry. Listen, we'll go to my house and work there, okay? You can call me on my cell if you need anything."

His arm stiffened under my hand. "Keep her away from me, that's all I need." He walked across the reception area to Gabe's side.

I turned. "Let's pack up and go to my house."

She was already closing up the computer. "He's never going to forgive me."

I wasn't so sure about that.

"Where's Fletch?" I asked Grandpa when Lola and I walked into the house.

The microwave dinged, and Grandpa headed into the kitchen while saying, "He left. He has an appointment with some guy to try wakeboarding."

I shook my head and dumped my purse and the laptop on the kitchen table. "Stubborn, isn't he?" Then I turned to Lola. "Want some coffee? Or water? Or a soda?"

"Do you have diet?"

I went to the fridge and pulled out two Diet Cokes.

Lola found a way to plug in Gabe's laptop all by herself and was booting it up. I set a Diet Coke in front of her and took a seat.

Grandpa went to his computer carrying his warmed-up coffee. His shoulders were hunched, and the stray gray hairs that clung to his balding head were ruffled. "Did you eat breakfast, Grandpa?"

He looked up with surprise in his blue gaze. "Yes, I did. And I fed Ali. I've been real good today."

At least he had his sense of humor. I opened my can of Diet Coke and caught him up on my chat with Nikki while Lola stuck the CD into Gabe's computer and started going through the files.

"Pregnant," Grandpa said in a sad voice.

He was thinking of my mother, of his own regrets. "She'll be okay. Rosy is there for her. And Nikki's a strong gal."

Grandpa sighed. "Sam, after you left, when we couldn't find anything on Bo, Fletch and I looked into Nikki."

I set my can down on the table. "Her bank account?"

He nodded. "Two large cash withdrawals in the last few days."

Oh Nikki, I thought helplessly.

15

Lola looked up. "Sam, these files are a complete time-line of Shane's shows, which magician's acts Shane spoiled, and interviews with some of the magicians."

I turned to look at Lola. She sat with her back to the sliding glass door that led to our backyard. The sunlight cascaded gently over dark, long hair pulled back in a tight ponytail. "Anything that points to a killer?"

She squinted at the screen. "Not exactly. But three of the five magicians whom Nikki interviewed said they knew ahead of time that Shane was spoiling their act."

I sat back trying to shift my thoughts from Nikki to what Lola was telling me. "How did they know?" And how could that help us find Shane's killer? Was the magician whom Shane planned to expose the killer?

Lola scrolled through files, her face a mask of concentration. "Tickets. Either they or someone around them was sent two free tickets to the show."

A shiver ran down my spine. Someone knew that Shane was going to expose their illusions. They had known all along. And they sent a hit man to stop him. When that didn't work, they came to Elsinore to do the job themselves.

Who was this killer? A magician that we knew?

Grandpa said, "That helps rule out Bo, right? He tried to break into Shane's prop trailer to discover if he was the victim."

I just didn't know. "Well he seems to have an alibi for the time of Shane's murder." Bo had already told Grandpa about it this morning.

He frowned and said, "And Nikki hired you to find out if Shane was exposing her, right?"

We all turned to look as the front door opened and Gabe walked in. He carried a cardboard box that had a few greasy stains on it.

Donuts. Cool. I think better when chocolate is involved.

"Nikki could have hired Sam to keep tabs on Shane Masters so she'd be able to find him and kill him." Gabe slid easily into the conversation as he set the box of donuts down on the table.

Ali fussed at the back door.

Gabe let her in, said hello, then got her a treat out of the cupboard. Then he poured himself some coffee and took a seat between me and Grandpa, who was at his computer. "Two people saw a slight figure in a baseball cap and hooded sweatshirt taking a walk around 12:30 P.M. That's all the description they could give me. It's pretty common for campers to take walks around the campground. Several people heard Shane's dogs barking furiously around that time too."

I took that in. "Slight figure? As in a woman?"

Gabe said, "Not as big as me was as definite as I got."

"So not Bo." Grandpa reached past Gabe and got a plain donut.

"But it could be Nikki." I got a chocolate buttermilk donut, then turned to Lola. "Help yourself."

Lola stared at the box, then she shrugged and picked out a big jelly donut.

I took a bite, then asked, "Lola, any idea whose show Shane was exposing?" Now that Shane was dead, she wasn't bound by the confidentiality agreement she had signed. And she had offered her help.

She shook her head. "I only worked for Shane for a couple months. I don't know a lot about magicians, except Barney and what I learned on the magician's assistants loop. All I can tell you is that I was supposed to be assisting Shane with vanishing flowers when I would disappear instead. He was showing how he keeps the audience focused on the flowers while I slip away through a hidden door in the set."

"Misdirection," I sighed, thinking that a truckload of magicians vanish their assistants. "What about props? Did you see a motorcycle? Did Shane use a whip as a prop?" That was Nikki's trademark.

"Shane had a motorcycle prop I've seen before, but I never saw it for this show." She looked around the table and said, "He had this down. He kept everyone he could in the dark. His main assistants know the entire show, I think, and his manager, although he's not in town. He was coming later. But the rest don't know anything. I'm sorry, I just don't know."

Gabe said, "What about the assistants who do know? Where are they?"

"Two left after they were cleared by Detective Vance. I tried to get more information out of them, but they are in shock and scared after being questioned by the police. I think they are afraid the killer will come after them." She looked up at us with her dark brown gaze. "I doubt they told the police whom Shane was exposing. And the third one, Michelle, is still here, staying at those little bungalows at the edge of the campground."

I was amazed at how Shane could keep such a big show a secret. I also saw Lola's point. These assistants were scared. If they told the police whom Shane was exposing, and that person was the killer, he might come after them too. "We should talk to Michelle. We might be able to get her to tell us whose show Shane was spoiling. Or at least give us some clue."

Gabe agreed. "I'm going to go to the office to check on things there. I'll call my source with the police and see what else I can find out." He stood up, and I went with him to the door.

"Have you talked to Cal?" I asked him.

He shook his head. "We haven't had time. I'll handle it once the painting is done. It's good for him to work, Sam. It'll help him focus on his options," he added. "Have you explained to Lola that we're not hiring her beyond her help on this case?"

"I haven't gotten around to it yet."

He arched an eyebrow.

"Shut up, Pulizzi."

"Babe, you are something else." He pulled me to him for a quick kiss, then left.

I walked back into the kitchen wearing a hot blush that probably matched my tangerine shirt. "Lola, let's go see if we can find Michelle."

She started packing up the laptop.

I turned to Grandpa. "You're coming with us, okay?"

"Because you need me to protect you two girls, not because you think I'm a defenseless old man, right Sammy?"

I smiled at him. "You bet, Grandpa. And Michelle might trust another magician more than a homicide detective."

We drove into the campsite and could see a little of the yellow crime scene tape that still surrounded Shane's motor home. I wondered when they would move the motor home. But I guessed they had to process the scene to determine exactly how the murder happened before they moved anything.

I parked close to the little row of one-room shacks at the left edge of the campground. The cabins butted up to the parking lot for the Jack in the Box where Grandpa spent so many of his mornings drinking coffee and gossiping with his friends. Lola went to the third cabin and knocked on the door. "Michelle?" she called out. "It's me, Lola."

Lola used a soft, reassuring voice, and it hit me then how scared all Shane's employees must be. They had been scared of him when he was alive, and now they were scared of his killer.

The door opened, and the first thing I noticed was her hair. Long and silver blond, it was stunning. It fell all the way to her waist. Beneath all that hair was a slender woman who stood a couple inches taller than me. She had very little coloring under her artfully applied make-up. Even her blue eyes were pale. She drew her eyebrows together. "Lola, what's going on?"

"This is Samantha Shaw, and her grandfather—"

Michelle nodded impatiently. "Barney Webb." She looked at Grandpa. "I've seen your shows. You are very good."

He nodded. "Thank you. We'd like to talk to you, Michelle. As fellow magic professionals, we are looking for some of your insight."

She was frozen to the spot. "Into Shane's murder?"

Grandpa said, "Yes. None of us are safe until we figure this horrible mess out."

I sometimes forgot how charming and convincing Grandpa was. Michelle actually looked relieved. "Come in. I've already told the police what I know."

The cabin looked like a one-room shack stuffed with a bed, TV, and chair, I felt sorry for the assistants. Shane hadn't been overly concerned about his employees' comfort. Grandpa sat in the chair and Michelle sat on the bed while Lola and I stood.

"Michelle," Grandpa began, "do you have any idea whose show Shane was spoiling?"

She looked tired. "Shane never called the magicians by name. He assigned them a number. He had a computer file that he kept locked—that file matched the number to the magician. This was magician number 111."

I asked, "As in the one hundred and eleventh spoiler show?"

Michelle shook her head. "Shane mixed the numbers."

Grandpa got us back on track. "Did you see a run-through of the whole program?"

She shook her head again. "I could tell you the portions of the show I appeared in, but we'd only be guessing. Shane was getting progressively more paranoid, especially with MTV in on this. What you need to do is crack his computer program and find out who he sent the free tickets to."

I wondered if she did know and was afraid to tell us. I looked toward the door that faced the campground and asked, "The computer was in Shane's motor home?" Would the computer still be in there? Or had the police removed it from the motor home?

She shook her head. "I'm pretty sure it was at his office trailer on the location. It's a laptop. Shane sometimes brought it back to the motor home with him. But he usually left it in his locked office trailer during the day. Besides," now Michelle looked in the direction of the motor home, as if she could see through the wall, "he only came home during the day to check his dogs if he didn't have them with him."

I thought about that while Grandpa tried to see what more he could get out of Michelle. Then we left.

"She's scared," Grandpa said as the three of us huddled by his Jeep. "I think she knows who the magician is, but she's afraid."

"Murder has a way of scaring people," I agreed.

Lola looked back at the little bungalow. "Maybe I should try talking to her by myself."

I could see how hard Lola was working to be useful. "That's a good idea, but let's leave her alone for a bit to settle down. Then you can talk to her as two women in the same boat since you were both Shane's employees."

Lola nodded. "So now what?"

"I'm betting that if Michelle told Vance the same thing, he's at the stadium right now trying to crack that computer." I looked at Grandpa. "Vance would be easier to convince than we are that Michelle didn't know whose show Shane was spoiling. He doesn't know much about magic."

Grandpa frowned. "But won't he get a fancy computer tech to try to get into Shane's computer?"

I thought about that. "Eventually. But how long would it take to get a tech? Budget cuts make everything hard on the cops. And Vance really needs to crack this case. I think he'll try himself first. And we are going to offer to help him since we happen to have a computer tech on hand, one who is also an expert in magic and magicians."

Grandpa grinned and laced his hands together, then turned them out to flex his fingers. "I am good, both at magic and computers. I could crack Shane's firewalls."

Lola perked up. "Tell you what, I'll drive and you call Vance. Barney can navigate." She took the keys from my hand.

Which meant I got to squeeze my buns into the backseat. I dialed Vance's number while Lola started the car. By the time she navigated out of the campground, I had Vance's voice mail. "Vance, it's Sam. I think we might be able to help you out. We need to see Shane's computer though. Call me."

"Turn right," Grandpa told Lola.

"Where are we going?" I asked. My cell phone rang before anyone could answer. "That was fast," I said, then looked at the screen. "It's Gabe." I put the phone to my ear. "Hi, what's up?"

"Sam, they've identified the hit man."

My breath caught in my throat. "Who is he?"

"Pete Olsen. From Las Vegas."

I went cold and looked at Grandpa. He was turned in his seat and watched me as I asked Gabe, "Anything else?"

"He's a two-bit thug and card shark who's been banned from a couple casinos."

Just the kind of dumb-ass criminal to try and hire himself out as a hit man, I thought to myself. "I'm going back to talk to Nikki."

"I'll meet you there," Gabe said. "I'm in my truck. I don't want you going in there alone. If Nikki's the killer, she's going to feel cornered."

I shoved down the automatic denial that tried to get out of my mouth. Gabe was being reasonably cautious. "All right." I hung up and said, "Make a left at this light, Lola." That would put us on Lake Street, then we could make another left on Machado.

Grandpa remained twisted in his seat to look at me. "What did he find?"

"The hit man. His name is Pete Olsen, and he's from Vegas."

"I am buying a magician's illusions from his estate. That's why I took the money out of my account in cash," Nikki explained.

We all sat in Rosy's living room. Old-fashioned paneling contrasted with the brightly colored rugs on the floor. Rosy had a big screen TV where the movie *Shakespeare in Love* was currently frozen.

Rosy was gone, so Nikki was alone. She sat on the floral couch, wearing a pair of cutoff shorts and a T-shirt that said, "Bite Me."

"Why cash?" I asked. I knew that magicians occasionally bought the illusions and apparatus of dead magicians to expand their own skills.

"The widow is having financial trouble and that's why she's selling. I'm giving her a very fair price. There are a couple illusions in there that are worth it though."

The cash tax dodge. Got it. "There's one more thing." Everyone else stayed quiet. Gabe and Lola didn't know Nikki, and Grandpa looked like he wished he was someplace else. So it fell to me. "What about Pete Olsen?"

She raised her dark eyebrows. "Who? Never heard of him."

"He's from Vegas," I prodded.

She curled her legs up under her and sat back. "I don't know him."

I looked at Gabe, out of ideas.

"How many magicians are there in Vegas?" Gabe took over.

"At any given time, there are quite a few. They come and go, appearing at the casinos, clubs, and dinner houses. I doubt anyone has an exact figure."

She was right. Hell, a magician could be in Vegas to negotiate a contract, apply for a job, catch a peer's performance, or even just to take a quick vacation. We weren't getting anywhere with this.

I kept coming back to one thing about Shane's murder. "Nikki, what can you tell us about Shane's dogs?"

She looked over at me in surprise. "Houdini and Blackstone? Not a lot. Shane never wanted me to get friendly with or pet them. He was possessive about them. I think he loved those dogs more than anything else."

Could Nikki have been jealous of Shane's dogs? Would a woman pissed at Shane take such care of the animals he loved? Going as far as lifting them up on the bed? They were not small dogs, and Nikki was pregnant, which made most women cautious about lifting heavy things. And if she had been jealous of the dogs—

Grandpa's voice interrupted my thoughts. He sat forward in his chair and looked into Nikki's face. "Nikki, how are you doing?"

She turned to Grandpa. "I didn't kill him, Barney. I know what I'm like, I know what people think . . . but I didn't kill him."

It broke my heart. Gabe shifted uncomfortably next to me while Lola studied the bookcases on either side of the big-screen TV.

"Honey, he did you wrong," Grandpa said. "You're scared. You have every right to be."

Nikki kept Grandpa's gaze. "I've always been scared. And I never killed anyone."

Grandpa stood up. "That's good enough for me." He leaned down and hugged Nikki. Then he said, "I think you are a talented magician and a good friend. Give other people a chance and you might find they think the same thing." He turned and shuffled to the door.

My cell phone rang again. I pulled it out of my purse and looked at the screen. Vance. "Hello?"

"This is a bad joke, right Shaw? I've had a full day, including an interview with Bo Kelly where he told me he went to your office first. Weren't you supposed to call me if he showed up?"

I think I may have promised that in the endless interview after Shane was murdered. But who could remember? I waved a good-bye to Nikki and walked outside. I wanted to believe in her like Grandpa did, but I wasn't going to take any chances by tipping our hand. I walked to the Jeep and got into the driver's side. "Let me ask you something Vance—have you been able to get into Shane's password-protected computer files?"

After a pointed silence, he growled, "How the hell do you know about that?"

"Investigative work." And sheer luck. "Vance, not only is Grandpa good with computers, he knows how magicians, and Shane specifically, think. Just let us take a crack."

The silence was annoying.

I added, "You'll be right there! You'll see everything we see. Vance, we have to find this killer." A horrible lump rose in my throat as my deep fear surfaced. "He knows Grandpa is looking for him. He might kill Grandpa next."

"Meet me at the stadium in twenty." He hung up.

I dropped back against the seat of the Jeep in relief.

"Hey."

I opened my eyes and saw Gabe standing there. I told him, "Grandpa and I are meeting Vance in twenty minutes."

"Take Lola too. I have to go back to the office. Blaine won't like it if I take her with me."

I nodded.

Gabe leaned closer. "Babe, we'll keep him safe."

"I know."

"I'm going to see what I can get on the hit man and see if I can find a connection to the killer. Go straight to the stadium, then call me when you are done."

"Okay." I stuck my phone back in my purse, then looked up at Gabe again. I kept thinking about the dogs. Nikki hadn't developed a bond with the dogs. She was pregnant, and the dogs were heavy. She might even have been jealous of the dogs' place in Shane's affections. Bo didn't like dogs. So who got the dogs out of the way with sleeping pills, enough to knock them out but not hurt them, then put them on the bed?

"Sam?" Gabe said.

"It's the dogs, Gabe." Something was hovering right on the edge of my mind. Right there. I gripped the steering wheel, trying to make it materialize.

He arched an eyebrow. "Yeah?"

Talk this out, I thought. "The key to who killed Shane. The dogs. Drugging them, putting them on the bed . . . it's not Bo."

"Plus he was in Orange County on his way to Hollywood at the time of the murder," Gabe added. "So Nikki? She's a good actress if she really did know who Pete Olsen was."

"She's a magician, she has to be good. But the dogs."

He reached behind my neck and rubbed my tight muscles. "What, Sam?"

It hit me then. Ali. She had ignored Bo and pouted because he didn't love her. But someone else did. I looked up. "Fletch."

His hand on the back of my neck froze. "Christ."

"Gabe?"

"Rookie mistake," he snapped.

I half smiled. "I am a rookie at this."

He did his lopsided grin. "Me. I meant me. Fletch has

been there all along, helping Barney, having issues, and being invisible. We didn't even look at him."

"It might not be him."

Gabe nodded. "Nikki had a point about magicians coming and going. We may have overlooked someone else hovering around town."

"Or they may be long gone." The depression settled over me at that thought. Once the dust settled, they could come back and kill Grandpa. Plus, if Nikki didn't kill Shane, she deserved to know who did and get on with her life and plans for her baby.

But I had to keep trying. I sat up. "Gabe, Fletch said that he went to the motorcycle shop on Tuesday. Wednesday was skydiving. He said he went up in the airplane but got sick. I never thought of checking it out. What if he didn't get sick from the airplane?" It was too awful to contemplate.

"You're saying he could have been sick from killing Shane?"

"He hates blood sports." I glanced out the window to see that Grandpa and Lola were talking to Nikki. Random pictures of Fletch and Grandpa over the years popped into my mind, and I remembered something. "Guns. Grandpa and Fletch joined the NRA, then blew up our garage. They both dropped out then. Fletch can't shoot." A giddy relief welled up inside me. Grandpa cared about Fletch; he'd be devastated if Fletch killed Shane.

"I can find out if he really did drop his NRA membership," Gabe said.

I shook my head. "I don't know what I was thinking. Fletch is a klutz. You saw his bruised leg from the motorcycle shop." I shut up when I saw Grandpa and Lola turn and head this way. The passenger side door opened. Lola got in the back, then Grandpa sat in the passenger seat.

"Nikki still wants you investigating for her, Sam. This is really important to her. She feels like she has to do the right thing, get on the right path, for the baby." He buckled his seat belt and asked, "What did Vance say, Sam?"

I really admired Nikki and hoped she wasn't a killer. I answered Grandpa's question about Vance. "We're meeting him in twenty minutes at the stadium."

He looked at me, then at Gabe. "What?"

I couldn't tell him that it might be Fletch. Not just yet. "Gabe's going back to the office to research the hit man."

"Okay if we keep the laptop for now?" Grandpa asked. "You never know, we might need it." He leaned past me a little bit and said, "It has the wireless modem, right?"

Huh? I turned to look at Gabe.

"Yes. I have accounts everywhere. You should be able to get online in Starbucks or any place that has the technology."

I could barely use my cell phone. I had no idea what they were talking about.

"Call me when you have something or are finished. I'll do the same." Gabe shut the door and stepped back.

I started the Jeep and backed out of the driveway. There was something about the way Gabe listened to me. He was done backing away. He was engaged and listening. That gave me strength to see this through.

To find the killer.

16

Shane had two trailers—a prop trailer and one that he used as an office. Vance was being testy and wouldn't let us in the prop trailer. *Evidence, chain of custody, yada, yada, yada . . .*

We walked across the black pavement of Storm Stadium parking lot to the office trailer. "Put these on," Vance ordered, handing us gloves. "Hurry." He unlocked the door.

Poor Vance was breaking his tried and true procedures, and he was not happy. He was so distracted that he barely even looked at Lola.

As I pulled on the gloves, I watched Vance unlock the door. He had on his nicely cut suit pants, but he'd taken off his coat and tie and rolled up the sleeves of his silk blue button-down shirt. He looked yuppie rugged.

He opened the door and ushered us inside. "Don't touch anything you don't have to." He came in and shut the door, then turned on a light.

This was another custom job. Built-in desk, small kitchen and bathroom, very nice. The laptop computer sat closed on the desk. Vance opened the unit and started powering it up. I walked over to watch.

He stood up, and we were chin to nose.

"I'm putting my career in serious jeopardy for you, Shaw. And if I go down, you are going with me."

His jaw was clenched tight, and his brown gaze bore into me. "We're just trying to help."

"Your grandfather better be as good as you say he is."

I lifted my chin. "He's better."

A vein in his temple throbbed. "Computer hacking is not something to brag about."

God. "Vance, you can't have it both ways."

"If you two let me through, maybe we could find out how good I really am," Grandpa said.

I tried not to blush. Vance just pushed my buttons. "Sure, Grandpa." I moved over to let him sit down. I stood back behind his chair next to Lola. Vance hovered over Grandpa like an old woman.

With a cute ass.

Caffeine withdrawal. That was it. I needed more coffee.

I had Gabe. He was all the man I could handle.

I focused on the computer screen. A dialog box popped up asking for a password.

Grandpa looked up at Vance. "Have you gotten past this?"

"No."

Short and clipped. Annoyed.

"What have you tried?" Grandpa asked.

Vance reached into his shirt pocket and pulled out his little spiral notebook. He flipped some pages, then set it down on the desk.

I looked over Grandpa's shoulder. There was a neat list in dark block printing. *Magic, show, spoiler, superstar . . .*

Grandpa turned the page, reading the entire list. "Does the computer lock up after a few attempts?"

"Three."

He nodded. "Shane has good firewalls," he said, and leaned back in the chair.

"What are you doing?" Vance demanded.

Grandpa answered, "Thinking like Shane."

This was going to take forever. I sat down on a leather couch.

Lola sat next to me. "Maybe I should take the car and run over to see Michelle again while he's working on this."

I didn't want her going anywhere alone. Grandpa sat up and started typing.

The computer beeped at him.

He typed again.

Beep.

A headache took root. I answered Lola. "Let's just sit tight for a little bit and think about Shane. What might he use for passwords?"

"Party clowns," Lola said. She looked over at Barney. "That's what he called a lot of magicians."

Grandpa had just rebooted the computer. He turned around to look at us and said, "He called magic 'party tricks' when we talked to him, remember Sam?"

I nodded that I did remember and suggested, "Try them."

When the dialog box popped up, Grandpa typed in "Party Clowns."

Beep.

I was ready to bash that computer with my purse.

Grandpa tried again. "Party Tricks."

Beep.

I could almost hear Shane laughing. It gave me the creeps. "That two-bit imposter," I muttered just to shake off the creepy feeling.

Grandpa said, "two-bitpartyclowns."

Beep.

The computer locked up.

Grandpa rebooted and was muttering nonstop. "You will not beat me. I was a magician before you were born . . ."

The computer was back up with the hated dialog box demanding a password.

Grandpa leaned forward. "What did Shane love?" He typed in "Houdiniblack."

The dogs, a combination of their names, I thought to myself, and held my breath.

No sound.

I looked at the screen. It was filled with icons. "You're in!" I stood up and smirked at Vance.

He gave me a look of supreme patience. "Just getting started, Shaw. I'm sure that he password protected each of these files. Shane Masters was the paranoid type."

I sat back down. "Grandpa got farther than you."

The next hour passed in agonizing frustration as we watched Grandpa painstakingly crack the passwords on four files. But each time, the files turned up nothing. The up-and-down roller coaster was wearing on all of us.

We all jumped when Vance's cell phone rang.

Vance answered the phone and walked to the other end of the trailer. When he returned, he was finished with the call. He swept his gold-dotted brown gaze over us, then looked at Grandpa. "We're done here. I have to go."

Grandpa typed faster. "I'm almost there. I know it."

Vance said, "We've opened four files, and they are all useless. I have work to do."

Grandpa looked up. "Fine. Let me shut this down. Just stop hovering over me."

I could tell Grandpa was tired and cranky.

And up to something crafty.

I stood up. "Vance, I thought you wanted to find Shane's killer!"

He took a step toward me. "I have a real expert coming in, Shaw. I'm not about to let him find out that I let an amateur try to get into the computer. As it is, I'll have to claim I was doing all this work. Experts can track a computer's usage history. Now, do you have anything else that might be helpful?"

"Yes." I didn't dare look at Grandpa. I was stalling so he could do whatever he was doing. But he was going to figure out my suspicion about Fletch when I told this to Vance. "Fletch Knight."

"Sam?" Grandpa said.

I ignored him. "He's a magician. He's been in town since Tuesday. I forgot to mention him because he's, well, he's Fletch. Besides, he has an alibi, or I thought he did." Quickly I told Vance about Fletch's skydiving plans and explained about his show at the House of Cards and that he'd been planning this visit with Grandpa for a while. I left out the part where they had once blown up our garage.

Okay, not blown up. But they could have. It had been a little fire that required a bomb squad to remove the unstable gunpowder.

"Shaw, I could strangle you." He reached over and snatched his notebook off the desk. He pressed his pen down so hard on the pages, I wondered why they didn't tear as he made notes.

I patiently answered his rapid-fire questions. Fletch was staying at the Night Haven Motel. Grandpa was his mentor. I didn't think Fletch had even met Shane, but I didn't know for sure. He'd been helping Grandpa look for a magician that hired a hit man in the professional magician organization that they both belonged to. . . . I was a fountain of information.

Until Grandpa stood up. "Let's go, Sammy. The detective's expert will crack this faster than I can."

Now I knew Grandpa had been up to something. We skedaddled out of there before a tired and harassed Vance caught on.

We all piled into the Jeep. Since we were literally just around the corner from the office, I headed that way and said, "What did you do back there, Grandpa?"

"I was trying to copy the files to a CD. I slipped it into my pocket." He pulled it out and held it up, then set it on the floorboard by Gabe's computer. "What's this about Fletch?"

I had to tell him, so I outlined the quick version of why I thought we had to look at Fletch as a possible suspect. As I parked the Jeep, I said, "But if we can establish that he was at the airport yesterday at the time of Shane's murder, we'll drop him." I felt guilty. We were suspecting all of Grandpa's friends.

Grandpa leaned down and picked up the CD and the computer. "Let's see if I was able to copy the password-protected folders." He looked at me. "Shane came here because of me, Sam. He was going to prove that he's the better magician."

"By spoiling the show of someone you care about in your hometown." I'd put it together while sitting in Shane's trailer as Grandpa worked to crack Shane's passwords. I reached out and touched his arm. "Are you okay?"

He nodded. "When you live as long as me, you know that some people will break your heart. Others, like you, will fill your heart. Let's get going." He turned and opened the door.

The smell of paint was still strong enough to scorch our lungs. The painters were all done. Gabe, Cal, and Blaine had fans set up to dry the paint and air out the fumes. I could hear noise from both sides of the offices, so I assumed they were cleaning up, moving furniture, and replacing hardware like the light switch plates.

I stood inside the door to the Heart Mates side and looked around. Taking out the wall between the suites had doubled the space. The cream paint gave it a fresh feel. It would look inviting and professional once the carpet was done and the furniture delivered.

Cal walked out of Gabe's side of the office. He had on his low-slung jeans, a T-shirt, and a tool belt. The scowl on his face made me wonder if he'd hit himself with the hammer. "Hi Sam. I'm going to replace the fixtures in your office."

I could see his was angry. "Cal, what's wrong?"

Gabe came out from his side and said, "You told me to talk to him. But he's not talking. He's got it all under control, isn't that right, Cal?"

Cal's shoulders went up two notches at the sarcasm. "Did it ever occur to you that I don't want to be a fireman anymore, Gabe?"

Lola said, "Uh, Sam, maybe we should—"

Cal cut her off. "Stay. I don't care who hears this." He strode up to Gabe so that they were nose to nose. Two furious Italian brothers. "I didn't need your self-defense lessons, little brother. And it's damned insulting that you think one man could do this much damage to me. But I don't really give a shit about your opinion of my fighting skills. I will not be a part of a brotherhood that hides men who beat their wives. So save your breath and leave me the hell alone." Cal pivoted, stormed into my office, and slammed the door.

The echo washed over us as we stood there dumbfounded.

Then Blaine stormed out of the interview room and right up to Lola. "What did you do now?"

"Nothing," she said softly. Then she firmed up her spine. "And stop being so damned mean to me, Blaine. I left you. I was wrong and I am sorry. But I'm not going to take your nastiness."

"So you'll leave?"

"No. I'm staying. Lake Elsinore is my hometown."

Blaine opened his mouth, then snapped it shut and huffed off back into the interview room.

Good God, what was wrong with these men? I focused on Gabe. He looked like he'd been gut punched. He stared at the door Cal had slammed, his eyes dark and stormy. I could see that he was thinking. I had to fix this somehow. I walked up and touched his arm.

He turned his gaze to me.

I had a sudden stomach cramp of worry that he would emotionally shove me away again. But I'd be a coward not to try. "He's just upset. I'm sure he'll calm down and talk to you soon."

Gabe held my gaze for long seconds. I was aware of Lola and Grandpa watching in thick silence. Finally, Gabe said, "Damn right he will, or I will handcuff his ass to a chair until he does."

"That's a step up from fighting, I guess."

Gabe's mask of anger cracked. "We weren't fighting. He walked in with a cut lip and black eye. I was giving him a refresher course on self-defense."

I rolled my eyes. His reaction to my own black eye and bruised cheek had been extreme too. "You are a violent man."

He actually looked proud. "When necessary." He looked over at Grandpa and Lola, then back at me. "Let's go into my office and you can tell me what you found out with the computer. I have coffee in there."

The magic words for me. I followed him, along with Grandpa and Lola. Gabe's office was rich with the light-pecan-colored walls. His desk was on the left side of the room facing out. His computer was on. He'd been working. The coffee was on a TV tray on the right. Gabe and I went to get two folding chairs from his storage area.

Away from the others, Gabe picked up both the chairs and said, "I need to know one thing about Cal, Sam."

I wondered if I should tell him everything Cal told me. "What's that?"

"Cal didn't attack Dirk without provocation, did he?"

His face was cop blank. He was trying to get information and see if he could build a defense for his brother. He could. "No. There were two others involved."

His face tightened. "I should have known."

"Cal has torn loyalties, I guess."

He nodded. "Let's get back in there. I'll fix this with Cal later."

I blinked. "Don't you want to go talk to him now?"

He shook his head. "He'll cool off. He has a right to be pissed. But he'll cool down. Cal never stays mad for long. Right now, we need to focus on Shane's murder." He turned and walked back into his office, carrying the chairs.

We got settled around his desk while Grandpa explained that he hadn't gotten anything off the computer yet but that he had copied the files to a CD.

Gabe sat in his chair and looked at Grandpa. "I'm doing some checking on Fletch."

Grandpa nodded. He sat across from Gabe and had the laptop open on the desk. It was still booting up.

Gabe went on. "I made some calls. Fletch was definitely at the motorcycle shop and did knock over a row of bikes.

That doesn't prove anything though, because the hit man wasn't killed until later Tuesday night." Gabe looked at me and Grandpa. "After the dinner at your house."

"What about skydiving yesterday?" I asked.

"I can't get any information on that yet. The owner is out of the office but will call me back later. In the meantime, I'm looking at a couple things. A man using Fletch's ID registered at a hotel in Vegas last week."

A shivery cold washed over me. "The hit man is from Vegas. What was Fletch doing there?"

"Could be perfectly innocent." Grandpa slid the CD he'd copied from Shane's computer into the laptop. "Vegas is a big spot for magicians."

Gabe let that go. "I'm still tracking to see if he dropped his NRA membership as you thought he did, Sam."

Grandpa turned and looked at me. "What does that mean?"

"Remember when you two joined the NRA and then tried packing your own bullets in the garage?"

A grin twitched his mouth. "Yes. I never actually joined the NRA, and Fletch gave it up after that little incident. We'd only taken the one shooting lesson."

"What if Fletch didn't give it up?"

Grandpa thought about it. "He hates blood sports like hunting. He hates most sports altogether. Maybe he'd do target shooting, but he would have told me."

I shook my head. "Not if he was doing it to impress his dad."

Grandpa sighed. "He would do that. But Sammy," he fixed his gaze on me, "he has his House of Cards show next month. Why would he risk that by doing all this? Sending a hit man after Shane, killing the hit man, and then killing Shane? This is what Fletch has worked for. It doesn't make any sense."

It really didn't. I frowned. "Shane's exposing all Fletch's illusions wouldn't affect his House of Cards performance, would it?"

Grandpa shook his head. "No. It's one of our highest honors, and we don't acknowledge spoilers like Shane."

I rubbed my forehead. "But who else could have killed Shane?"

Lola said, "So where is this Fletch right now?"

I looked up. "He's supposed to be doing his wake-boarding thing, right?"

"That's what he said," Grandpa affirmed. "But let's find out." He pulled out his little cell phone, scrolled through his numbers, and dialed. "Hi, Fletch. How'd the wake-boarding go? Did you get the video?"

We all sat there and held our breath.

Grandpa said, "Oh. Well how's that for disappointing? So how long will you be there?"

Where? I wondered.

"Okay. Bye."

We all stared at him.

"Fletch is in the emergency room getting a fishing hook removed from his foot. Apparently there was one on the boat floor, and he stepped on it."

"So where does that leave us?" I tried to bring this all to-gether. "Someone killed Shane, after sending a hit man that failed. We think it was a magician, one who had enough to lose to try and kill him to stop him. Bo had his cartoon, Nikki may have wanted revenge, and Fletch?" I tapped my nails on Gabe's desk trying to see it.

Grandpa picked up his Styrofoam cup of coffee. "From Shane's point of view, he'd go after Fletch to spoil his show."

I stared at him, seeing the pain etched into his craggy face. But his blue eyes were clear and determined. "Why?"

"Fletch attained the one thing Shane could not—a legitimate recognition. And Shane blamed me for removing him from the Triple M. So he came to my town to humiliate my protégé by doing a spoiler on Fletch's act."

That made perfect sense. It fit with Shane's huge arrogance. "But that still doesn't explain Fletch trying to kill Shane. Why not laugh it off, or file a lawsuit even, if he knew that's what Shane was going to do?" I frowned and tried to think like Fletch. He was a talented comedy magician who was goofy enough to try extreme sports and videotape his attempts to use as a backdrop for his shows. All to impress his dad.

His dad.

Omigod! I sat up straight and said, "Grandpa, can you get into the other computer files from Shane's computer?"

He shook his head. "They didn't copy. His firewalls are excellent. I only got the ones I had opened with a password." He looked serious. "I need to get back into that computer. I can crack those passwords, I know I can. If Vance hasn't moved the computer, I'm going to try and get back in." His balding head darkened with frustration and anger.

"No!" I shook my head. "That's . . . tampering or something serious." I didn't want Grandpa arrested!

Gabe said, "Barney, you can't break into a police crime scene. Besides, Vance most likely logged the computer as evidence for the computer expert. They don't usually make crime scene calls but work out of their offices."

Grandpa set his chin and squared his thin shoulders. "Where would that be? At the police station?"

Jeez! "Grandpa! You aren't breaking into the police station! I'll think of another way." My mouth was dry. I took a sip of coffee.

"Humph," Grandpa said.

But Gabe zeroed in on me. "Another way to do what, Sam? What are you thinking?"

I met his dark gaze. "Fletch's motive for going after Shane. Remember that Lola found that, at least for some of the magicians, Shane sent tickets to the magician or someone close to them?"

Grandpa jumped in. "That's the whole reason I'm trying to get into Shane's computer."

I turned to Grandpa. "I know. But what's the worst thing that could happen to Fletch, Grandpa? Or let me put this another way—if Shane did his spoiler on Fletch's show, who is the one person that Fletch would go to any lengths to prevent from seeing that show?"

Grandpa's milky blue eyes widened with comprehension. "His father."

I nodded, feeling a heavy sadness envelope me. "That could motivate Fletch to murder."

Grandpa sat back in his chair. "We have to find out if Fletch's dad had free tickets sent to him."

I nodded. "There has to be another way. . . ."

Lola sat forward. "How come you don't just call his dad and ask him?"

All three of us turned and looked at her.

Well, duh.

17

"Lola," I said from where I sat between her and Grandpa at Gabe's desk, "you are both *smart* and *useful.* We'll call him!"

Gabe said, "We can do a White Pages search in a search engine and see if his address and phone number turn up." He signed onto his Internet service and pulled up the Web site he wanted. "Name?"

"Jim Bob Knight," Grandpa answered.

Gabe pulled his mouth tight as if trying to hide a smirk. "We'll try James Robert Knight." He typed that in, then he looked at Grandpa. "What state?"

"Montana. Don't remember the city."

"Okay." Gabe typed, then waited. "Four of them." He hit a button and his printer started spewing. "We'll do a little pretext calling and find our man."

"Pretext calling?" I probably should learn these terms if I was going to be a private investigator. *If.*

"Lying," Gabe answered. "It's developing a story that gets the mark to tell you what you want to know. For instance, if I wanted to know if Barney lived alone, I might call and say I was doing a survey for health insurance, then ask a few questions including how many people lived in the household and how many of those people were covered by insurance."

"That's just creepy," Lola said. "It never occurred to me that a survey taker might be lying."

Gabe turned to look at her. "Never give out personal information on the phone. Ever. Not even what kind of car you drive. Simply hang up. Your bank does not call you and ask you your social security number or account number. They already have it. And no one is calling you to give you something for free."

I hid a smile at Gabe's passion, but his speech gave me an idea. "We should hold safety talks like this for my female clients," I said. "Or all my clients. Men can have their identity stolen."

"Babe, I sell my services, not give them away. Now, let's figure out our pretext. Our goal is to find out who Shane sent free tickets to for this weekend's show. We have to assume that Jim Bob," his mouth twitched again, "has heard that Shane is dead."

I thought about that. "So we can't say we are making sure the tickets arrived. With Shane dead, there won't be a show, so no one would care if the tickets had arrived or not."

"Right."

Grandpa said, "What if we were letting the ticket holders know the show is cancelled?"

"That could work," Gabe said. "We want to get his attention and get him cooperative. So we'll say we are calling Mr. Masters's special guests to let them know the show is cancelled. We'll use one of my throwaway cell phones."

I tried to figure the reason for that.

But Grandpa was ahead of me. "Caller ID, right?"

Gabe nodded. "We never want our subjects to know they were contacted by a PI. And remember, we are looking at his son for a murder. Down the road, Jim Bob might figure a little revenge is in order."

It all made sense. And damn, Gabe was good at this. I asked him, "Are you going to call?"

He pulled a cell phone out of his desk and handed it to me with the printed list of the four James Robert Knights. "No, you are. Men tend to think secretaries and assistants are female. And they are usually less threatened by a woman's voice on the phone."

I took the phone and tramped down on the bundle of nerves that woke up in my gut. I didn't want to screw this up. We needed to know if Fletch's dad received free tickets from Shane or someone in his organization.

Gabe watched me. "Write down what you are going to say, if that helps you."

I set the phone down, picked up a pen, and jotted down a few notes on the paper with the phone numbers. Then before I could dwell on it, I picked up the cell, turned it on, and dialed the first number on the list. I held my breath as it rang, then went to the answering machine.

I hung up and dropped my shoulders in both relief and frustration. "Answering machine."

All three of them stared expectantly.

I used the pen to make a note of getting the answering machine by the first name. Then I took a breath and dialed the second name.

"Hello?"

"Uh, Mr. Knight?"

"I'm not buying."

Panicked, I practically yelled, "No! Mr. Knight I'm not selling anything." I talked faster. "I'm Shane Masters's executive assistant. It's my understanding that you've been sent some complimentary tickets to the show this weekend and—"

Click.

I sighed and said, "He hung up." My hand was sweaty. It took a concentrated effort to unclench my fingers from around the plastic base of the black phone. I shifted the phone to my other hand and wiped my hand on my pants.

"Try the next one," Lola said next to me.

"Right." I dialed the next number. It felt like I was growing cotton in my mouth as I put the phone to my ear.

"Yeah?"

The voice was thick and rough. "Hello, this is Shane Masters's personal assistant. I'm looking for Mr. James Robert Knight."

"You got 'im. I heard on the news that Shane got himself killed. So what about my tickets?"

My heart kicked up. The cotton in my mouth doubled in size. "Uhh, yes, well that's what I'm calling about, Mr. Knight. You received the complimentary tickets that Shane sent you, correct?"

"And the plane ticket for tomorrow. Can I cash them in for money?"

Hell if I knew. Or cared. We had our answer! If this was Fletch's dad. I just wanted to verify that. "I will look into that for you, Mr. Knight. But in my records there's a note that you were planning to bring your son, a Fletch Knight, with you to the show. Is the information correct?"

"Damn right I was gonna. The boy might of learned something. How do I cash in the show and plane tickets?"

I looked at Grandpa and felt a wave of sadness. "I'll call you back with that information. Thank you for your time." I disconnected.

"What did he say?" Grandpa asked, his voice low and quiet.

"Shane sent him two tickets for seats and a plane ticket to fly out here."

His entire face sank. "Fletch." He shook his head.

My heart broke. I put my hand on his arm. "Grandpa, it's not your fault. If Fletch did all this, he made the choice. Not you."

He put his hand over mine on his arm. "Don't worry about me, Sam. Now that we suspect Fletch is behind Shane's murder, and the hit man's murder, we need to tell Detective Vance before more people are hurt."

I stared at the man I'd loved all of my life. I hoped I'd be like him when I grew up. "I'll call him."

Gabe said gently, "Would you like me to call Vance?"

I kept my hand on Grandpa's arm and turned to look at Gabe. "I'll do it. I talked to Fletch's dad so I can describe the conversation better."

Gabe leaned across the desk and touched my hand resting on the paper with the phone numbers. "Good."

It was all he said, but his intense dark eyes showed pride in me. Gabe had a remarkable sexiness about him. It was part in his hero streak that would rush in and fix things for me if I needed it, but the other part of him respected my ability to do things for myself, even if I screwed it up the first or second time. His gaze told me that he had complete faith that I'd get it right. That kind of belief from the hot and sexy ex-cop, for me the small-town soccer mom, was sexy as hell. I slid the disposable cell phone to him. Then taking my hand off Grandpa, I dug my own cell out of my purse on the floor. I had Vance's number programmed in there.

I got his voice mail. Naturally. "Vance, it's Sam Shaw. I

know who Shane Masters sent the free tickets to. Call me ASAP." I ended the call and said, "What now?"

"What about Michelle?" Lola said. "I think she knew it was Fletch's show all along that Shane was spoiling."

I turned to look at her. "Would Fletch know that? *How* would he know that?" I was trying to think it out and determine if Michelle was in danger.

"I can answer that," my mom said.

I swiveled around in my seat. My mom stood in the doorway of Gabe's office wearing linen pants and a black silk blouse with an exquisite scarf draped around her neck. "Mom! What are you doing here?"

She walked into the office. Her wedge-cut blond hair barely moved, but her brown gaze swept around the room and finally landed on me. She reached into her purse and pulled out what looked like a check and handed it to me. "This is for your skirt that security brute ruined."

I took the check and looked at the amount. "A hundred dollars! That skirt didn't cost that much!"

She stood at my left shoulder and looked down at me with her shrewd businesswoman gaze. "Samantha, there's your mileage and time in buying a new skirt to be considered."

"Sheesh, Mom, you're a shark."

"Thank you," she answered, nodding as if it were a compliment. "While I was at the security company's offices discussing your skirt, I also got some other information. They had a man there today asking all kinds of questions, particularly about Shane's trailers at Storm Stadium, and if they knew where Shane's office computer was. He pressed the security people to find out if the contents of the trailers had been removed by the police, if the trailers were scheduled to be moved, stuff like that."

Gabe made a noise. "The security detail isn't privy to police information."

My mother nodded. "Indeed. However, the description of the man asking the questions matched Fletch. I was curious about that and tracked down Louis."

"Louis?" Gabe and Grandpa said at the same time.

I was too busy staring at the woman who had invaded my mother's body. "You tracked down a grounds maintenance person?" My mother, the snob who refused to acknowledge that she grew up in a trailer? Later, Grandpa had built the house on the land, but for many years, they all lived in a trailer.

"Louis was working on the grounds of Storm Stadium when Samantha and I were there yesterday. And yes, Samantha, I tracked him down. I am not a private investigator, but even I can see that Dad is in danger here." She put her hand on Grandpa's shoulder.

My mom rarely showed affection. Who was this woman? But I knew, this woman was scared that Grandpa was going to get hurt or killed. She didn't show affection easily, but I never doubted that she loved us—Grandpa, me, TJ, and Joel. My mom had some deep scars, I understood that. It made her constantly try to change our lives to fit her view of a perfect life, and it was frustrating and annoying. But she did love us. "Sorry, Mom," I muttered. "What did Louis have to say?"

"He's cleaning up all those leaf piles at the stadium. He said that the policeman who guarded the trailers had to run off a man lurking around."

"And that man looked like Fletch?"

My mom nodded. "So to answer your question about how Fletch might know about whoever this Michelle is, I'd say he's been conducting his own investigation."

My insides went icy. Unease crawled up my back. "Then Fletch isn't at the hospital like he told you on his cell when you called him, Grandpa."

Lola stood up. "I'm worried about Michelle. I'm going to go over there."

Grandpa got up. "I'll go with you."

"Hold on," Gabe said. "First, no running off half-cocked. We need to plan this out. We'll get Vance up to speed, then Sam and I will go check on Michelle. In the meantime, Barney and you," he turned to Lola, "can try to find out where Fletch is by phone."

I looked at my watch. It was one-thirty. "Joel gets out of school in a half hour. Then TJ will come home on the bus an hour after that."

My mom spoke up. "I'll get the boys."

Relived, I looked up at her. "Thanks, Mom."

She smiled, a real smile that reached her eyes and softened the businesswoman shark into a grandma. "*That* you don't have to thank me for. I'll head over to Joel's school now. You be careful," she said, then left.

I looked at Grandpa.

He shrugged. "That's Katy. But she'll watch out for the boys."

Vance returned my call while we were in Gabe's black truck on the way to the campground. I told him how we'd come up with the idea of calling Fletch's dad and that we found out he had received free tickets from Shane to his show. Then I added what my mom had learned about Fletch nosing around.

Vance said, "Okay. I've been by the motel, and Fletch is not there. We'll track him down. What are you doing?"

"Gabe and I are on our way to the campground to

check on Shane's assistant, Michelle. She seemed really scared earlier today."

"Why didn't you call the police to check on her? Damn it, Shaw, this could be dangerous."

I winced and pulled the phone an inch from my ear. "We're just checking. And I did call the police—I called you."

"Is Pulizzi armed?"

I had seen Gabe unlock his glove box and strap his gun to the small of his back, then add a long-sleeved shirt over that. I was pretty sure he had a permit to carry. "Yeah."

"Be careful and call me as soon as you check on her."

"All right."

"And Shaw."

Gabe was turning into the campground. I looked around, half expecting to see Fletch running out of the row of little cabins. "What?"

"Let Pulizzi go in first." He hung up.

Men.

I pushed the button to end the call. "It's that cabin." I pointed to the one that Michelle was staying in. Gabe parked the truck, and we got out.

Gabe stopped a few feet back from the door. "Sam—"

"I know," I said with a sigh. "Let you go in first."

He cracked a smile. "Vance?"

"Men. You're all alike."

Gabe stilled in the peculiar way of his. It was like his body stopped moving but all kinds of powerful energy hummed below the surface. "Vance wants you because he can't have you. I want you because you are a strong, sexy, and scary woman who isn't afraid to think for herself. Vance and I are not alike." He turned away, then looked back over his shoulder. "Stay to the side of the door until I clear the cabin." He knocked.

I moved to the side of the door on some kind of automatic pilot. Then I stared at Gabe's hard profile as he watched the door with his head slightly cocked. He was listening.

I tried to push Gabe's words away and listen too.

But *strong, sexy, and scary* played over in my head. What did that mean?

Gabe looked over at me. "Hear anything inside?"

I shook my head. I didn't hear anything but my thoughts.

He reached out and slowly turned the knob. It was unlocked. "Stay there." He whispered the warning. He reached behind his back and took out his gun. Then he eased the door forward and went into the room.

I heard him moving around while my heart pounded out a worried beat. How long did I stand there? It felt like forever.

"Sam."

I knew that tone in Gabe's voice. Something was wrong. I sucked in a deep breath of air and went around the door frame into the room.

Michelle was splayed on her back over the top of the bed. Her slack face seemed to sink back into the pool of platinum blond hair. "Is she breathing?"

"Yes. Call 911."

I pulled my cell phone out. "Vance said to—"

"911, Sam. Now."

I turned away and dialed. I gave the 911 operator all the information. When she told me to stay on the line, I told her I had another call to make and hung up.

Probably that was stupid.

I turned around and froze. Gabe was doing CPR. "I

thought she was breathing!" Hysteria built up below my breastbone.

He ignored me and worked on forcing air into her lungs.

I lifted my hand clutching the cell phone and punched in Vance's number.

He answered, "Vance."

"It's Sam," I said, my mouth full of words I was desperate to get out. "We're in Michelle's cabin. She's unconscious. Gabe's doing CPR."

"Did you call for paramedics, Shaw?"

"911." I choked on the word as I watched. I wanted her to be okay. Had Fletch done this? But how?

"I'm on my way. Don't touch anything other than what's necessary to help the woman."

The next few minutes passed in a blur. The paramedics and cops arrived and pushed us out of the way. Vance arrived just as the ambulance was loading Michelle in. He had a quick word with the crew, then the ambulance screamed away, blaring lights and sirens.

18

Gabe and I stood outside the little cabin at the edge of the campground. We were both quiet, trying to figure out how Michelle had become unconscious. Vance strode up to us and said, "They think Michelle has a good chance."

I was thankful for that. But what happened to her?

Gabe said, "I didn't see any bottles of alcohol or any pills. No drug paraphernalia. Nothing that would indicate she was a user who overdosed."

Vance made a note in his little pocket-size notebook. "We'll do a search."

I hated what I was thinking. "Do you think Fletch tried to kill her?"

Vance looked at me. "Do you? You know him."

I shook my head vigorously. "Not this side of him. I never would have thought he'd kill. He just seemed like a goofy comedy magician who adopted Grandpa and desperately wanted his father's approval." But it was that very desperation that finally made me see him as a possible killer. "I just never realized how desperate, I guess."

Gabe reached over and took my hand.

The warm skin-to-skin contact anchored me. I tried to think of something to describe Fletch. "It's his need for approval from his dad. He'll do extreme stuff like making a skydiving video to add to his show to prove his manhood to his dad, and to prove that being a magician is manly."

But there was more, and it had to do with Grandpa. How did I get it across? "For some reason, he's focused on Grandpa too. He's important to Fletch, I guess because he can get Grandpa's respect and approval. He always jokes about marrying me, but I think he would marry me just to get Grandpa in the bargain."

Vance nodded. "That indicates something a little stronger than focus. More like obsession. Where do you think Fletch is now?"

I shrugged in frustration. "Don't know. If he hurt Michelle, why?" Then I remembered. "Lola, Grandpa, and I thought she knew whose show Shane was spoiling. Fletch must have figured she knew too."

"Cleaning up loose ends," Gabe said.

"He appears to have some agenda to keep him here in Elsinore," Vance said.

I looked around. Why had he stayed in Elsinore? Once he killed Shane, shouldn't he have left? It didn't make sense. He'd been helping Grandpa. . . . I looked up. "Maybe he was trying to stay close to the investigation to find out what was going on? Then he figured Michelle was a threat? Would he think anyone else is a threat?"

"Anything's possible. Many killers stay close by to keep tabs on what's happening in the investigation. All right." Vance snapped his little notebook shut. "I'm going to go take a look at the scene."

Gabe said, "Any problem with us leaving?"

"Keep your cell phones on," Vance said, and walked away.

Gabe tugged on my hand. "Come on. We're going to get you some hot coffee and something to eat."

His concern made me realize that I was being selfish. It was Gabe that found Michelle first. Gabe had been the one giving her CPR and fighting to keep her alive. At the front of his truck, I stopped. "I'm fine. But how about you?"

The cop-ice glaze cracked. Gabe pulled his mouth thin and tight. "She had better live. I hate it when they die after I work that hard to keep them alive."

Interesting. *She* had no name. It was *she, they,* or *them.* He distanced himself automatically. And that was partly how he handled it.

"Let's get some coffee, stud. Then we'll see what we should do next."

We went over to Hunny's restaurant. It was tucked back from Riverside Drive right next to the Kentucky Fried Chicken and a laundromat. After finding a slot for the truck on the bricked parking lot, Gabe and I went inside. We took a seat at a booth that had a window facing the street.

The campground was a little ways down and across the street. The lunch crowd had emptied out, and we had the place practically to ourselves. There were TVs that played the Keno numbers mounted over the bar. A waitress in a shorts-with-nylons uniform took our order. Gabe had the beefeater sandwich, and I had French onion soup and corn bread.

After the waitress left, I looked at Gabe. "What do we do next?"

"You, Barney, and the boys will stay at my house. We'll

check in with Nikki and Bo and make sure they are safe. Fletch may be gone, Sam."

"What about his dad? Would Fletch go home to Montana?"

"That's a possibility."

We stopped talking while the waitress brought our food and checked our coffee. When she left, I shook my head. "I can't believe he was in our house, helping Grandpa, and he was the killer the whole time." I looked down at the soup. My stomach tightened into a knot. "TJ and Joel, he could have hurt them."

"Don't do that, Sam. They are fine. Your mom has them."

I nodded, staring at the cheese and bread at the top of my soup. "Do you think Fletch is really gone now? On the run? He had a rental truck; has he turned it in? Taken it? Stolen something else? Bought something else?"

Gabe took a bite of his sandwich, then picked up a french fry and pointed it toward my soup.

I picked up the spoon and cut a chunk of the thick, spongy bread and a glob of cheese. I set it back down and drank some coffee. Then I cut a piece of the corn bread and moved it around.

Gabe set his sandwich down. "What?"

I looked up. "He's not done. Fletch, I mean. He's got some other purpose here."

"Hmm. Okay, what?"

"I don't know. It's just that he was determined enough to kill Shane to keep Shane from humiliating him in front of his dad. Or I think that's why he did it. But he stayed around Grandpa the whole time."

"He didn't expect the first hit to go wrong. And then

Shane demanded that Barney help him find the magician who ordered the hit," Gabe added.

"Right. Fletch could have been doing damage control by keeping an eye on what Grandpa found. Maybe he was even attempting to protect Grandpa since he never meant for him to get involved. It was Shane that dragged Grandpa into this." It just seemed like it was more than that with Fletch.

Gabe reached over and cupped his large hand around mine. "But?"

I used my free hand to break off a piece of corn bread and stuffed it in my mouth while thinking about Gabe's question. *But what?* Fletch was bent on impressing his dad. He had added fireworks to his show a few years back for that reason. His latest scheme was the video backdrops of extreme sports. I swallowed the bread and said, "Fletch's dad is a blood sport kind of guy. A hunter. What if Fletch thought that killing Shane would impress his dad?"

Gabe kept his gaze locked on me. "Twisted thinking, but murder usually is. So okay, he's killed Shane and thinks he killed Michelle because she knew something, so now he'd be finished, right?" He took his hand back to eat more of his sandwich.

I ate a bite of soup. What was bugging me exactly? Gabe was right that if Fletch killed Shane to keep from being humiliated in front of his dad, and/or to impress his dad, then he'd be done and likely take off.

But I didn't think he was done. What was it Fletch had said about Shane? I thought back to the morning Fletch had come over before Grandpa got back from dropping the boys at school. Fletch had seemed worried about my poking around in Shane's business. He said that he understood Shane . . . that was it! Fletch said, *Shane's the magician that went bad. I'm the one who is succeeding. I understand a little better how Shane thinks and how Shane's betrayal is a black mark on Barney's stellar career.*

I set my spoon down. "Fletch said that Shane was a black mark on Grandpa's career. Shane was the magician that had gone bad while he was the success."

Gabe wiped his hands on a napkin. "Sort of like the good son and the bad son?"

"Right." I sipped some coffee. The hot soup and coffee were doing the trick, helping me to calm down and focus. So what was Fletch doing?

"Did Fletch know Shane? I mean personally? He knows Bo, right? They seemed familiar with each other at your house when Bo cooked dinner."

Gabe was trying to help me get to the thing that was bugging me. "You know, when Grandpa was toasting Bo for his cartoon character the night Bo made jambalaya for us, Fletch dropped his glass of wine. At the time, he looked dejected and miserable. I thought he was upset that he ruined Bo's moment."

Gabe pushed his plate away. "But he could have been purposely ruining Bo's moment. Because Fletch is supposed to be Barney's shining star."

My nerves flared to life, and the muscles in my neck and shoulders clenched tight. "Gabe, could he think that Grandpa belongs to him? Is that what kept him in Elsinore?" Worry rushed at me, suddenly making me anxious and antsy.

The waitress came by and asked if we wanted anything else, then left the check. I reached for my purse.

Gabe pulled out his wallet. "We'll go back to the office

and check on Barney, then we'll see." He pulled fifteen dollars out and left it on the tray. "Let's go."

I got up and held out the money for him.

Gabe looked down at it, then back up at me. "You are insisting on paying your way at work, and that's fine. I get it. But I can buy you lunch without it being a big deal. Now let's go."

We had just gotten into Gabe's truck when his cell phone rang. He pulled it off his belt, looked at the display window, then answered with, "What's up?"

He looked over at me as he listened. Then he said, "We're closer to the house, but go. Are Blaine and Lola with you?" He started the engine and backed out of the parking space.

What was wrong? I had to bite down on the inside of my cheeks to keep from demanding to know what was going on.

Gabe said, "Stay together and keep an eye on Lola." He hung up.

"What?"

Gabe turned out on the small street that led to Riverside Drive. "Rosy came by the office and said something about Nikki being sick. She seemed upset. Barney told Cal he was going to walk her to her car. It was ten minutes before Cal realized they both left in Rosy's car." He made a right onto Riverside, then gunned it up to Lincoln where he made another right.

"That makes no sense. Why would Rosy come get Grandpa if Nikki was sick? He's a magician not a doctor." I squeezed my hands together, then I grabbed my phone out of my purse. "I'll call Grandpa's cell." I hit speed dial and waited through the rings. "No answer. Something's wrong." I fought to breathe. Raw fear fogged my brain. What was going on? "Could it have been Nikki all along? Was Rosy in on it, somehow trying to save her granddaughter? But why get Grandpa to go with her?"

Gabe said, "Call Vance. We're only a minute from Rosy's house if that's where they were headed."

I had to clutch the phone to steady my shaking hands, but I found Vance's number and hit Send. I knew he was probably still at the campground. I got his voice mail. Trying not to cry or scream, I said, "Vance, it's Sam. Gabe's brother just called. Rosy Malone went to Heart Mates and said something about her granddaughter, Nikki Eden, being sick. Grandpa left with her. We think something is wrong and are on our way to Rosy's house to check." I hoped I made sense, and hung up. "What if they didn't go to Rosy's house?"

Gabe made a hard right on Machado. "We'll find out in a second." He went a little ways down the street, passed Rosy's house, then did an illegal U-turn and parked where a large bush hid the truck from anyone looking out the front window.

"That's Rosy's Grand Am." I pointed to the brown car parked on the half-circle driveway. "And that's Nikki's car." I didn't see any other car. Maybe Nikki really was sick. "What do we do?"

Gabe looked over at the house. "What's in the back of the house?"

I tried to see the house in my head. "There's a sliding glass door and a kitchen door in the back. And there's a slider in the master bedroom."

He looked around the neighborhood. There was a school a little ways up the street. They had let out already, so that was good. "I'm going to try and get in from the back." He settled his serious, dark gaze on me. "Why don't you stay here and wait for Cal?"

I had another idea. "I'll go to the front door and knock. That will distract anyone from realizing you are coming in the back."

"No, it's too dangerous. We don't know who is in there. Sam, Nikki might be the killer. Maybe it was revenge all along and Fletch's show being the target of Shane's show was just a coincidence."

I nodded. "Then I'm going with you. It's my grand-father."

He reached out and took my arm, pulling me closer to his face. "I am not going let TJ and Joel lose the only par-ent they have. You are staying here."

He didn't understand. "He's my grandfather." Tears pricked my eyes and pissed me off. My throat hurt. "I have to help him. TJ and Joel need him as much as I do." I lifted my chin. "I'm going. He's my family." He accused me of not understanding family. Well, I understood this— I loved Grandpa and would do anything for him. He needed me.

Still holding my arm, he relented. "Do you have your pepper spray? And can I trust you not to spray me with it?"

He understood. "Yes, and only if you stop ordering me around."

He flashed a grin, then went back to serious. "Does Rosy have a dog?"

"No."

"Let's go. Stay behind me."

I fished my can of pepper spray out of my purse, then shoved the purse under Gabe's seat. I got out and shut the truck door softly like he did. There was a long hedge that divided the yard from the empty lot next door to it. To get to the gate leading to the backyard, we had to run along the house side of the bush. We made it to the six-foot-high wood fence painted a cream color.

I prayed the gate was unlocked.

Gabe pulled the string quietly, and the gate unlatched.

I sighed in relief, and we both went through. Rosy had a roomy half-acre lot. She had a large patio that gave way to gardens with walkways, benches, a butter yellow gazebo, and a toolshed. Her bedroom was on the gate side of the house and faced the gazebo in the back. We found the sliding door. It had vertical blinds that were closed.

Was anyone in there?

My ears buzzed with the high rush of adrenaline pumping through my body. I lifted my hand to touch the window and realized my hands were numb. I was hyperventilating. I forced myself to breath in and out to calm down.

Grandpa was in the house somewhere.

Was Fletch there? If so, how did he get there? I hadn't seen his yellow rental truck in the front of the house. Or was Nikki the killer and Rosy was helping her? But what would they want with Grandpa?

Or was it something innocent like Nikki being sick?

Gabe put his hand on my arm and pushed me behind the protection of the stucco wall. Then he tugged slightly on the sliding door.

I heard the click of the engaged lock resisting. Damn. It had been maybe a minute and a half since we had gotten out of the truck, but it felt like forever. What do we do now? I looked at Gabe.

He moved past me. Next was the kitchen with the regular door, then another sliding glass door, but it was too risky. Someone could see us.

Gabe went past the door, then stopped before the slider.

I slid up behind him and saw that the vertical blinds were pulled closed there too. Gabe hurried past that, and I followed him.

There were two bedroom windows that faced out to the back of the house. They were about chest high to me. Gabe passed the first one and stopped at the farthest window.

It was opened about two inches.

We both listened. There were muffled, long-distance sounds and occasional voices. But we couldn't make them out, which meant they weren't at this end of the house.

Gabe pulled out his keys and used the edge of one to slide in the screen track and pop the screen off. After he set the screen down and put away his keys, he gently slid the window back. We both looked in the opened window. A guest room. The bed wasn't made, and there were clothes piled around. It must be the room Nikki was using. The bed was across the room. Right below the window was a square upholstered chair with a TV remote sitting on the cushion.

How was I going to climb in that window?

But Grandpa was in there. I had to get inside.

Gabe grabbed the edge of the window and hoisted himself up so that he supported his body weight on his hands, arms, and shoulders. He lifted one leg over the windowsill and must have found the chair. He got his balance, let go of the windowsill, and pulled himself the rest of the way in.

All very quietly.

Shit. I looked around. The lawn furniture was the heavy wood kind that would make a lot of noise to drag over. I turned back around and noticed something.

Gabe was gone from the room.

Damn it! He had realized I couldn't climb in the window and left. *Quick, think!* I reached inside and dropped the can of pepper spray onto the chair. Then I grabbed the edge of the windowsill, trying to haul myself up like Gabe had. I got my ribs high enough to touch the windowsill, then I lost my hold, and my ribs and breasts scraped down the track. *Ouch!* My ribs, boobs, and hands burned. I looked down and saw that my tangerine silk shirt had dirty, gray tracks and a couple tears. My hands were a mess.

Fury rocketed through me. I had to get in there.

I turned and looked around the yard again, desperate to get inside.

The shed! It was tucked back into the corner on this side of the yard. I ran over there. The door was partway open, and I slipped inside. I could smell rich dirt, fertilizer, and other tangy scents.

There was a workbench for repotting plants built against the far wall. And there was a stool! It was the kind I thought of as a Grandma stool, where the seat lifted up to reveal a two-step stool. I grabbed it and hurried back to the window.

Still no Gabe. But I didn't hear any sounds of a confrontation. I climbed up on the stool, held onto the bars of the metal back of the stool, and lifted one leg over the windowsill. I felt my foot land on the arm of the chair. I grabbed the window on one side, the wall on the other, and pulled myself through.

Success! I was through.

I put my foot down to stand on the cushion when a loud rap song suddenly blared out.

What the hell? Startled, I jerked and teetered on the chair. Frantic to keep my balance, I tried to grab the windowsill. My fingers brushed the sill just as I tumbled off the chair. My right shoulder and hip hit the hard carpet. I bit my lip to keep from grunting.

The noisy music filled the room.

Desperate not to be discovered, I pushed up to my knees. Where was the music coming from?

I saw the TV across the room. A music video rocked across the screen. I realized I must have stepped on the remote control that had been on the chair.

Good God, they probably heard all the noise as far as the school down the street! Quickly, I reached to the chair and ran my hands over the flowered chair cushion until I found the remote. I turned to the TV on the far wall and hit the little red power button.

The music died away.

Just the pounding of my heart echoed in the room— and my ragged breathing.

I had to pull myself together. My pepper spray! I kept expecting people to burst into the room. I needed some protection. I dropped the remote on the carpet and, while still on my knees, I searched the carpeted floor for the pepper spray. I found it a couple feet away where it had rolled. I scooped it up, stood, and turned expectantly to the door.

It was closed.

Gabe must have closed it when he left. Had the closed door kept anyone outside the room from hearing? What was going on? I went to the door and pressed my ear to it.

I could hear raised voices. I thought one of the voices belong to Grandpa.

How long had we been here in total? I looked at my watch. Five or six minutes.

I reached down, turned the knob, and pulled the door open. The voices were clearer.

"Put it on, or I'll shoot her."

It took me a second, then I realized that was Fletch's voice. God, what was Fletch doing? I had to get out there. Where was Gabe? I edged out into the hallway. There was a bathroom and the door to the garage on the right side of the hallway. I ignored those. Slowly, I went past the other bedroom. At the edge of the hall, I saw them in the living room.

Nikki was about ten feet from me, in front of the big-screen TV and tied to a kitchen chair. Obviously someone had dragged the chair in and used duct tape to secure Nikki to it. Fletch held a gun to her head and had his back to me.

Grandpa stood closer to the front door. I could see his face if I peeked around the corner, but I didn't think he saw me. He was focused on Fletch and Nikki. He had something that looked like a cross between a vest and a life jacket in his hand. Slowly, he slipped one arm in. "Fletch, you got me here. Now leave Rosy and Nikki alone. You don't need them anymore."

Where was Rosy? I didn't see her in the living room. I looked left, through a doorway that opened up to the kitchen. I could make out Gabe bent over, but that was all. What was he doing? Helping Rosy?

Fletch kept the gun on Nikki's head and looked at Grandpa. "They *know*, Barney. As soon as we leave, you'll forget all about them."

He was kidnapping Grandpa! And what was that vest thing Grandpa put on? It seemed to have wires and—I inhaled sharply. *A bomb!* It was a bomb on Grandpa!

Fletch whirled around. He'd heard my intake of breath.

I took a step back and flattened myself against the wall. I held my breath and willed my body to be silent. I lifted my gaze, saw Gabe stand and look at me, then melt away out of my line of vision.

Nothing happened.

Then suddenly Fletch stepped past me, going backward so that he could see me and the room at the same time while he held the gun. He looked at me, his face tight and determined. He didn't look anything like Tobey Maguire anymore, but more like that Chuckie doll. "Who else is here?" he demanded.

"No one." I had the can of pepper spray in my left hand by my leg.

"Won't matter." He lifted his other hand. In it he held a remote control of some kind. Fletch looked around the room, then back at me. "You never deserved Barney." He used his thumb and pushed a button.

Something exploded in a loud percussion as a whoosh of light flashed then died. I smelled of gunpowder or something like that but couldn't make sense of it. My wits scattered, and it took me seconds to recover. I blinked and looked around.

Where was Fletch?

I pushed off the wall, stepped out into the living room, and spotted Fletch running toward Grandpa.

I rushed after him. Gabe got there before me, his gun in his hand, but he pulled up to a stop. I halted right next to him when I realized Fletch held a gun on Grandpa. "Don't do this!" I pleaded.

Fletch shoved the remote control device into the pocket of his blue-checked shirt and looked at me. "The vest Barney is wearing is rigged to explode. I did it myself. Just as I rigged up the bombs in this house."

"Bombs?" Nothing was making sense. This was Fletch— what did he know about bombs? "You don't want to hurt Grandpa!"

"It's up to you if he gets hurt or not, Sam. I'm taking him." He narrowed his blue eyes, the freckles standing out against his pale skin. "I'm a magician Barney can be proud of. You didn't even care enough about him to learn magic. You're almost as bad as Shane perverting magic with his spoiler shows."

"What?" What the hell was he talking about? "I love Grandpa! He knows that!" I turned my gaze to Grandpa, frantic to think of a way to save him.

"Sammy, I love you too." Grandpa's milky blue eyes were full of that truth.

Fletch pushed the gun into Grandpa's side and forced him a step closer to the opened door. He glared at me. "If you force me to, I'll blow him up, then neither of us will have him."

"No!" It felt like sharp claws were digging into my heart and lungs. I desperately tried to think, tried to keep Fletch here so we could stop this insanity. I couldn't let him get away with kidnapping Grandpa strapped into a bomb vest. "How do you know about bombs? You blew up the garage when you tried to pack bullets!"

"I've learned since then. The pyrotechnic experts who work on my shows have taught me everything I need to know."

He was crazy. "Fletch, what about your dad? He's going to be mad if you do this!"

"He'll be proud. I'm making him proud. Shane tried to humiliate me and I stopped him. I'm a real man." He nudged the gun deeper into Grandpa's side, driving him out the front door. I saw him reach to his front shirt pocket and pull out that black remote control again.

I stood there frozen in horror. Some part of my mind registered that I smelled fire and heard the crackle of hungry flames, but all I cared about was Grandpa. "Don't do this, Fletch!"

He didn't even look back.

Another explosion rocked through the house.

19

Even as I heard the explosion, all I could think about was that Fletch kidnapped Grandpa and was getting away. I had to stop him! But before I could take a step, Gabe got his arm around my waist. "He'll kill Barney, Sam." His voice was loud and urgent. "The house is on fire. We have to get everyone out."

I fought to clear the rage and panic. Nikki was duct taped to a chair. "Go get Rosy!" I yelled, then ran to Nikki. Her face was pale with splotches of red anger. There was a piece of tape across her mouth. I yanked that off so she could breathe.

"Grandma!" She croaked the word out.

"Gabe will get her." I fought with the tape. Her arms were down to her sides, and the tape was wound all the way around her entire body and the ladder-back chair several times.

Fletch meant to kill her.

Oh God. It was hot and smoky, the flames making horrible snapping sounds. My fingers slipped on the tape.

"Get out, Sam!" Nikki yelled.

"No!" Tears filled my eyes, my lungs burned, and it hurt

to breathe. I was aware that Gabe ran past me. I think he was carrying Rosy, but I couldn't see. The smoke had thickened and invaded every part of my body. All I could think about was that I had to get the tape off Nikki! I couldn't let her burn to death.

Grandpa would be mad.

My fingers slipped and a nail tore. I scratched at the tape, desperate and dizzy.

Suddenly, two large hands landed on my shoulders.

"No!" I knew it was Gabe. He'd make me leave her. Grandpa loved Nikki. "No!" It came out a croak, and I coughed but kept my fingers working the tape.

Gabe pulled me away, lifted me up, and took me outside. I couldn't even see the door. Suddenly, there was light and air. I sucked in a huge lungful of air.

Gabe set me down on my feet at the bottom of the yard by the street. Fire trucks were racing toward us, along with an ambulance and a police car. Sirens, loud engines, and people yelling directions swelled around me.

I looked back and saw Rosy's home engulfed in flames. The horror liquefied my stomach. I grabbed Gabe's arm. "We have to tell them to get Nikki!"

Cal strode up. "Sam, we got her out. She's okay." He pointed to the spot where the ambulance was parked.

I looked over there. Nikki was still taped to the chair, and a cop and Blaine were trying to cut the tape off. A paramedic had oxygen on her and was asking her questions. I realized that Cal and Blaine must have gone into the house, picked up Nikki and the chair, and got her out. "Thank you," I told Cal. "What about Rosy?" I didn't see her.

Cal's eyes darkened with anger. "They already have her in the ambulance. Fletch held Nikki hostage and made

Rosy bring Barney to the house. But once Rosy did that, she knew Fletch was going to kill them and tried to attack him. He hit her with the gun. She needs a couple stitches, but she'll be okay. Right now, though, she's pretty upset. She begged me to tell you that she's sorry."

Sorry because some animal tried to force her to choose between her pregnant granddaughter and her friend? I let go of Gabe's arm and rushed to the ambulance. As I passed Nikki, I saw that they had her free of all the tape and that Vance was talking to her. So Vance was here too.

But I had to see Rosy. I climbed into the ambulance and found her on the bed in a sitting position. Her head was wrapped; it looked like the wound was over her right ear. A paramedic was taking her blood pressure.

I moved up and took her hand.

She looked at me with hollow, tortured eyes. "I'm sorry, Sam! I . . ."

"Oh Rosy, none of this is your fault. Don't blame yourself. It's Fletch's fault. And mine. He was around the whole time and I didn't even realize—" I stopped talking and swallowed hard. This would get us nowhere. "Rosy, you take care of yourself and Nikki. I'm going to find Fletch. I'll bring Grandpa home."

"She's pregnant," Rosy said, referring to Nikki in a brittle voice.

I nodded. "She's okay. Gabe's brother and Blaine got her out. But she wouldn't be okay if something happened to you." The pressure to get moving, to hurry and find Grandpa, built to a ferocious force inside me. As the paramedic took the blood pressure cuff off Rosy, I bent over and kissed her cheek. "Nikki's going to need you."

"Go on, Sam. Go find Barney."

I hurried out of the ambulance, becoming aware of an

ache in my ribs. It was either from trying to jump up on the windowsill to get into the house or from falling off the chair. I'd worry about that later.

Vance caught my arm and stopped me. I winced, then turned to look at him. "We have to find Grandpa!"

"They took Rosy's car. I have units out looking for a brown Grand Am all over the city. I've notified Highway Patrol. We're doing everything we can."

It wasn't enough. "Let go of me. I'm going to look for him."

Vance's handsome face tightened, and he clenched his jaw. "You have blood coming through your shirt and you look like hell. Go to the hospital."

Was he serious? "I screwed up in there. It's my fault he got away with Grandpa. If I'd let Gabe handle it—"

Vance cut me off. "The end result would have been the same. Once Fletch got that vest on Barney, he had you and Pulizzi under control. That's the fact, Shaw."

I blinked back tears. "Find him, Vance."

He nodded, his brown gaze filling with gold specks. "Pulizzi's putting together search teams. He thinks Fletch has a plan and that he holed up somewhere safe with your grandfather where he'll wait until later to try and get out of Elsinore. Any ideas where he'd go?"

I tried to think. "What about the house you found the hit man's body in?"

Vance shook his head. "He'd know we'd look there."

I didn't know. The horrible failure tortured me. "I don't know. Another house? Have you looked in his motel room?"

"Clean. He's got his stash of guns, etcetera, somewhere else. The room was just a front." Vance unclenched his hand from around my bicep and slid his palm up and over my shoulder. "Keep thinking about it and call me if anything comes to mind. Work with me, Shaw. Trust me. I'm going to do everything I can to get your grandfather back."

I shuddered from so much emotion mixing with the contact of his hand and words. I believed him. "I will call you. I just don't know, but I'll try."

He nodded and took his hand off me. "And stay with Pulizzi."

I walked away, looking for Gabe. I didn't have time to figure Vance out. I found a bunch of people spread out in the street by Gabe's truck. Blaine, Cal, Lola, several of Blaine's friends, and, to my surprise, Bo were gathered there. Gabe was breaking everyone into teams and then spreading the teams around the city to look for Rosy's brown Grand Am and Grandpa. He gave them the descriptions and instructions. Because of the vest on Grandpa, no one was to approach them but was to call Gabe or Vance.

Bo spotted me, and before I could catch my breath he folded me into his strong arms. "We'll find him, darlin'."

I nodded against his T-shirt. Then stiffened my back and looked up. "Thanks, Bo. How did you know?"

He let go of me. "Lola called and asked me to help."

Lola stood between Blaine and Cal with a large tablet of yellow paper and a pen. It looked like she was matching up teams and writing down cell phone numbers. She looked much more like a resourceful friend in a crisis than a useless sexy siren, as Blaine had accused her of being.

Another large car crawled down the street, then stopped. Four old people inched out. Hank, one of Grandpa's coffee and gossip friends, shuffled over. "We're here to help find Barney."

Tears filled my eyes. Did Grandpa know how much he was loved? "Thank you, Hank." I went up and put my hand on his arm. I felt a tremor, either age or anger at his friend being kidnapped. Lola walked up. "Sam, get going. I'll get these folks set up to help us."

I hugged her and walked a couple feet to Gabe.

Gabe swept his gaze down my length. "There's a first aid kit in my truck. Let's go."

I didn't argue. I went around to the passenger side. Cal was there. He opened the door, then looked down at me. "I'm heading out too. Lola will stay here and coordinate to keep up with Detective Vance. Then she'll go to Gabe's house and work from there."

I nodded.

He touched my hand. "Hey, Gabe'll find him. Your job is to make sure Gabe doesn't kill Fletch unless necessary."

"Shut up, Cal. Get in, Sam." Gabe was already in the driver's seat.

I climbed into the passenger seat.

Cal leaned in. "Gabe."

Gabe had the engine going, but he left the truck in park and turned his full attention on his brother.

Cal said, "Once you get Barney back, we'll talk. I'm going to need your help."

My heart skipped a beat. Something powerful passed between Cal and Gabe. I could literally feel the emotion, or connection, that made them brothers. Even with all the anxiety and urgency, the air hung still in the truck for a few seconds.

Then Gabe said, "You got it, Cal."

Cal stepped back and shut the door, and Gabe put the truck in gear and took off. "The first aid kit is under the seat. Your stomach is bleeding."

I reached down and pulled out my purse that I had set down there before we went into the house. Then I felt around and came out with a plastic first aid kit. "Where are we going?"

"Your house first. Just in case Fletch goes there."

I tore open a couple antiseptic wipes, then pulled up my shirt. Ugh. Scraped and ugly, but not serious. "Then?" I dabbed at the blood and sucked in a breath at the sting.

"We're going to look everywhere we can think of. Lola has people spread out all over the city."

I put the first aid kit away and looked at Gabe's profile. "But?"

"Fletch doesn't seem stupid or ready to get into a chase with the police. I think that whole scenario at Rosy's house was just about delaying us and the police long enough to get to a safe place."

I thought about that. "If he had wanted to make sure we died, he would have shot us." That did make sense. "So he had some place ready close by." My thoughts tripped over themselves trying to figure it out.

Gabe nodded.

"Maybe an abandoned house like he killed the hit man in? I asked Vance about that. He said he wouldn't go back to the same one." Something else Vance said surfaced. "He said that the motel room was clean and looked like a cover, that Fletch had his guns and other stuff somewhere else."

"Makes sense."

Dread slammed into me. "Are we going to find him?"

Gabe turned into the dirt lot in front of my house. Dust kicked up around us as he drove up to the porch, then parked. I heard Ali frantically barking in the backyard. Gabe barely stopped the truck before he opened the door and jumped out. He came around to my side and opened the door, then gently pulled me out of the truck. He looked down at me. "If it's possible, we are going to find him."

His hands were hard and secure on my waist. I could smell the smoke and sweat on both of us. "Fletch thinks I let Grandpa down by not becoming a magician."

"That's bullshit and you know it. You love him. You love him so much you are afraid I'm going to make you choose between him and me."

"You knew that?"

"I know *you*. And I'd never ask you to leave Barney alone, Sam. If our living arrangements ever change, Barney will come too. We'll always have a place for him. But right now, we are going to go out there and find him. So take a deep breath and hold it together, babe. We can do this."

Something vicious eased in my chest. "Okay, let's do it."

He leaned forward, just brushing his mouth over mine. Then he turned, pulled his gun out of the back of his pants, and headed for the front door.

Ali's bark turned to pitiful frustration. I felt for her, but I stayed behind Gabe as we went into the house. I knew no one was there as soon as we reached the living room.

The house felt empty.

But Gabe did his cop thing, quickly working his way through the house while I went to the sliding glass door and let Ali in. She came right to me, licking my hand and whining.

She knew something was wrong.

I dropped to my knees and hugged her. "I won't leave you here alone. You'll come with us." I stood, and Ali ran off to check in with Gabe.

I went to Grandpa's computer and rifled through his notes and printouts. There was the list of magicians whom Shane had victimized with his spoiler shows, along with notes on the financial searches that Grandpa did.

Nothing indicated some kind of hideaway.

"Come on, think," I told myself.

"Nothing there?" Gabe asked, coming up behind me with Ali.

I shook my head and said, "Empty buildings, that's where he'd go, right? Maybe a place he has a car stashed?"

"Yes." Gabe stood next to me, looking through the same papers I'd just rifled through.

But I had an idea. "Then we have to call my mom."

Gabe put the papers down. "Would she know what houses and businesses are abandoned?"

My heart kicked up. "She's the real estate queen. I'd bet she keeps lists of those to get the owners to sell. My mom is relentless in business." I pulled out my cell phone and dialed my mom's cell. I wasn't sure where she was, but I knew she had the boys with her.

She answered, "Samantha, any news?"

"Mom, where are you?" I realized that of all the people Blaine and Lola had called, no one had called my mom. She didn't know that Fletch had kidnapped Grandpa.

"At home. TJ and Joel are bickering over what to have for dinner."

My stomach lurched. TJ and Joel—they loved Grandpa. As did Mom. But at least they were safe in Temecula. I prefaced telling her the situation with, "Mom, listen but don't tell the boys, okay?" I launched into the fastest explanation I could manage.

"That weasel—" She cut herself off, probably remembering the boys. "I see," she replied in her clipped business voice. "What do you need?"

I was grateful to her for sparing TJ and Joel from finding out. If we were damn lucky, I'd tell the boys after we had Grandpa back safe with us. Then it would just be a cool story, not a terrifying ordeal. "I need a list of abandoned or foreclosed and empty properties where Fletch could be lying low until he can get Grandpa out of town."

"No problem."

I looked at Gabe and nodded.

"Damn," he said softly in a complimentary voice, then said, "Let's start with the properties closest to Rosy's, then fan out."

I relayed that to my mom.

"I'm starting with a five-mile radius. It'll take a minute to sort the program."

"You can do that?"

"Get your real estate license, Samantha. Then you will be able to—here we go. Turn on Grandpa's printer. I'm going to fax this."

I reached over and hit the power button.

"Thanks, Mom."

"Samantha, keep checking in with me."

"I will. I'm with Gabe. You can call his cell if you can't get through on mine." I gave her the number.

"Find him." She hung up.

I started to shake my head at my mom, but the printer began spitting out the fax.

Gabe grabbed the first sheet and studied it. Then he looked at me. "Your mom is scary, you know that, right?"

"Hey, I've met your mom. She carries a gun and smacks you with a large spoon." Good God, I was defending my mother.

He reached for the second sheet and handed me the first. "What do you think?"

I looked over the list. "The houses off Machado are very close to Rosy's, but they are in a tightly packed neighborhood. Too easy to be spotted." I looked down the list. "Up here by our house, in the old Woodhaven tract, is possible."

I took the second sheet of the houses that were a little farther away from Rosy's house. I tried to picture Fletch thinking this out. Fletch had a plan all along. Kill Shane, and if no one ever knew, then he would go on as Grandpa's star protégé. But his backup plan was to grab Grandpa and hide. So he must have scouted out at least two abandoned houses—one house to give the hit man the deadly dose of sleeping pills and alcohol and the other to hide in. The hit man was found up in Elsinore Hills, quiet, rural properties spaced out a little bit more. Several abandoned homes. "Elsinore Hills." I looked at Gabe.

He nodded. "Let's go, we'll start there."

I followed him to the door.

Ali beat us there and looked at me with her liquid brown eyes.

I looked up at Gabe. "She knows something is wrong. She's coming with us."

Gabe opened the door, and Ali raced for his truck. She settled between us, and we pulled out. I looked over the list.

"Should I call Lola and have her send teams to start canvassing these other abandoned or foreclosed spots?"

"Have her send Blaine and Cal. They both are armed, and they both can handle a bad situation. But Barney's friends could get hurt." Gabe turned the truck left out onto Grand and raced up to Lake Street. I called Lola and gave her the information.

She listened carefully, then answered, "I'll call Cal and Blaine. We've had two sightings, but neither panned out."

"Thank you, Lola. I don't know what we'd do without you."

"Anything to help, Sam." She hung up.

I set the phone down on the seat under my leg and petted Ali as she rested her head in my lap. We were on Lake

Street, and Gabe made a left onto Gunnerson. I had lived in Lake Elsinore all my life, so I knew these hills that over-looked the valley and the lake pretty well. I directed him through the streets, some paved, some still dirt. The homes up there varied in age—some decades old, some completely remodeled, and a few newer ones. There used to be an old country club up there that had been condemned for decades but it burned down, which still made me sad. It was such a telling piece of Lake Elsinore's history, a grand attempt to turn Elsinore into a resort town back around the 1920s, before the Depression hit.

"There," I pointed to a dirt road. "Turn left."

Gabe wove through the back roads, easily maneuvering the truck over the uneven hills and road. We came to a stop at the first abandoned house. The driver's side door faced its driveway. It was a one story crumbling Spanish-style house surrounded by a crumbling wrought iron gate. Chunks of the roof tile littered the grounds. The sides had been tagged by punks with spray paint. I reached for the door handle, but Gabe caught my arm.

I looked over at him. His eyes were cold and fixed, his mouth tight. I could feel the anger rushing beneath his firm hand. "What?"

"Ali and I are going in first."

"I'm going with you."

"You are staying outside with the cell phone."

I opened my mouth to argue, but then I remembered the disaster I'd caused at Rosy's. Gabe might have man-aged the situation if I hadn't gotten Fletch's attention. Guilt twisted my insides. At least if I stayed out here, I could get help. I nodded but I couldn't say anything.

"If there's trouble, I'll send Ali out to you. Call for help and drive away. Got it?"

My guts twisted tighter, and I forced out the words pounding in my brain. "I won't leave you."

His face hardened. "Yes, you will. For TJ and Joel, you damn sure will leave. You'll get help, and you'll stay safe."

Stubbornness wasn't going to get the job done. "I'll do what I have to."

Gabe put his hand on my face. "I never doubted it. We'll be back in a couple minutes." He dropped his hand and said, "Come on, Ali."

She barked once, apparently thinking that Gabe had a terrific idea. Gabe left the engine idling and the driver's side door open as he got out of the truck. Ali jumped lightly to the ground next to him. He pulled out his gun in his right hand, and Ali positioned herself at his left thigh. The two of them disappeared through the broken wrought iron fence to check around the back of the house.

I sat there for three or four minutes, my muscles clenched into knots as I strained to hear any sound and stared through the opened driver's side door.

Then Ali and Gabe walked out through the gate. He met my gaze and shook his head.

My muscles sagged in disappointment, even though I was relieved that Gabe and Ali were okay.

Ali jumped in first and settled close to me. I put my hand on her neck as Gabe got in and shut the door. "Next house," he said.

I still had the paper in my hand. I looked down and directed him to a two-story house. There were some wood stairs that led from the driveway up to the front door. The house sat on a hill covered in brown weeds and littered with debris. There was a dirt area left of the garage that looked like it had RV access, but I didn't see a vehicle back there. The front window and the windows of the rooms over the garage were broken. The paint might have once been blue, but now it was a dusty, peeling gray.

The house looked like it had been abandoned for years.

Gabe stopped the truck on the street. We were risking being seen if Fletch and Grandpa were in there, but time was a problem. There just wasn't enough time to sneak up on every house. If Fletch was holed up in a house, he probably had a car ready to escape.

"Call Lola and see if anyone has called anything in."

I nodded.

"Let's do it again, Ali," Gabe said. He left the truck idling for a fast escape, and he opened the door and got out.

Ali stepped to the seat's edge to jump out and froze. She sniffed, her long German shepherd nose twitching as she checked out the air. Then she jumped to the ground and ran up to the warped garage door and sniffed again.

She lifted her head and barked, using her right paw to scratch at the garage door. In seconds she grew increasingly agitated and determined.

My heart ramped up to high-speed pounding. Had we found Grandpa and Fletch?

20

I stared at Ali struggling to get through the garage door of the abandoned house. Was Grandpa in there?

"Ali, come," Gabe said.

She stopped barking and whining and looked back at Gabe with uncertainty confusing her beautiful fur face.

I leaned across the truck toward the opened driver's side door. "Ali," I said softly, knowing full well she could hear my voice. "Come here." We didn't want Fletch to hear us if they were in there.

She paused for one more long second, then turned and ran back to us. She sat down by the opened door of the truck and whined softly.

Gabe had his gun out. "Keep her here with you."

Every cell in my body urged me out of that truck and into the house to find Grandpa. I didn't know what to do. "Wait, Gabe." I had the phone in my hand. What was Cal's phone number? "Let me call your brother, or Vance or Blaine!" Panic, the need to move, to do something, had my breathing in overdrive. But I didn't want Gabe hurt or killed either.

"Let me check it out." He walked toward the house.

I scooted over to the driver's side and watched him. He moved up to the garage, then stayed close to the wall until he got to the stairs. He stood there for a few seconds, looked up the straight flight of stairs, then moved up. He went carefully, one step at a time, keeping to the shadows of the wall with his gun held down in both hands.

Then he disappeared from sight.

I put my hand on Ali's head. She shivered, with her muscles tense and ready to pounce. I knew exactly how she felt.

A few minutes later Gabe came back down the stairs. His face was grim, set hard with his mouth thin. There was a pumping anger in his walk.

My heart stopped. I couldn't breathe. Pain bloomed in my chest, and all I could do was stare at Gabe. He wore a careful mask on his face, but I could read the anger.

Oh God.

Helpless, I wanted to run, to escape what he was going to tell me.

But I couldn't run. Couldn't breathe.

He stopped next to where Ali sat.

"What?" The word hurt all the way up my throat.

"They were here. Rosy's car is in the garage. Fletch used this house to make the bombs he set off at Rosy's, the vest he forced on Barney. . . ."

I couldn't stand it. "Is Grandpa in there?"

His face shifted. "No. Sam, no. Barney's still alive. There was no sign of his being hurt. All they did was come here to switch to another car."

"They're gone?" It was a better option than Grandpa being dead, but my mind was trying to catch up. I began to realize Gabe was pissed because we were too late, not because Grandpa was dead.

I asked, "What now?"

"We call Vance." He reached for the phone in my hand. I let him have it.

He made the call. I'm not sure how he got patched through, but he talked to Vance. He described finding gunpowder, wires, and caps . . . things I didn't understand. No guns, he said. No sign of blood and no sign of any struggle.

Then Gabe said, "Once a uniform gets here to secure the scene, I'm going to go get gas. Then we'll be back." He ended the call.

"Gas?" I stared at Gabe and repeated myself in confusion. "Gas?"

He handed the phone back to me. "For the truck. It makes it go."

I blinked. Grandpa was kidnapped, and getting gas seemed unimportant.

"Ali, in," Gabe said.

I moved over and Ali jumped in. Gabe followed her and pulled the door shut. Then he looked over at me. "I want to be ready for what comes next. Running out of gas wouldn't be a good idea."

That made sense.

A police car roared down the street with flashing lights. Gabe got back out of the truck and went to talk to the cop. Then he returned and slid into the seat next to me. He put the truck in gear, did a three-point turn, and headed through the streets toward the main road. "There's a chance they've gotten out of town, Sam."

I nodded. "He couldn't get on an airplane dragging Grandpa as a hostage. Wherever they are going, they are going to have to drive." Getting gas made more and more sense.

"To Montana?" Gabe made the dangerous left turn from Gunnerson onto Riverside Drive.

"That's a long drive." I had to force myself to think, to set aside my worry and guilt over Grandpa and think like Fletch. "He's proving something to his dad, but that doesn't mean he has to go to Montana, does it?"

"I don't know. You know Fletch better than I do."

"I thought I knew him, but I was just looking at the surface, at the goofy comedy magician." Right now, the fact that I could be that shallow wasn't my biggest problem.

"Expand on that, Sam."

He was right. I had to try. I was the best hope of finding Grandpa. I knew a lot of things about Fletch. "Fletch's dad seems to be the driving force behind his decisions, maybe more of an influence than I realized. Fletch loves dogs, and he got that from hanging out with his dad's hunting hounds. His dad used to get furious at Fletch for making the dogs *soft.*" I let my thoughts string along, adding up the details. "His dad is a bit of a survivalist. Fletch probably picked up all kinds of skills from him. He might try living on the run somewhere. Although he hates rough living." I was contradicting myself, but I had to look at every angle, see all of Fletch, not just the surface.

"Where does he usually live?" Gabe asked.

I knew that answer. "Reno. That's where he does most of his shows."

"He may have a cabin or something. I'll start running checks, and I know Vance will do the same." He turned left onto Collier Avenue, and we passed the Lake Elsinore Outlet Shopping Center on our right. Coming to Nicholas Road, Gabe turned into the gas station.

That made sense. A cabin would utilize some of the survivalist skills but minimize the rough living. Ali's whining interrupted my thoughts. "She needs to go to the bathroom. I'll take her while you're getting gas."

Gabe nodded as he got out. "Stay where I can see you."

Ali and I got out and walked away from the gas station, toward the dirt hill that led down to the parking lot at the end of the outlet center. At the top of the hill, I stopped and waited.

Ali edged partway down the hill, sniffed a plant, then snorted and ran the rest of the way down the hill.

Guess she didn't want to pee on an incline. I sighed and followed her down, trying not to slip in my boots and end up sliding down on my butt. When we got down to the blacktop, there was a sea of cars and a line of motor homes parked up against the brick wall. On the other side of that wall was the 15 Freeway.

Ali and I walked across the asphalt to a large tree in a planter that decorated the parking lot. From his position above us at the gas station, Gabe would have no trouble seeing me moving among the parked cars.

I stopped at the first tree planter, but Ali ran ahead. "Ali, come back here." She went to the next planter a couple parking lot rows over, closer to the brick wall, and sniffed. Then she relieved herself.

I looked back at Gabe. He was standing at the truck, pumping the gas and watching us. I turned back and saw that Ali had run to the next tree planter, closer to the row of motor homes.

She was just letting off the excess anxiety, but we didn't have time right now. "Ali—" I started to demand she come back.

But Ali suddenly lifted her head and started barking furiously. She ran flat out toward the motor homes. A green SUV had to swerve and lay on the horn to miss hitting her.

What the hell was wrong with my dog? I ran after her as fast as I could in my boots. "Ali!"

She raced around the motor homes, weaving in and out, stopping and sniffing, then taking off again. After a minute or so, she picked out a midsize motor home. It was the fourth motor home in the row from the gas station side. She ran agitated circles around the motor home, barking furiously.

I stopped at the back of the motor home. Ali raced along the door side of the home, around the back, and up the other side. "Ali." I dropped my voice to a whisper as I turned to watch her. "Damn it, we don't have time for this. We have to—" The hair on the back of my neck stood up.

Idiot!

The obvious slammed into me all at once. The house we knew Fletch had been in had RV access. Shane had a motor home. Successful magicians often traveled in motor homes. A motor home was the perfect answer to a man who had survivalist skills but liked comfort.

Oh God.

I started to turn so that I could look toward the door of the motor home.

"Don't move. I have a gun."

It was Fletch's voice. Ice crusted my skin as sharp fear slithered over me.

Ali's deep growl rose from farther behind him.

He poked me in the back with what I assumed was his gun.

"Tell her to stop or I'll blow up the vest on Barney. You know I'll do it, Sam."

Terror for Grandpa wrapped around my throat and I croaked out, "No, Ali." I tried to swallow past the constriction around my neck and asked, "Where is he? What have you done with Grandpa?"

"He's inside the motor home. He's going with me. Barney always believed in me. He will come to understand what I did for him. I couldn't let Shane come to Elsinore and humiliate him, or me. I've made both of them proud."

"Both?" What was Fletch talking about?

"Barney and my dad. My dad got tickets to Shane's show and he laughed. Laughed! Said that I never stood up for myself against real men. Well, I stood up to Shane like a man. He was a bully, and I fought back. And I protected Barney by stopping Shane from humiliating both of us. My dad will see now that magicians are not sissies but tough and brave."

Oh God. His dad had finally pushed him over the edge. Fletch was trying to earn his dad's approval while keeping Grandpa's support and affection.

Ali made a low and threatening growl.

"Make. Her. Stop." He poked the gun into my back.

The icy crust paralyzing me cracked, and hot tears filled my eyes. My brilliant dog had tried to tell me Grandpa was in the motor home, and I screwed it up. *Again.* I had to keep her safe. "Ali, sit. Stay." I fought to breathe, and said to Fletch, "Don't hurt her. Let her go." Fletch loved dogs, but if he was willing to blow up Grandpa, then I had to believe he'd kill my dog.

"You're going to lock her in the bathroom inside the motor home. Now turn around slowly."

I looked around. I saw a mother pushing a baby stroller. She was across the huge parking lot. An older couple was walking to their car about six or seven rows over. I swept my gaze up to the gas station. From this distance I could see over the dirt hill.

I didn't see Gabe or his truck.

Had he seen where Ali and I went? Could he help us and Grandpa? I knew Gabe wouldn't leave me. I doubted Fletch realized he was here. How could he?

"Now," Fletch ordered.

I just had to stay alive and keep Grandpa and Ali alive until Gabe could help us. I turned around, facing the space between the door side of Fletch's motor home and the back of the one parked next to it. Ali sat, but she let out another growl. Her hair stood up on her back in a stiff row of pure canine rage. Her lips were drawn back in a vicious mask of huge teeth. I had never been afraid of Ali, but at that moment I didn't know if I could control her. She was not going to let her people be threatened. She knew Grandpa was in the motor home, and she meant to get to him.

"I'll shoot her if I have to," Fletch said behind me. He shoved the gun hard into my back.

"Ali, stay," I said in the calmest voice I could manage. I thought that the idea of shooting Ali was stressing Fletch even more. Now that he was the *real man* his dad wanted him to be, he'd have to shoot her if she got in his way.

"Inside, Sam," Fletch said. "Open the door."

I went to the door and opened the latch. I carefully pulled open the door, unsure what to expect.

"Tell her to go in."

"Are you sure? Wouldn't it be better to leave her out here?" I really didn't know if I could control her.

"No, she'll alert someone. Get her inside. Now." His voice was as brutal as the gun jamming into me.

"Come on, Ali. Let's go see Grandpa."

She got up and raced into the motor home.

"Now you."

I stepped up on the built-in ladder, then into the interior. It was warmer and smelled like closed-up air and old food. I looked around. The motor home was much less grand than Shane's.

I spotted Grandpa on the right. He sat at a table that

butted up to the cab of the motor home. Across from him was the small kitchen. Over the cab was a bed. Grandpa sat at a table and reached out to pet Ali with his left hand. His right hand was handcuffed to a bolt of some kind that had been anchored into the wall next to a big red fire extinguisher. He still had that vest on. He looked up at me. "Sam, we heard Ali barking. What are you doing here?"

Seeing him in that vest and handcuffed choked off my air. But I refused to cry and forced myself to remember that Grandpa always boasted no handcuffs could hold him. And I would find a way out of this. I had to. I saw the pain shadow and age Grandpa's blue eyes. He was afraid for me. But he also trusted me to lie. "I was looking for Rosy's car. I didn't know what else to do! I couldn't just sit home and wait." I started forward to reassure Grandpa.

Fletch said, "Stop. Call Ali and get her in the bathroom."

I assumed the bathroom was at the other end of the motor home. "Ali, come here girl. Let's go this way." I turned. Fletch backed up while holding the gun. He was smart enough to keep me between him and Ali.

I took the time to study Fletch. His blue eyes were bright and focused, and his face was tight with strain around his mouth. But his hand holding the gun was steady. I was pretty sure Fletch had stayed in the NRA and leaned all about guns, just like he'd learned about pyrotechnics and explosives from the experts that worked on his shows. The determination in his gaze and the steadiness of his hand assured me he would shoot Ali or me if he felt he had to.

I dropped my gaze to his blue-checked shirt with the pocket. I could see the top third of the remote control device sticking out of the pocket.

I had to get it somehow. I knew part of the reason he

had Grandpa handcuffed was that Grandpa had the skills to pickpocket that remote without Fletch realizing it.

I didn't have Grandpa's skills.

I didn't have any magic skills. Now I wished like hell that I did.

Fletch backed up past the bathroom door. "Turn around slowly, then step back to stand in front of me and tell Ali to go into the bathroom."

I turned around with my back to Fletch and took another step back. Ali stood there and watched us both. She was leaning forward slightly on her powerful shoulders, as if she were ready to attack.

Would she go into the bathroom? God, I hoped so.

"Ali, go in." I swept my hand toward the tiny little bathroom. It consisted of the basics—a sink, toilet, and tight little shower. There was just enough room for her to lie down and wait once we shut the door.

She growled in response.

"Ali, stop that." I tried to reason with her. "Just go in."

She sat down.

Damn. "Ali, what's the matter with you?" I looked past her. "Grandpa, tell her to go in."

He looked up from his shackled hand resting in his lap. "Ali, go in."

She turned her neck around to look at Grandpa. Then she turned back to me and stared.

I knew Grandpa was up to something. It was true that no handcuffs could hold him, but what could he have found to pick the lock with? I didn't want to give him away so I didn't dare look at him again. Instead, I sighed and looked over my shoulder at Fletch. "I can take hold of her collar and tug her in there."

Fletch stabbed the gun hard in my back. "Stop playing games!"

I yelped and took a half step forward to get away from the pain arcing through my sore ribs and stomach.

Ali barked and growled, then lunged toward us.

Fletch got his left arm around my waist and jerked me hard. It hurt like a bitch and I struggled to get away, but we both fell backward. I landed on Fletch and lost my breath in a haze of pain rolling across my middle. His hand dug into the scrape on my stomach.

Fletch screamed, "Get her off me! She's biting me!"

I wasn't biting him, so it had to be Ali. Where was the gun? Had Fletched dropped it, or was it still in his right hand? I tried to move, but his arm stayed locked around me. Every twist shot another wave of pain through me.

"Call her off!" he screamed in my ear.

I lifted my head, fighting to ignore the soreness in my middle, and saw that Ali had her jaws clamped around Fletch's right calf. "Ali! Let go!" He'd shoot her if he had the gun. And if he didn't have the gun, he could have the remote that would blow up Grandpa's vest.

I forced my head up a little farther to see Grandpa.

He was gone.

Before I could make sense of it and figure out where Grandpa was, Fletch screamed in my ear,

"I'm going to shoot her!"

My brain put it together that Grandpa had escaped the handcuff. He was gone. We were on the floor in the hallway with the door around the corner about even with our knees. I prayed Grandpa had gotten out. Maybe he could get the vest off, but I couldn't risk it. I didn't see any other choice. I had to get that remote control device. Struggling to keep my back away from Fletch's chest, and the shirt pocket where I hoped the remote still was, I brought my right arm up and drove my elbow hard into Fletch's side.

"Ooff." His body bowed up underneath my back, and he let go of me.

I rolled to the right, away from that remote control device in his left breast pocket. Then I got to my knees and reached for the remote while my brain tried to figure out if he still had the gun.

Fletch clamped his right hand over my right wrist. "You're dead." He brought the gun up in his left hand.

Time slowed to a sense of surrealism.

I saw the gun coming at my face and thought, *Damn magicians! That gun had been in his right hand.* Then I saw the fury and pain on Fletch's face change before my eyes—

Into the intent to kill me.

In my peripheral vision, I saw Ali let go of his calf.

From my far right, a stream of foam shot straight over Ali, past me, and hit Fletch in his face.

Instinctively, I used my left hand to shove the gun away from me.

It fired, rocking the motor home with the report.

My ears rang, and adrenaline pumped thick and fast through my veins. Specks of foam hit my face and chest. I didn't know where it was coming from. All I could think about was getting the remote and not getting shot. I looked at Fletch's shirt pocket.

The remote was still there.

Fletch roared in fury, and his hand tightened in a bone-breaking hold on my right wrist. He used the back of his gun hand to wipe foam from his eyes and face.

I ignored the crunching pain in my wrist and kept my focus on the black remote sticking out of his shirt pocket.

I had to get it before Fletch remembered it and killed Grandpa. I reached my left hand over and got my slippery, foam-spattered first finger and thumb on the remote. I had it!

Don't drop it.

Don't think about the pain in my wrist or around my middle.

Don't think about killing Grandpa if I make a mistake.

I bit my lip, struggling to hang on to the remote. I pulled it out of his pocket, every cell in my body centered on that remote. My finger and thumb slid a little on the black plastic casing, but I kept my grip and moved it farther away from Fletch.

I turned.

Grandpa stood there in the horrid vest holding a fire extinguisher. He stopped spraying once I had the remote. With my right wrist in Fletch's grip, I couldn't reach very far across my body to give the remote to Grandpa.

I knew Fletch was going to shoot me any second.

Grandpa started to take a step toward me when there was a loud noise.

For a horrid second, I thought Fletch had fired the gun and one of us was dead. Grandpa had frozen midstep.

Then behind him, Gabe, Cal, Blaine, and Vance burst into the door of the motor home. It hadn't been gunfire we'd heard, but the door bursting open.

My relief turned to panic when I remembered the remote. "Wait!" I screamed. "The remote. It's in my hand!" With Fletch's hold on my right hand, I strained my muscles to reach farther across my body and away from Fletch. I didn't want to drop it or accidentally push the button that would blow up the vest.

And I knew Fletch still had the gun.

It all happened at once, in fast-forward speed.

Blaine reached for Grandpa, moving him out of the way.

Cal rushed in and took the remote from my fingers, grabbed Ali's collar, then got them both out of the way.

Gabe and Vance stormed in with their guns drawn, filling up the small space.

Fletch brought the gun in his left hand up.

Vance and Gabe fired.

The gun flew out of Fletch's hand, and he screamed.

Then Gabe was there. He slammed his right foot down hard on Fletch's right bicep.

Fletch screamed again and let go of my wrist.

Gabe kept his foot anchored over Fletch's arm and looked at me. "Get up, Sam."

My right wrist hurt like a bitch, and I didn't dare look to see if Fletch even had a hand left. I dragged myself to my feet. The motor home spun. I got to the corner and leaned against it as Vance moved in with a couple uniformed cops.

I concentrated on breathing. We were alive. Grandpa was safe. Ali was safe.

Then Gabe was there next to me. He slid his arm around my shoulders and pulled me into his body. "I got you, Sam."

21

It was a night of magic. Nikki, Bo, and a few other magicians joined Grandpa to put on a spectacular magic show at Storm Stadium in place of Shane Masters's spoiler show. The evening had concluded with a standing ovation.

Afterward, friends and family gathered at the new offices of Heart Mates and Pulizzi Investigations to celebrate. We had platters of chicken wings, cheese and fruit kebobs, cookies, brownies, coffee, and wine set up on the round desk in the center of the new offices.

I moved through the people, trying to thank everyone for pitching in to help make the magic show work. I paused where TJ and Joel were talking to Bo about his upcoming cartoon character. "I'll see if your mom will let me take you to the studio where we do the voice-overs of the characters," Bo said.

I looked at the excited faces of my two sons and smiled. "It's fine with me."

Bo turned around. "Hey, Sam. These two," he tilted his head toward the boys, "did great tonight."

Pride filled my heart. Joel loved magic and had been

terribly excited to assist Bo and Grandpa in different acts. TJ pitched in to help Nikki. He wasn't as big a magic fan as his brother, but he was a huge fan of Grandpa, and he knew how much this night meant to him. "Yes, they did. And you were wonderful too. The audience loved you."

Bo grinned. "Everyone needs a little magic in their lives. And I had a great time. It's been years since I've been onstage with Barney."

His chocolate-colored eyes shined, and I knew he was sincere. I opened my mouth to tell him how much he meant to Grandpa when my mom's voice cut me off.

"Samantha, I have a client interested in your half of the suite." She slid up between Bo and me.

Bo, TJ, and Joel knew when to make their exits, and they melted away. I drained my glass of wine, then said, "Mom, I'm not selling out my lease."

She pulled her mouth tight. "This is a perfect opportunity to change your life. You can work for my real estate office answering phones and filing while getting your real estate license."

That was my mom. Even though she helped on this case, she was still determined to get me on the path she thought was best for me. I tried for patience. "I don't want out. I love Heart Mates."

She raised her perfectly penciled eyebrows. "And private investigating?"

I hadn't been sure for a while there. Change was overwhelming and a little frightening. But, "Yes, and private investigating."

She shook her head. "I've gone to so much trouble, Samantha, to get all the key people here tonight. People who could help you—"

I laughed. "Oh please, mother. Sure, you talked the city leaders into hiring Grandpa and his friends to put on the magic show in place of Shane. And they are grateful to you for saving their collective butts. But I've seen you pass out at least two dozen business cards between the magic show and the party. You will probably parlay that goodwill into a half-dozen home sales."

She glared at me. "And why is that funny? It's good business, Samantha."

"Yes, it is. But real estate is not my passion, it's yours." Before my mom could figure out how to convince me otherwise, I reached out and put my hand on her arm. "I never thanked you for coming to get me the night I called you at the police station."

She looked down at her black pants and brushed a speck off them and cleared her throat. "Don't be ridiculous. You're my daughter. Of course I came to get you."

I knew I made my mom uncomfortable. The truth was that in my growing-up years, my mom might not have come to get me. Not if she had a new boyfriend on whom she had been focusing all her energy. She would have told me to call my grandpa. In those years, I had come in second to some driving need in my mom to catch a man.

I was pretty sure that need came from something that had hurt her deeply. Grandpa knew it. And I knew it. I was sure it had to do with my mystery bio-dad. I intended to find out what that mystery was.

One day.

When I was ready.

My mom looked up. "He's going to hurt you."

I knew she meant Gabe. "Maybe, but I'll survive it."

She sighed and put on her critical gaze. "That skirt is a little short. You really don't have the thighs for it. A nice calf-length black skirt would look more slimming, polished, and professional." She walked away.

I felt my left eye start to twitch.

A voice behind me said, "That skirt is short. And with black boots, it sends a certain message."

I blinked and turned around. "Vance! What are you doing here?" He was dressed in boat casual—tan slacks and a black knit shirt that graphically outlined his swimmer's shoulders.

A group of guests drifted toward us, stopped and said hello, then faded away to join another group. Vance watched them move away, then answered, "I had to see for myself. So you are really hooking up with Pulizzi?" He looked around.

We stood on my side of the reception area. The pale rose paint trimmed in white molding on the walls and the rose, tan, and cream blended carpet made the area feel soft and romantic. I had the brown leather couch my best friend Angel had given me against one wall, and two chairs in a soft rose facing them. Right now Nikki, Rosy, and several others sat around the waiting area and chatted. Gabe's side of the reception area had several brown leather chairs but no couch. In between was Blaine's round desk covered in the food trays and drinks. I turned my gaze back to Vance.

"Yes, although I'm running my dating service and just working for Gabe part time. Rosy and Nikki were happy with our work. In fact, now that the case is solved, Nikki is in talks with a TV station to do a special on Shane and spoiler magicians."

Vance shook his head. "You are something else, Shaw."

I looked down, adjusting the thin gold chain looped around the waist of my skirt. "I don't think that's a compliment." What message did Vance think my outfit sent? My black skirt covered about two-thirds of my thighs. I probably didn't want to know; besides, I had a more important question. Looking up, I said, "How is Michelle?" Shane's assistant had nearly died from an overdose of sleeping pills that Fletch forced her to take.

Vance said, "She's very lucky you and Pulizzi found her in time. She's been released from the hospital and will be fine."

I still had trouble believing everything Fletch had done. "Do you know how Fletch drugged the dogs and got into Shane's motor home?"

Vance looked around, then said, "Can we talk in your office?"

I nodded, then turned and walked to my office and opened the door. He followed me in and closed it. I sat on the edge of my desk and said, "Why the secrecy?"

Vance sat on the arm of the chair facing my desk. His left knee was inches from my right thigh. He answered, "Normal caution. We always keep some information back, so I don't want other people to overhear. Where's Pulizzi?"

It took me a second to follow his shift of topics. "Gabe is on his way. He's been in Los Angeles helping his brother out with something." They had tracked down two witnesses who had seen Dirk and his two firefighter buddies jump Cal. That put an end to the assault charges against him. Gabe had been trying to get back in time for the magic show, but then Cal asked him to go have a beer. I knew Cal needed to talk to Gabe. He had career decisions to make. I told Gabe to take all the time he needed with his brother. "So tell me how Fletch did it."

He flashed his deep dimples, revealing the sun-god handsomeness he often kept locked up with his hard cop stare. "Bathroom window, which is kind of disappointing since he was supposed to be an accomplished magician. Fletch knocked out the screen in the little window over the shower and tossed in meatballs laced with sleeping pills. The dogs gobbled them up. Most guard dogs are trained not to take food except from their handlers. But—"

I knew the answer. "They are still dogs. Left alone without Shane around, the meatballs were too tempting. And Fletch knew animals. He knew they'd probably eat them." I picked up the length of chain that hung down from the waist of my skirt and played with it. The dogs had always bugged me. The first hit man hadn't known Shane had dogs, which meant Fletch hadn't known. "How come Fletch didn't know about the dogs when he hired the hit man in Vegas?"

Vance watched me fingering the chain. "Best as we can determine, when Shane stayed in hotels, he didn't have his dogs with him. He brought his motor home to Elsinore because we don't have the swanky accommodations that he's used to. But in Vegas, he had his pick of high-end hotels. Fletch apparently went to Vegas to confront Shane about the tickets sent to his dad."

I sighed. "Shane was in Vegas to see Nikki. Once she told him she was pregnant, he dumped her. He wasn't a nice man." But that didn't mean he had deserved to be murdered. "So once Fletch came to town and learned about the dogs, he devised a way to murder Shane but spare the dogs."

His dimples flattened to cop serious, and he stopped staring at the chain dangling over my thighs. "So it seems. Once he had the dogs sedated, he picked the cab door lock on the driver's side of the motor home and went in. All he had to do was wait for Shane to come in."

I shook my head. "He couldn't kill the dogs, but he could shoot Shane in cold blood." A shiver ran through me.

"He's lawyered up, but that's what it looks like. Did you

know he parked the truck a couple blocks away from Rosy's house and blew that up too? He set it off around the same time as he set the bombs off in Rosy's house."

I nodded; Gabe had told me. "To delay police and fire so he could get into hiding. Once he dropped off Rosy's car at the abandoned house he hid in and picked up the motor home, he thought they were safe. Then to be sure, he had been going to wait at the outlet center, right by a freeway on-ramp, until everyone gave up looking for him and Grandpa. All he had to do was drive away." And we would never have known but for Ali. *My hero dog.*

Vance reached over and tugged the chain from my hand. He wrapped his fingers around the links and looked into my face. "You have the damnedest luck, first stumbling onto him like that with your dog, then not getting killed. I don't know why he didn't shoot you."

I tried to tug the chain from his grip. "He didn't want to kill me or Ali. He just wanted Grandpa."

He held on. "There's something about you Shaw that drives men to insanity."

I could hear voices and laughter from outside my office door. But in here, it was warm and dangerous. I tried to think of something safe to say. "Even you?" Uh-oh, that wasn't safe. That was inviting trouble.

He stood, still holding the end of the chain, and hovered over me. "Even me," he answered in a husky voice. "You make me want to do insane things. Like in a romance novel. A very hot, sexy, downright sizzling romance novel."

No! Danger! My brain screamed warnings, but his voice and words stirred my nerves to a searing curiosity. I couldn't tear my gaze away from Vance. I didn't really even know him, I desperately reminded myself. But I did know that he secretly wrote romance novels that crackled with sexual tension. He knew the language of women, and he wasn't afraid to use it. I stiffened my spine and said, "Save it for your books, Vance."

He smiled and dropped the end of the chain. "We're going to keep running into each other. Wouldn't it be better to get it out of the way?"

Huh? "Get what out of the way?"

He leaned down. "Sex. Lots of pleasure and orgasms. Then we move on."

"You think so?" He thought a quick roll in the sheets would extinguish the sexual tension between us? *Men.* I stood up, forcing him to step back, and went to the door. For once, just this once, I was going to get the last word. "Won't happen, Vance."

He smiled at me. "Afraid, Shaw? Maybe you'll find out what it's like to make love with a real man?"

I shook my head. "No. You'll find out what it's like to make love with me." I turned the knob but didn't open the door. Then I looked back. "And Vance, with me— once would never be enough." I opened the door and walked out.

I heard a choking noise behind me.

I walked fast, heading toward Grandpa, where he was chatting with Bo and Lola by Blaine's new desk.

A hand caught my wrist and I ground to a halt, then looked over to see Gabe leaning against the wall behind Blaine's desk. He wore butt-hugging jeans, a molded T-shirt, and an expression I couldn't define. How long had Gabe been there? "Uh, hi."

"Why were you locked in your office with Vance?"

Oh boy. "He was telling me stuff about Fletch."

Gabe did a slow and very thorough body search with his gaze. Then he said, "Do I have to shoot him?"

I relaxed. "No."

He pulled closer. "You look hot."

He smelled of male heat and soap. Very Gabe. Very sexy. "Really? 'Cause I've had some complaints."

"Your mom?"

I laughed and nodded. "'Fraid so."

"No complaints here." He leaned closer, brushing his mouth over my ear. "I want to peel that top and skirt off you. We'll keep the boots on."

My heart kicked up to raw-lust speed. "Gabe! There's a party going on."

"If I behave now, promise to keep the boots on later?"

Swear to God. I thought I might burst into flames. "Yes."

He lifted his head and smiled. It was a wicked grin. "I'll hold you to it."

"Gabe." Grandpa came up to us and said, "How's your brother? Did you tell your mother hello for me?"

Gabe let go of me and answered, "Mom says hi back. Cal's fine. He's taking a little time off to decide his future." He looked at me. "And he said to tell Sam thank you."

I was surprised. "Me? What for?"

Gabe arched an eyebrow. "He didn't tell me the specifics, he just said the two of you had a talk and it helped him sort some things out."

Cal must have meant the night he came into my bedroom after Shane was murdered. He'd been the one who told me where Gabe was, told me how much Gabe loved me, and gave me the courage to go after him. "He helped me too."

"Yeah? Good." That was all Gabe said. Didn't ask, didn't push. Just accepted me into his family. Then he turned his attention to Grandpa. "Sorry I missed the show, Barney. Sam said it was videotaped."

"You can see the tape anytime. Family comes first." Grandpa reached out and squeezed my arm.

Blaine walked up. "The party is breaking up. I think I'm going to head home."

I nodded. I had apologized to Blaine for bringing Lola on as a client without talking to him. She wasn't a client any longer. The problem was that she thought she was working for us. All night, Blaine had ignored her.

But it was time to resolve the issue. "Where's Lola? I'll talk to her now and tell her she's going to have to find another job."

"Not tonight, Sam," Blaine said.

I blinked. "Why not?"

He rolled his shoulders and looked around, not meeting my gaze.

Grandpa answered, "Blaine's probably thinking that Lola worked hard to help pull off the magic show tonight. She's been helping us all. Then she worked as my assistant, and she was darn good. Let her have the glory tonight."

"Humph," Blaine said.

Was he agreeing? I stared at Blaine, but he appeared extremely interested in the new paint on the wall behind me. Every time Lola and Blaine crossed paths in the last couple of days, there had been a flare-up between them. I thought Blaine couldn't wait to be rid of her.

Yet he wanted her to have her night of success.

Hmm. "Okay, I can talk to her next week."

"Humph," Blaine repeated, and wandered off to leave.

I looked at Grandpa.

He shrugged. "Romance is your business. Magic is mine." He leaned forward and kissed me. "Thanks for making this night happen, Sammy. Night."

I hugged him. "I love you, Grandpa. Good night." I watched him gather up the boys and leave. All three of them were laughing and chatting as they walked to the Jeep.

We saw the rest of the guests out, then I had one thing left to do. I looked at Gabe. "Let's go see your conference room."

He closed the new miniblinds over the windows and locked the door. Then he turned to look at me. "Lead on. I like the view from behind you."

I rolled my eyes and turned around to walk past Blaine's desk and Gabe's reception area, while trying not to be self-conscious. I was a thirty-something soccer mom with two teenage sons and cellulite.

Gabe was a smokin'-hot ex-cop. No fat on him.

I turned left into the hallway and then right into the conference room.

It was long and rectangular, with a sink, small refrigerator, and a coffeemaker. The table was actually something I found at an estate sale. It was long and mahogany, very strong. I had managed to get eight matching chairs. I doubted Gabe would need more than eight chairs. The walls were painted a light pecan like his office.

The wall behind the door had four pictures I'd spent weeks hunting down and having made for him.

Gabe stopped behind me, taking it all in.

I had trouble getting my breath. My stomach tightened.

"Where did you get those pictures?" he asked softly, his voice brushing over my hair.

He still stood behind me, hadn't moved. "Old newspapers. Grandpa helped me search them out online. We bought copies, then I had them enlarged. Your father was in the newspaper a few times." They were prints of his dad fighting fires. I'd found four black-and-white prints in old newspapers that looked pretty good once I had them enlarged, matted, and framed.

Did he like them?

He stepped past me and stood in front of the prints. He didn't say anything.

I walked up to stand next to him. "You can take them down; do whatever you want with them." Maybe it was too personal for him. Or too painful. Or maybe it was a silly, female thing.

Moments passed.

Gabe tore his gaze away from the pictures and turned to me. "I want them exactly where you put them. They are special." He reached for me, pulling me into his arms and kissing me. "You are special."

Gabe was not a man of words, so these words had a quality to them. A magic. "You like them?"

He smiled. It was a rare smile for Gabe, soft and full of something poignant. "I do. I'm blown away that you knew how much I would like them."

It was my turn to smile. I had no idea how all this was going to work out. Combining offices, training for my PI license, running Heart Mates, loving Gabe. The potential for pain was tremendous. But right now, this moment gave me, us, magic.

I let go and stepped back. "It's my night to give you what you like." I stuck out one leg and looked down. In a teasing voice, I asked, "Now what were you saying about my boots?"